# "You confuse me," she said, clearing her throat of its huskiness.

"Last night you broke into my home, threatened my life and made me afraid that you'd rape me. Today you're taking over my chores, making free with my home, digging a trench. You're acting like a...like a neighbor, friend, hired hand, what? I need some rules."

"You are a plain-speaking woman."

"Lies never served anyone. I can't abide a liar. You know what I said was the truth."

"Would you have given me shelter if I had knocked on your door?"

"You alone? I would have offered the barn, but with your sons, my home."

"My sons make you feel safe?"

"Yes."

"And I do not?"

His steady, probing gaze holding her own, even with the evidence of fatigue in those cinnamon-colored eyes, robbed her of the will to lie, the will to fight.

"No...."

Dear Reader,

This month we're giving you plenty of excuses to put your feet up and "get away from it all" with these four, fantasy-filled historical romances.

First, Theresa Michaels is back! And she's outdone herself with this heart-wrenching Western, *The Merry Widows—Sarah*, the last book in her MERRY WIDOWS trilogy—although you needn't have read the others to enjoy this one. It's about two wounded souls who find each other and fall in love. Rio Santee, half-Apache, rescues his sons from a mission school, only to become a fugitive until Sarah Ann Westfall, a widow, reluctantly lets the trio into her home—and heart!

*The Rancher's Wife* by Lynda Trent is about a "pretend marriage" that turns real when an abandoned wife moves in with her widower neighbor in order to care for his infant daughter. Rising talent Lyn Stone returns with *Bride of Trouville*, the story of a young widow forced to marry, who must hide her son's deafness from the husband she has grown to love.

If those aren't enough reasons to curl up with a book, then perhaps Irish rogue and rebel Conor O'Neil will entice you in Ruth Langan's latest Medieval, *Conor*, when he teams up with a beautiful noblewoman to unravel a plot to murder Queen Elizabeth. Don't miss it!

Whatever your tastes in reading, you'll be sure to find a romantic journey back to the past between the covers of a Harlequin Historical®.

Sincerely,

Tracy Farrell
Senior Editor

Please address questions and book requests to:
Harlequin Reader Service
U.S.: 3010 Walden Ave., P.O. Box 1325, Buffalo, NY 14269
Canadian: P.O. Box 609, Fort Erie, Ont. L2A 5X3

# THE MERRY WIDOWS
## Sarah
### THERESA MICHAELS

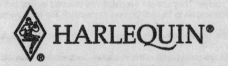

HARLEQUIN®

TORONTO • NEW YORK • LONDON
AMSTERDAM • PARIS • SYDNEY • HAMBURG
STOCKHOLM • ATHENS • TOKYO • MILAN • MADRID
PRAGUE • WARSAW • BUDAPEST • AUCKLAND

ISBN 0-373-29069-1

THE MERRY WIDOWS—SARAH

Copyright © 1999 by Theresa DiBenedetto

Visit us at www.romance.net

Printed in U.S.A.

**Books by Theresa Michaels**

Harlequin Historicals

*A Corner of Heaven* #104
*Gifts of Love* #145
*Fire and Sword* #243
*\*Once a Maverick* #276
*\*Once an Outlaw* #296
*\*Once a Lawman* #316
*†The Merry Widows—Mary* #372
*†The Merry Widows—Catherine* #400
*†The Merry Widows—Sarah* #469

*The Kincaid Trilogy
†The Merry Widows

Harlequin Books

*Renegades* 1996
"Apache Fire"

# THERESA MICHAELS

is a former New Yorker who resides in south Florida
with her family, including three "rescued" cats. Her
avid interest in history and her belief in the power of
love are combined in her writing. She has received the
*Romantic Times Magazine* Reviewer's Choice Award
for Best Civil War Romance, the National Readers'
Choice Award for Best Series Historical and the
B. Dalton Bookseller Award for Bestselling Series
Historical. When not writing, she enjoys traveling,
adding to her collection of Victorian perfume bottles
and searching for the elf to master her computer.

**For all my readers**

# Chapter One

On a late January night when thick, ugly clouds hunkered across a full moon, Rio Santee crouched on a rooftop of the newest Indian mission school.

He had relearned the lessons of childhood that night was his friend, but it was a cruel moon. A hunter's moon. The cruelty lay in that it made all things vulnerable—the hunter and those he hunted.

They were victims, all.

But his need was such that he could not abide a longer delay. The men who hunted him might know he would come here. Even now, they could be waiting outside the box canyon. He had lost them two weeks ago, then come here. Two weeks when he had hidden by day, and by night prowled the mission seeking what he had lost.

He had watched and waited with the infinite patience that was his people's legacy. No longer would he walk the white man's path as his Irish grandfather had taught him.

For behind the stone walls, within one chamber, was

where his heart lay. His life, all reason for living was locked within the walls.

Tonight he would steal back what had been stolen from him. A hunted man had little choice but to become a thief.

Rio was no more than a shadow as the biting winter wind sent clouds scudding across the sky to dapple the adobe and stone buildings on the canyon floor. He seemed oblivious to the cold in his thin wool shirt and buckskin pants. He was one with the darkness.

Yet, moving or stilled, there was an intensity that set him apart. Like all night creatures, his senses were fueled by fear and excitement.

He was aware of every breath, of the pulsing in his veins, a raw quickening that indicated the end of his yearlong search was near.

One year. He wanted to howl his grief, his denial of stolen time. A bloodlust filled him as powerfully as the smell of his own warm sweat. His hand swept down to touch the handle of the knife sheathed at his side.

He couldn't fail. Not as he had in the past. But that was a thought path he refused to walk. The way was clear before him. It was time.

With a lithe roll he went over the edge of the roof, his fingertips hugging the rough stone as he hung for a moment, then silently dropped to the ground. He turned immediately and drew his knife.

The wooden shutter he faced was poorly made, the gap wide where the inside bar secured it shut. He used his knife to raise the bar. It wedged an opening for his fingers to slip inside. He caught and held the bar up as he eased open one side of the shutter. Sliding the knife into its sheath, he peered into the room.

There wasn't enough moonlight to cast a shadow on the interior of the room. The darkness was absolute.

His breathing was shallow but controlled, and so at odds with the thudding pounding of his heart. A cloth headband absorbed his sweat. If he were caught now, he would be killed and everything lost to him.

With extreme caution he lifted the bar free and set it on the ground. Like the shadow he had been likened to he slid over the windowsill. There in the dark he stood for a few moments, listening to the sleeping breaths of twenty young Indian boys.

Among them were his two sons. Half-breed Apaches forced to live among those of other tribes who hated them.

His soft-soled moccasins helped him move silently into the center of the room. He counted off the wooden bedsteads until he came to the first one he wanted.

Rio closed his eyes briefly. He was afraid to utter a prayer. The overwhelming emotions of standing this close to his firstborn son in more than a year stole his strength.

They had stripped him of everything—beloved wife, children, home and his wealth of horses. Memories flooded his mind until he stood and shook like an aged man with a wasting sickness.

His pride, his dual heritage and the precious peace he had fought to gain and believed his, were all gone.

But he could give those gifts back to his sons.

Now was not the time to savor the thought, or dream of what would be. Now was the time for the warrior.

From his cloth belt he removed strips of rawhide and a length of cloth. His hands trembled as he leaned over his sleeping son and covered his mouth.

The twelve-year-old's struggles were no match for the man and were quickly subdued.

Rio could not take the chance to whisper to his son and calm his fear. He cursed the thinness of his child's body as he gagged and bound him in minutes. Wrapping the boy in his blanket, Rio carried him to the window where he lowered Lucas to the ground. Every move he made had been planned without wasted motion.

He hadn't planned on the pain it caused him to bind and gag his child, yet he made his way back to the bed where he quickly bundled the boy's clothes. Another trip to the window to set the bundle outside and then he searched out his younger child's bed. His was closer to the door.

With the lightest of touches he discovered the boy still slept belly down, arms and legs flung to the four bed corners as if he would embrace all he could, even in his sleep.

Rio's body tensed with the effort to hold back his need to gather this smaller boy to his body and just hold him. Delay was deadly. Once more he quickly set about gagging then tying him, too.

Soft mewling noises escaped the gag. Rio froze. In

the next bed the boy mumbled in his sleep, then rolled over, facing away from them.

Fear raked Rio like roweled spurs, to be so close to winning their freedom. He tossed clothing on the boy's legs and wrapped him in a blanket, hurrying to the open window. While he lowered his son to the ground, the boys in their bed stirred as the cold night air filled the room. Urgency to be away filled Rio.

Still without speaking he made two trips to take each boy outside the high-sided canyon to where he had hidden two horses. Stolen, like everything he possessed. But these were horses first stolen from him.

He searched the shadows, forcing himself to patience. He had to be sure there was no one waiting to shoot them down. But the night wind whispered only of its biting cold.

Rio hunkered down before his sons. He untied their gags, speaking softly to them as he then worked to free their bonds.

"Lucas, I have come for you as I promised." He offered the boy the canteen. "We will travel quickly and in silence." He saw Lucas nod as he sipped the water. "Dress now."

While Lucas obeyed without question, Gabriel, the younger, threw his arms around his father's neck. He pressed his lips against Rio's ear.

"I told him, Father, that you would come for us. I told him over and over, but Lucas did not believe me."

"But I am here now, and he knows you spoke the truth." Rio felt the child's smile form against his cheek. He held the boy tight for a moment more, then gave in to the need that forced him to set the child away. "Dress quickly now. We ride hard and long this night."

Lucas, taller, thinner than Rio remembered, turned from him without a word.

Rio needed no words to know his son blamed him. He thought he knew the depth of his rage, but it had been smaller measured against the feeling that swept through him now. He helped his sons to mount double. He tucked the spare blanket around them to cut the chill of the wind and tied their bundled clothing behind the saddle.

He touched each boy's shoulder. A little over a year, and in that time, the trust between them and his oldest son had been destroyed. He was helpless to stop himself from thinking about it, just as he had been helpless to stop it from happening.

He mounted his own horse, a mountain-bred mustang mix, its steel-dust color and the boy's dun of the same strain, animals barely a year away from their wild range. He could depend upon the horses to warn him of danger. He fought the urge to set his heels against the horse's sides and race away. He kept both animals to a walk. A loose stone in the silent night would make a sound that carried far. Nor could he have the horses go lame.

Rio kept to the deepest shadows against the towering upthrust of rock. He hated the fear gnawing inside him.

Rio glanced behind him. This had been too easy.

He couldn't trust his own timing and planning. He had expected someone to be waiting for him to try to free his sons. The men that hunted him knew of his boys, knew he would go to them.

True, it had taken him almost a year to discover which mission school they had been sent to. But those who trailed him had been led to many such places, no matter how carefully, how cunningly he laid false trails for them. He wished in all this time they had grown tired of hunting for him, but it was a wish born without substance. They would never give up until he was dead. He was the only one who stood against their greed and murder.

Darkness was his only friend, the only aid he had to their escape and to keep them hidden. Darkness and silence. Later he would have time to talk to his sons, later the healing would begin.

But would his sons forgive him? Would they ever understand the grief that had stolen his reason and for a while, his very will to live?

He had no answers, for they were questions he dared not ask his sons now.

Despite the biting cold wind that cut through his clothing, sweat broke out on his skin. He rode on with a growing belly-tightening anxiety that gripped him in its fist without a sign of easing as time and miles slowly passed. He rode with a numbing exhaustion, his constant companion for months. How much of an alarm the mission school would raise over the two missing boys was anyone's guess. There was no choice but to keep moving.

Briefly then, his hand touched the wooden stock of the rifle, secure in the saddle boot. This and his knife were the only weapons he had to protect his sons. He glanced behind at them, saw they were riding with eyes closed.

The faint dawn tinting the sky saw them through the Zuni Mountains west of Alamitos on the northwestern side of the New Mexico territory. Within an hour they reached the edge of the Malpais lava beds. The trail through the treacherous beds led south.

Rio pulled up. He scanned the land around and behind him. Once through the territory, he could cross to Mexico. There in the Sierra Madres, or a hundred miles east to the Candelaria Mountains, he would find a safe camp. These Mexican mountains offered sanctuary to Victorio, Geronimo and, long before, to other bands of Apache warriors. No, the whites called them renegades, and the men who hunted him would see him branded the same.

Victorio had died down in those mountains over a year ago. But there were others who raided on both sides of the border. None, he admitted to himself, cut the bloody swath of death that Victorio's revenge had taken. He could well understand what led Mangas's war chief to split the band and leave the reservation for good. If he had found women and children dead on their gathering forages, scalped for the bounty paid on their Apache hair, he too would have sworn to avenge them. The promised beef never came, nor the blankets, and with their weapons taken, the warriors could not hunt for meat, had no skins or furs for warmth. They had to watch their women and children perish. All for the broken promises made to them.

He had never lived on the reservation or with any of the roving bands. War had never been his path. His grandfather had seen to that. There was no reason for his rancheria to be attacked, all that he loved destroyed. His place of peace, where he loved, was gone.

With a start, Rio turned aside the dark thoughts haunting him and once more studied the land. His glance showed both sons watching him now, and he smiled to show his pride in their silences.

He led off on a path that followed a dry, sandy watercourse. The sand left only a vague depression of their horses passing, which the wind and coming rain would wipe away.

Off to the east the wall of the mesa rose, towering black against the light of a cold, gray dawn. Huge black blocks of lava tricked the eye into believing there was no path through the lava flow, but he knew of a path few men alive could find.

At the path's end were trees and water in a hidden island of grass. While the eruption of El Teinero and Mount Taylor had desolated the country with its river of fire, there were a few places where the lava flow had split into separate streams. It was there that the islands were formed.

Rio pulled up to study the land around him. He needed more light, for one misstep would send the horses plunging through blisters of apparently solid rock that might be eggshell thin. The broken lava that

lay beneath the surface in vast caverns could slice man
or animals to shreds.

And he didn't trust the silence.

The growing light revealed land like an ugly,
twisted snake, enormous ropelike rock that wound
south for miles. It was a dreaded place, and he hoped
for those who followed him, it would remain so.

Rio studied the trail, then slid from his saddle, drop-
ping his reins to ground-tie his horse. He motioned to
Lucas to remain quiet as he stepped away. The path
was narrow, one made by animals. Deer, antelope,
bear, his eyes skimmed their tracks as he walked carefully, searching for any sign that another man had
passed this way.

Caution was part of his nature, always, from his
earliest memories. Now that caution meant his life and
that of his sons.

The twists and bends of the path took him out of
sight of the horses. There was brush, stiff, wiry, filled
with thorns, clumps of prickly pear and a few scattered
pines. He walked another hundred yards or so before
he was satisfied that no one had recently passed this
way.

On his return, he saw that Gabriel still slept. Lucas
had his dark brown eyes fixed on him as he made his
way to the boy's side. Rio gazed into blank, staring
eyes with no expression for a father to read. His shorn
hair, darker than Rio's straight brown hair, was the
same thickness and shade as his mother's. Lucas had
her eyes, too, both in color and shape, but his nose,

straight and thin as a blade, was Rio's, as was the boy's mouth.

Rio stood there. One hand held the reins to his own horse, the other hand clenched at his side. He tried to think of something to say, but his parched throat and the ache within would not allow him to speak. His heart was full, his gaze—unknowingly—pleaded with his son.

The boy continued to stare at him.

Rio turned away and mounted. Agony rode with him as he followed the path.

*There comes a time when a man believes everything is finished. That is a false belief. It is only the beginning.* His grandfather's words. He had thought of their meaning a great deal this past year. It was all he wanted. A new beginning.

His grandfather had also told him that time was a healer. But time was a thief, too. Time had robbed him of years, and of memories with his sons.

Judging by the look in Lucas's eyes, Rio didn't think his son was going to forgive him. Not that the boy had a choice. Rio had taken that from him and from Gabriel.

Time. He needed time and a quiet place where no one hunted him.

He constantly looked over his shoulder to search the rim as they dropped down into a hollow. There was no sign of life. That didn't mean someone was not there. He wished he had his father's field glasses. He wished for many of the things he had counted as his, but they were gone, and all he had was himself to depend on.

Lost in his thoughts, Rio almost missed the opening. He had gashed a mark low on the boulder opposite a crack in the lava. The brush screened the angled opening. From where he sat on his horse, it appeared too small to allow a horse through.

Once more he studied his back trail. He was uneasy. Every sense told him they were safe. His eyes saw no movement. He heard no sound above the howl of the wind. He inhaled deeply several times but caught no scent of smoke indicating a fire nearby.

He did not know of any man who would travel the lava beds unless he was running from something. If he had been driven to the lava itself, he would be lacerated by the glasslike shards and die there.

Rio stared once again at the crack in the wall. A note of added caution whispered through him. He watched the horses, for their mountain-bred senses could be trusted more than his own. Neither horse showed alarm.

His gaze traveled up to where the rock appeared to curve over the slitted opening. It would shield those below from any gunfire from the rim. But the way before him was narrow, in some places so narrow he had to ride with one foot free of the stirrup.

It was the quiet that added to his unrest. He had no choice but to go forward. Inside, where water had hollowed out a cave, he had food and blankets cached. There was wood for a fire within the green oasis. The horses needed rest as much as they did. He needed a chance to explain to his sons where they were going and why.

But sometimes a man's senses pick up sounds or a glimpse of something not strong enough to make an immediate impression, but strong enough to affect his thinking.

Rio's instincts prowled with warnings that all was not right.

He motioned for Lucas to stay. With a gentle touch he started his horse toward the opening. Nothing. He walked the horse a few steps more. His nostrils flared as he caught the faint smell of dust. Surrounded by the sheer, towering walls of lava, there was no wind here. The dust could only drift from the green oasis.

Were he alone he would chance going forward, but he had the lives of his sons to think about before he made any move. Old as life itself was a man's desire for sons to walk upon the earth of their father, and that of his father before him. Having lost his sons once, he would do nothing that would endanger them or risk having them taken from him again.

Now the mustang's ears pricked forward. Rio heard the sound at the same time. It was a scraping noise like something brushing against rock. A noise a man might make if he grew impatient with one position too long and moved to ease a cramp in his leg.

Rio listened for long minutes but there was no repeat of the sound. With firm hands on the reins he touched his heels to the horse's flanks and backed him out of the defile. Once clear, he motioned for his son to follow as he took the faint trail south.

They rounded a twist in the trail when a shout sounded behind them. Without looking back, Rio spurred his horse, with the other keeping pace, as he led the way out of the lava beds that should have offered him shelter and safety.

Acoma, on the other side of the Ceboletta Mesa, was the closest town. Rio thought the men hunting him would expect him to head there for food. But no man could reckon on his need for freedom. He headed for the North Plain.

Within an hour, black thunderheads piled high in the north sky. Rio eyed the building storm as he left his sons and rode his back trail to see who was following them.

There was no sign of pursuit.

That didn't mean they would not follow. Rio rode back. Off to the west was the Divide. He thought of trails that would take him over the mountains, then south through the Arizona territory into Mexico. But without needed supplies, and a desert to cross, he knew they would have little chance of succeeding. All he wanted now was a small canyon where they could build a fire and rest with a measure of safety.

He rejoined his sons and, keeping silent, they pushed on once more. Twice he veered away from box canyons that would be death traps.

In a broken wash where rain had collected in the stone depressions, he called a halt. There was barely enough water for the horses to drink. Gabriel complained of hunger. Rio shared venison jerky with his sons.

"The men who stole our horses are still hunting me. We will keep riding," Rio told his sons after each had a drink from the canteen.

"The men who burned our house? The ones who killed Mother?" Gabriel asked, pressing his small body against his brother's.

"The same. Only now they are three."

"You should have killed them all."

Rio shot a long, hard look at Lucas. The accusation in his older son's voice and gaze sent a fresh wave of pain through him. Rio was the first to look away.

"We will try to outrun the storm."

"And the men?" Lucas asked in a taunting voice. "Will you outrun them, too?"

The whine of a bullet stopped Rio's reply. Sand kicked up in front of his horse. He slapped his palm on the rump of the boys' horse, yelling at them to ride south. He barely managed to keep his seat as his horse reared. Twigs flew from a shriveled, dried shrub less than a foot away. Rio quickly drew his rifle and laid covering fire, before he too rode on.

There were men who would brand him a coward for running, but those men had no fear of having everything they worked for destroyed for no better reason than a taint of blood. Apache...hell. He knew the ways of the people, but he had never followed their war trail, never killed for the joy of battle, never counted coup against his white enemies. He had killed two men who had destroyed his life. Only two of five. And still they named him a renegade, a half-breed renegade they would shoot or hang on sight because he dared to fight back.

He thought of his wife and wondered if she watched over him and their sons? Did the dead know how the living fared? He shook off the black, despairing thoughts.

Running…even his son thought him a coward.

He caught up with his boys, motioned for them to keep to low ground as the storm began with great, fat raindrops plopping on the dry and thirsty land.

Rio had lived through his share of torrential rains and flash floods, but never experienced anything like the sudden, insane storm that smashed with howling, bansheelike winds strong enough to blow a man down. The hard-driven rain struck him like the lash of a lead-tipped whip. He heard Gabriel cry out, and Lucas quickly hushed him.

Rio cursed the storm for hurting them, but blessed it, too. The rain hid them from their enemies.

No sooner had the thought come than his horse went down. Between the rolling burst of thunder and the searing flashes of lightning, he never heard the shot that killed his horse.

Rio managed to kick free of the stirrups before the animal went over. He grabbed hold of his canteen and the rifle. He cried out to see Lucas swing his horse around to come back to him.

At a run, Rio grasped the reins, turning the horse. He slipped, for footing was already treacherous, but his only thought was to find safety for his sons. Not until later did he think of the saddlebags he left behind, and the ammunition for his rifle.

He veered from the trail, heading over rocky ground that would take them through the Black Hills, then south into the mining towns. He needed a horse, supplies and a chance.

Just one chance and then, freedom.

But the Apache Coyote, the trickster all men feared or hated, was laughing at his meager attempts to run.

Lightning created a dance of destruction over the land. Wind struck them like a solid wall, the rain lashed their clothing. The horse shied, and Rio used his strength to stop the animal from bolting.

Rio had a nightmare glimpse of bleached deadwood off to their left just as the lightning struck and turned it into flame. The horse reared, and the reins were ripped from his hand. He felt the sting of a bullet skinning his knuckles. Rio reached for his sons as the horse reared and then, in the howl of the bitter, cold wind, was gone.

They were afoot. Without shelter, food or ammunition. And the hunters were closing in.

## *Chapter Two*

Sarah Ann Westfall awoke with a start in the hours past midnight on the seventh night of a raging storm that swept Hillsboro and the surrounding New Mexico hills with an icy ferocity. Constantly battling the force of the wind and the flooding to get to the barn to feed her horses had left her with bone-deep aches.

Was it truly a noise she heard above the rolling thunder?

Or was this more of the vague unaccountable restlessness that had marked the past week?

She released a breath she did not realize she held and listened again. With one hand she clutched the quilt, but the other already gripped the loaded rifle she kept near her bed since Catherine had left on her marriage trip months ago.

The lurid flashes of lightning illuminated her sparsely furnished bedroom for a few seconds. Were she a weak-minded woman, she would indulge in a bout of pity for her lonely state.

But long ago, she had vowed to never be weak

again. She had kept that vow. Still she caught herself wishing for either her cousin Mary's comforting presence, full of practical reason and the warmth that was the very essence of the woman herself. Or if not Mary, then friend Catherine's unfailing good humor to laugh away the feeling that something was wrong.

The two widows who had shared the house with her were gone, both remarried with Sarah's good wishes for the love each woman had found.

There were no regrets for herself. Once again she lived alone. She just wanted a reason for the panic that was holding her still and frightened in her single bed.

"It's just the storm winds wreaking havoc again," she whispered. She remembered that two days ago a deadfall limb had been ripped from the cottonwood tree close by the house and smashed the side parlor window.

But that had happened during the daytime, gray and gloomy as the hours since the storm began. Night had a way of making every creak of wood in the old frame of the house into a flight of wild imaginings.

She lay there for long minutes, blaming the storm for the ragged nerves that set her mind on fire. The only cure, she knew, was to get up and go downstairs to reassure herself that she was indeed alone in the house.

Lightning danced beyond the windows as she untangled her nightgown and pushed aside the quilt. She did not light her lamp. She wanted both hands free for the rifle. The floor, despite the bedside rag rug, was chill and damp to her bare feet. She hefted the rifle and walked out into the hallway.

The door where once Mary and Catherine had their bedrooms stood open and empty. The stairs were lit with brief, indirect flashes of light, then instantly shrouded in darkness.

Sarah stood at the top of the staircase and listened. She could not identify the noise that woke her, and now it was impossible to hear over the growing howl of the wind and slashing pound of the rain.

By the very act of taking charge, she lost some of her fear. But she remained cautious, too. Keeping her back pressed to the wall, the rifle cocked and ready to fire, she made her way down slowly. Drafts crept beneath her nightgown. She shivered from the chill, but fought against an inner cold, too.

Telling herself she behaved with foolish caution did not lend the courage to step boldly into the parlor.

Here she hugged one side of the wide doorway. From the two front windows came the flickering lights or rapid strikes close by that revealed the room was empty. A few coals still glowed in the fireplace.

When she stepped into the hall again, a stronger draft of cold air swept over her bare feet. The weight of the rifle, the very tension of her grip, seemed to pull her arms downward. She did not understand why she hesitated. But her mind quickly took advantage to supply tales told over the years of women alone who were terrorized by men without conscience.

Her rough head shake sent the long, single braid of

straight black hair swinging against her back. This was not the time to be afraid.

She sensed something, someone motionless and most dangerous, beyond the darkened doorway to the kitchen. Alarm gripped her as she sought to steady herself. Her senses all were alerted. She smelled the wet mustiness of rain-soaked cloth. No wild imagining. From where she stood, she could see the lightning flashes that showed the large round table, the chairs and part of the back door.

The draft was no longer chill, but cold, icy cold. Goose bumps raced over her skin. She forced a swallow, thought about calling out a demand to know who was hiding, but the sudden dryness of her mouth spread to her throat. No amount of swallowing sent moisture to aid her.

A few steps more. Sarah couldn't seem to take them. She thought of Rafe and Mary's visit with the children at Christmas and Rafe's insistence that she get a dog. She had refused, as she refused his offer to hire someone besides young Ramon to help with chores.

She was Sarah Ann Westfall, who had survived a marriage made of rosy bowers that quickly slid into hell. She needed no man. She didn't want one.

She had her precious breeding stock, the horses she loved, and the home she had struggled to gain and keep. No one knew the price she had paid for it. Not her dearest cousin Mary, or friend Catherine. She had made a life for herself, alone, and it was enough. It was peace.

She refused to allow fear to send her scurrying to the safety upstairs. Living the way she did, isolated from neighbors and far from town, with no one but herself to depend on, she could not afford to quake and hide at every noise. She was not about to let someone steal from her.

She pressed against the wall at her back, sliding her bare feet along the floor so not to make a sound.

But she heard her own shallow breathing, felt and listened to the racing beat of her heart.

Inches from the doorway, she stopped again.

There! On the kitchen floor near the back door were wet, dark spots. They were there and gone in the few moments of flickering lightning.

Damp palms and dry throat. Goose bumps and cold sweat. Fear quaked inside her slim, hard-workened body.

Sarah shifted her hold on the rifle, bringing the barrel up and taking a firmer grip. She was not about to walk through the doorway leading with the barrel, only to have it yanked from her hands.

She forced herself to calmly think of the kitchen, with the corner cupboard off to the left, the pantry door to the right, dry sink beneath the windows, wood box and stove against the outside back wall. Then the door. In the middle were the table and chairs. If she were hiding in there, the pantry would be the most logical choice.

There grew within her a fierce need to step inside the room and confront whoever waited. Above the increased drumming in her ears, the storm outside retreated to a muted roar. She reminded herself she came from hearty stock. Her grandmother protected her home from Indians when she had come to the territory as a bride, her mother stood in defense of the town when the marauding bands of soldiers turned loose after the Civil War had raided the Mexican rancheros along the Rio Grande.

Courage. She had inherited it in abundance. Or so she often claimed.

One step. Two. Caution or a bold entrance?

Sarah let caution win. The strength of danger she felt waiting had increased until she breathed its essence.

Her foot slid a little where water had puddled on the floor. She froze. Someone had stood there. Stood in the doorway and looked out into the hall. Watching her? All this time? Her teeth clenched to stop the inner trembling from making an audible sound. She felt him close. But where?

Dear Lord, was there only one?

Please, let there be only one.

Her night-adjusted eyes swept over the once-familiar kitchen. Now, with the eerie flashes of lightning, the room took on a frightening gloom that formed shadows where none should be.

Sarah made a half turn and stared at the partially closed pantry door. She leveled the rifle, her index finger coming to rest on the trigger.

"Come out. Come out or I'll shoot." She surprised herself with the firmly delivered demand. She edged around the table, gently squeezing the trigger.

There was a second when the overpowering sense of someone's presence swept over her. Before she could react, her wrist was manacled by iron-hard fingers that ripped her steading hand from the rifle's barrel. The ceiling beam splintered with the blast of one shot, and then the rifle was jerked from her hand.

A cold steel blade flashed before her eyes, descending toward her throat. She didn't move. Couldn't breathe. A powerful anger tore through her fear. She had vowed never to be helpless again.

Sarah threw herself backward and to the side, away from the wicked blade. She kicked out and heard a grunt of surprise. If there was pain she didn't feel it.

She was no longer thinking, but reacting with an animal need to escape danger. She swirled to yank open the back door, and escaped into the storm.

Instantly soaked, the gusting force of the wind made her stagger. Cold, primitive fear ran through her mind. The water was inches deep in the yard, and beneath it, the ground had churned into a treacherous sea of thick mud.

She could not begin to think of where to run. The road to town was flooded. She had seen no one this past week. The barn offered a hope of safety. But what if there was more than one? She could trap herself.

She slid and fell to one knee. Her hands found no purchase to help her to rise. The sodden weight of her long nightgown dragged her down. If she couldn't run, she'd crawl.

The intense, needlelike rain pierced the thin cloth and beat against her skin. She couldn't see. Her braid hung like a chained weight over her shoulder, but she kept crawling. Whatever hindered her, hindered her attacker. If she could make it to the trees, she could lose him.

Sarah felt nausea roil her stomach and send bile to her throat. She choked it back down. Her hand closed on rock, and she bore the sting of a cut without crying out. Strength flooded her body as she rose. She ran for the trees when lightning showed her how close she was to them.

Underbrush tore at her gown and welted her skin already prickling with fright. A limb slashed across her face. Sarah ignored it all in her panicked flight, seeking only to escape. The entangling long grasses beneath the water told her she was through the first line of trees and into a small clearing.

She could not hear the noise of pursuit over the raging fury of the storm, but that only served to increase her fear. She knew she was being stalked like prey.

Sarah ran blindly on, stumbling then falling over a deadfall tree. Her stomach was driven against her spine. Breath left her in a whomping rush, but she tried to lift herself frantically. Pinpricks of light danced before her eyes as she struggled to her feet, lungs sucking at air she could not find. She tore her nightgown free from the branch and took a staggering step.

She was driven down again by a hard body from behind.

Sarah lay stunned, still out of breath. Her hands and face burned from bleeding welts. She lay on the sodden ground, sobbing now, as she tried to regain her breath, helpless beneath the body of her attacker.

Her body was lifted from the ground and turned over. She lay very still on her back, and tried to see the man looming over her. The lightning denied her need to see his face. If it struck, it was too distant for her to make out anything about him.

"For you escape is impossible. I am Apache."

Words spoken with assurance. Soft and grating on already frayed nerves. Terror seized her. Less than two years ago, the Warm Springs Apache war chief Victorio had led his band of raiders on a bloody rampage throughout the territories in retaliation for the scalp hunters who killed women, children and old men for the hair that the Mexican government paid bounty on. Victorio was killed by the Mexican Rurales, but there were others who had taken his place.

And there were the survivors of acts too brutal to remember. And for Sarah, a woman's worst fear lived in these moments.

Her chest hurt, but air was beginning to creep into it again. Her hands clawed at the muddy earth. She swallowed painfully. Her vision was suddenly clear as his looming, dark mass blocked the rain and he bent closer to her. Darkness. Danger. The words to plead for her life waited to be said.

She filled her hands with mud and slammed her fists against his cheeks, pushing upward as she twisted and rolled away from him.

A yank on the back of her nightgown brought her up short. She gagged as the cloth neckline cut across her throat, choking her. And still she lunged, desperate for freedom. On her knees in the mud, she dug her fingers deep to aid her bid to flee. The sudden release of the pressure at her throat came as the well-washed fabric ripped from her body. Sarah used the last of her strength and rolled free.

But her escape was short-lived. He tackled her again, and this time held her down with her arm painfully shoved up between her shoulder blades.

She opened her mouth to scream, but another hand, callused and muddy, clamped over her mouth. A frantic, guttural sound, like that of a trapped animal escaped her lips.

She was flipped to her back and once more lay still as he knelt over her.

"To move now is to die." And Rio Santee, who had never raised his hand in anger to woman or child, released his hold on his prisoner.

Cold, muddy rain dripped from his shoulder-length hair onto her face. She closed her eyes, fighting to stay calm. She felt his hand brush her cheek, touching the welt there.

"You hurt yourself by running."

"Only a yellow dog attacks a woman."

She stiffened as he leaned closer, his hands spread across the ground on either side of her shoulders. His knees pressed tight against the sides of her thighs as he bent his head lower. If she moved upward, she would touch him.

"No!" she cried out against the implied threat.

"No," he repeated harshly, shaking his head from

side to side, spraying her with rain. He could taste her fear, it was that strong, that real, and he hated himself for intensifying it.

"You will deny me nothing. I hunted and found prey. Just as the whites have hunted my people. So many slain. And none thought to spare our women or children. We are a proud race. But sadly diminished in numbers. Does the living child care if the body that nurtured it was willing or unwilling?"

"They hang white men for rape in this territory. You they would castrate. For a start."

"Only if you lived to tell." With his upper body weight braced on his arms, he shifted so that one knee pressed between her thighs. Naked and trembling, Sarah listened to the voice of reason that warned her not to provoke him.

"Get up." His move was swift and graceful, despite the mud, and he stood tall above her, then jerked her to her feet.

Sarah shivered with a bone-deep chill under the icy sting of the rain on her bare skin. She was glad the lightning wreaked its havoc on the far-off hills. She had no desire to see him gazing at her naked body.

He caught hold of her sodden braid with one hand and threaded his fingers through the loosened plait. She stared at him as he bent down to retrieve her torn nightgown. If only she could grab hold of his knife...

"No more fighting. And you would be wise to obey." Rio handed over the drenched cloth, pushing it into her hands when she made no move to take it.

"Give me no more trouble and you will not be harmed."

She opened her mouth to reply angrily, but no sound came out. Not harmed? What did he think he had done to her, running her to ground like the prey he had called her?

After a moment she jerked her braid free of his hold and turned away, hugging the nightgown to her. She stiffened as his hands came down on her bare shoulders.

Sarah felt the trembling that seized her legs. She realized her flight and struggles had only succeeded in wearing her out. She needed to regain then conserve her strength. He couldn't watch her all the time. She ignored his other threat.

But as she started the long walk back home, she admitted to herself that she was afraid. He could rape her, he could kill her, and no one would know what her fate was until the storm was over and the floodwaters receded.

It was a chilling, sobering thought. She had only herself to depend upon. If she tried...no...when she made her next escape, it would have to be a good one.

Much as it went against her nature to appear docile, she pretended to be just that. She offered no protest or struggle as he guided her back to the house. Several times she staggered, and twice fell to her knees, but each time his strong, callused hand caught hold of her arm and lifted her to her feet.

It was only now that she fully understood how flight

had depleted her strength. She needed time to recover and plan.

When she fell a third time, he lifted her into his arms as if she weighed nothing. Sarah used her iron will to stop the scream welling in her throat. She pushed weakly against his firmly muscled chest, distressed to note that he was not breathing hard even after their mad race through the rain.

Beneath soaked cloth, his flesh, as rain beaten as her own, still retained a great deal of heat, which warmed her along one side. She did not want to acknowledge his strength, or the way he curved his upper body over her to take the brunt of the storm. She clutched her ruined nightgown with a fierce grip as he shifted suddenly and opened the door.

The storm winds renewed their fury. The door was ripped from his hold and slammed open. They entered the kitchen in a rush, and he swung around, still holding her to push the door closed.

Sarah expected to be put down. It came as a shock that he started for the hall.

"You'd better let me go. My husband—"

"No lies. There is no man here."

"You can't know that." Her voice rose on a shrill note for he unerringly headed for the stairs.

"I know. I know all about the widow woman who dresses as a man, does the work of two and lives alone."

"Who are you?"

He paused on the stair. And even in the dark, Sarah

could feel the penetrating heat of his gaze as he stared down at her.

"Who are you?" she repeated in a softer, and to her horror, weaker voice.

"I told you. I am your worst nightmare, white woman. I am Apache."

# Chapter Three

For long minutes, Sarah said nothing as she struggled to make sense of the impressions she had unknowingly gathered. She felt only a mild shock when he went directly past the other rooms to her own at the end of the hallway.

He stepped inside the room where no man had been. Sarah renewed her struggle, then, without a word, he set her on her feet.

She backed away from him, still clutching the nightgown, for it was the only thing she had to cover her nudity.

"For an Apache you speak English too well. And don't make idle threats of killing me. If that was your intent, I'd be dead."

"For a woman there are worse things than death."

"*You* have already committed one of them. You have violated my home by breaking into it."

"Be thankful to your God, *iszán*, that until this moment, that is all I have done."

"Do you curse me in your heathen tongue?"

"I used the Apache word for *woman*. Had I wished to curse you, I could do so equally well in English, and Spanish, as well as my heathen tongue."

"Then you said it to remind me you are Apache."

"No. I called you *iszán* to remind myself."

There was a distinct difference to his voice. Sarah shivered in reaction, and it had nothing to do with the chill left from the rain. She judged him taller than she first supposed, but it was the smooth, dangerous quality in his voice that caught and held her attention.

Smooth, like the aged whiskey that Judd had been too fond of when he could afford it, and dangerous like a coiled rattler. For all that he had spoken softly, Sarah was not deceived. She thought he could be whipped into a fury with the slightest provocation.

Sarah had no intention of provoking him to find out if she was right.

She backed up to the wooden wardrobe. With one hand she reached in behind her and took a shirt from a hook. She had drawn one arm through the sleeve when he lit the lamp.

She stared at the puddle of water on her wooden floor surrounding his moccasins. Her gaze rose to his knees where the soaked leather ended, and went no farther. Inwardly she cringed. She fought the very strong instinctive feminine urge to cover herself, and to seek the darkest corner of her room to cower in.

She won over the urge, but she was not courageous enough, or bold enough, to face him. With as much dignity as she could summon, she turned her back to him and finished putting on the shirt.

The hem of the shirt covered her to mid-thigh. It was an old, well-worn wool shirt that had belonged to Judd, one he wore before his taste and pocket allowed for a gambler's fancy linen or ruffled silk shirts. The shirt was also one of the few things of value she had from her deceased husband, or for that matter, from her disastrous marriage. But that was a closed door she refused to open.

Sarah ignored her trembling fingers' struggle to match button to buttonhole. All the while, she dreaded to hear his order to turn around.

The order never came.

She withdrew a pair of pants from the wardrobe.

"No. No men's clothes. White women pride themselves on their layers of female trappings. That is what you will wear."

Sarah squeezed the rough twill cloth in her hands. She bit back the words to tell him she would wear what she damned well pleased.

"You have a choice. Wear what I say or wear nothing at all. You will not wear a man's clothes to make running easier."

Somehow it did not surprise her that he knew her intent. He would do the same himself. But she would not give in so easily.

"You said it yourself. I do the work of two. These are all I have to wear."

"No."

Rio waited out her stillness and her silence, noting the white-knuckle grip she had on the cloth. The lamp threw a small circle of light that left her partly in shadow where she stood against the far wall.

Her hair, dark, near black, he thought, and as straight as his own, no longer resembled a neat braid. The wet, tangled hair soaked the back of her shirt.

Looking at her, ignoring his own chilled flesh, Rio felt her pride and strength come against him, and was momentarily taken aback. Instantly his anger heightened, while at the same time he became increasingly aware of her beauty. Not the delicate beauty he associated with pale-skinned women, but the beauty he could find among the Apache maidens.

*She is no maiden.* Rio did not need the reminder. If they were in Apacheria there was a law that no girl must be taken by a man except in marriage. When a woman was widowed or divorced she had no warrior to hunt for her or protect her. Her only way of repayment was the gift of herself. Her body would be for the asking of any warrior not married. The fact that she was no longer a virgin made the giving of her body not a sin but a duty. Following the warpath kept the death count of males high, and all women of childbearing age were urged to bear children to replace them.

Unlike the whites, adultery was all but unknown, and to take a maiden against her will was a crime punishable by death or partial dismemberment.

*But this one was a widow.* And he had been too long without a woman. And he reminded himself that he had not followed the tribe's ways for many years.

He could not take his gaze from her. She stood tall

for a woman, and moved with the suppleness of a mountain cat in a slim, wild beauty. His breath came faster, and he spoke harshly to hide that fact.

"I warned you to obey and no harm will come to you."

"Yet you fill my home with your threats? Why have you come here? What is it that you want?"

"Food and shelter. For now."

Sarah snatched her robe from the wardrobe's hook, slipped it on and belted the tie tight. She was almost overcome by the sudden weakness of her legs, a weakness that quickly spread throughout her body. Food and shelter, he said. Such simple, basic needs. But it was the threat of that only being the beginning that made her turn around to face him.

He stood outside the pool of lamplight. She saw he had made no move to dry off. The windows rattled as the storm's renewed fury brought eerie sheet lightning flickering its bluish tongues into the room. The howling wind seemed alive, like a ravening beast intent on destruction, intent on finding a way inside.

Where it should have been safe. But it wasn't. Not with him standing in her bedroom, making the room appear smaller than it was.

Her gaze went to the knife he held. She knew the terror of prey with its predator close by. But she had nowhere to hide.

Sarah's chin came up. Mentally she braced herself. She refused to show him how the intimidating sight he presented affected her.

Her eyes tracked the length of his sinewy arm, revealed by plastered cloth up to a curved shoulder. Broad and muscled. She would be no match for his strength.

The determined square chin with the hint of a cleft as much as told her it would be a foolish waste of time to argue with this man. There was a fullness to the shape of his lips, making them both sensuous and cruel. A straight, narrow nose, nostrils flaring as if her staring triggered some primal hunting instinct.

And then she looked into the most chilling pair of eyes she had ever seen. Clearly defined dark brown brows slashed above those eyes watching her with an intensity that made her fear he could look into her soul and know her every secret.

She fought off this thought. He could not do it. No one could. And she had secrets. Secrets she had never shared with anyone. Not even her dear Mary, and never with sweet, innocent Catherine.

"Who are you?" she asked.

The hard, set line of his lips lifted at one corner to form a smirking smile. He was enjoying her fear and that made her furious.

"And don't tell me again that you are Apache. If you are, you are not a full-blood. Your features are too refined, and you're too tall."

Rio's smile deepened before he answered her.

"Mangus, hereditary chief of the once-powerful Warm Springs Apaches was taller, and bigger. He was called handsome by many. But Victorio, ah, there was a warrior that even your army men thought to be physically perfect and handsomer than many, many men."

"That doesn't answer my question. And if you're seeking to make me afraid with the mention of those names, don't bother. They are dead. And I thought it was taboo for Indians to mention the names of the dead for fear of their ghosts coming back."

"As you said, I am not full-blood. I follow no man's path but my own." He spoke the lie calmly but inside seethed for saying it. He walked a path forced on him by those men who hunted him. And he would do well never to forget it.

While he spoke, Sarah still stared at his eyes. They seemed to have no necessity to blink, because he stared right back at her without movement. She came to with a start. Those steadfast brown eyes had held her attention far too long. She shrugged.

"Answer me or not. It really doesn't matter."

"Rio. Rio Santee."

Was that a true caution she heard behind his whisper of his name? Sarah couldn't be sure. "Rio is Spanish for *river*." His smirking smile was back, and she wished she had not spoken. She was standing in her bedroom in the middle of the night with a drenched, dangerous half-breed, commenting on his first name? Shock. That was all she could blame it on.

No, that was not entirely true. There was something uniquely formidable about Rio Santee with his high-cheekboned face, smooth of hair, as most Indians were, the straight brown hair held by the red cloth band tied Apache-style around his head, and those narrow, staring eyes the color of cinnamon.

Her judgment went beyond the sheer physical size

of him, though that was enough to intimidate, with the way the drenched shirt, cloth belt and pants outlined his strong, lean, muscled body.

Sarah was not sure of the right word—a stillness perhaps—whatever it was, it set him apart from anyone she had ever met.

She had to take back control. She had lived alone a few years before her marriage when she lost her grandmother to illness and her father to a storm such as the one that swept the land tonight. And then there were the best forgotten years of her marriage with Judd Westfall without having any say.

Until the end. She had found the courage at the end when it was too late.

Sarah closed her eyes briefly and wrapped her arms around her waist as if she could contain the painful memory. In the hollow pit of her stomach the too-familiar acid spewed its burning path up to her throat. She swallowed repeatedly, but the burning remained.

Yes, she had regained control over her life at the end. She had needed to be strong enough to go on living when all she had wanted to do was die.

But death had not wanted to claim her. She had slowly built a new life for herself, one she had shared with Mary and Catherine. Having control was the solid cornerstone of this life. She would not allow anything or anyone to disturb the peace she had found. It had been too hard won. For these few minutes, lost in her thoughts, she felt the old raw and empty feeling of helplessness.

Never again. It was a vow made and paid for in blood. She would die before she broke it.

"You said your name as if it should mean something to me. It doesn't. There are too many loose renegades—"

"Yes, there are some who call me that."

Sarah didn't want to be drawn in, she didn't want to know him, or care, even if some of her sympathy went to the Apaches forced to live where little could survive.

"I don't want to know. I've gone several times to the reservations with the Ladies' Aid sewing circle to bring clothing. I've seen the hollow eyes, the shrunken, starved bodies. We've complained to the army and to the Indian agent. I know I've looked at the remains of a once-proud warrior race whose most heinous crime is to roam and hunt the lands of their fathers. But I've seen firsthand the atrocities that have been committed by both sides. Both are wrong, and yet both are right. It is a question without an answer. The problem is broken trust, and violence, and will likely end that way."

She could read nothing in his stare or the hard set of his mouth. Nor did he respond.

"Look, you said you needed food. I've never turned away a hungry man. Take what you want. As for shelter, you can stay in—"

"No. You will not do the telling of how it will be. It is against the harmony of life for a woman to act as a man." Rio had done some assessing of his own and added it to the little he knew of the widow woman who bought wild stock from whites and Indians alike, paying fair prices, then Indian-gentling the horses to the saddle while living alone. He frowned and searched his memory for some talk that there had been other widows here not long ago. But that did not concern him.

Sarah cast a quick look toward the window. Water fell from the roof in solid gray sheets. Thunder shook the house as if to remind her what waited outside. Wind whistled through the cracks of the old two-story frame house.

"You should have let me finish. Take the food, and you can wait out the storm in the barn. It's dry there and warm if you light the woodstove in the tack room. I'll get you some blankets. You need to dry off. I'm sure you don't want to get sick and linger here longer than necessary."

Head high, she walked to the doorway. He stepped aside to allow her to pass. At any moment she expected to hear his order to stop, or to have him physically do it. He didn't come after her and said nothing as she went out into the hallway landing to the linen closet. For a wild moment she toyed with the idea of racing down the stairs and fleeing. But to where? The barn. She could. Her mare would ride out into the storm if Sarah asked it of her. But then? The roadway was flooded with every creek and stream, and the rivers overflowing their banks. It was the last news she had had.

And he would come after her. No, she had to deal

with him with reason, not show how afraid she was. Either that, or she had to disable him.

That still left the problem of where to go.

Sarah opened the closet door and reached up to the shelf where she kept the spare blankets. Only there weren't any. She searched for the quilts. They were gone, too.

The noise! The sound that woke her earlier. It wasn't the storm at all. Then she wasn't sure, but now...Sarah whirled and found Rio standing in the doorway of her bedroom, watching her.

"You've already taken the blankets." The import of her accusation hit her. "You stole up here earlier and took them. Where are they? What did you do with them? Who..." She had to stop and swallow against the sudden dryness of her throat. "Who else is here with you?"

He stalked her. There was no other way Sarah could describe the pantherlike walk of his coming toward her.

She held her place, but not with any great surge of bravery. It was the fear that he was not alone that shook her.

# *Chapter Four*

"Answer me!" Panicked and shrill, her voice rose on the last. She despised herself for giving way to a new fear.

When had he unbuttoned his shirt so that it was almost opened to his narrow waist? Dangling to mid-chest from a chain worn around his neck was an intricately worked silver disk set with chunks of turquoise, and from a piece of rawhide hung a small leather pouch. A medicine bag, she thought.

With mounting anxiety, she willed her heart to settle down and stop drumming against her ribs. Her palms were damp. She scrubbed them against the sides of her robe. A cold sweat broke out over her body and that she could do nothing about.

He reached out and slammed the closet door closed.

"W-what are...you...oh, Lord, what are you doing?"

He spun around and pinned her between the door and his unyielding body. She stared at his lips as he closed his hand around her throat just under her chin and bent his head down low over hers.

"What is your fertile white woman's mind thinking that I am going to do?"

"I...don't...my mind thinks the same way any white or Indian woman's would when threatened by the likes of you."

She turned her head away and he let her, but he did not let her go. If anything, he moved closer, lewdly pressing himself full against her, imprisoning her against the door with his hardness and his strength.

Sarah drew a sharp breath. She squeezed her eyes shut, unable to stop the whimper escaping her lips before she bit down hard on the lower one. His long, tapering fingers stroked her throat, while she was bathed in fear and humiliation.

She was afraid to move, afraid to breathe deeply, afraid, too, that he would stop his fingers moving up and down in a sensual rhythm on her throat and touch her in far more vulnerable places.

"It has been a long, long time since I have been with a woman. The territory jail does not offer much comfort for the likes of me." He said the last with a mocking taunt for her earlier words. His fingers slid down the center parting of her robe. He toyed with the top button on her shirt. She held her breath. His face was too close. His shoulder-length wet hair touched her cheek. She felt his breath warming her skin. The button popped open. She released her breath only to inhale sharply, hating him for forcing her to the intimacy of breathing the very air he expelled.

"Take this warning to heart. Behave, *iszáñ,* or you will set my mind on a path you would never willingly walk."

She heard the silken sound of his voice and then realized what he had said. She looked at him, at those intense eyes of his. Their gazes clashed, both a meeting of strong wills, and a small male and female battle of tempers. The moments stretched as they took each other's measure, probing beyond for the weaknesses and the strengths.

Suddenly he backed away from her. Sarah was so relieved she almost collapsed on the floor.

"We understand each other now."

She hadn't the strength to argue with him. But she didn't understand anything about him.

He threatened her, verbally and by his forceful masculine presence, and yet, when he had her well and truly cornered, vulnerable as only a woman alone can be, he suddenly backed off.

Sarah had to believe what he said. He wanted food, rest and shelter from the storm, and then he would leave. She wanted so badly to believe that he would not hurt her.

Could she believe anything he told her?

She needed to get away from him. The violence of the storm, her mad dash for freedom, the incredibly tense minutes that had just passed, all had drained her. She had amassed confused impressions about this man. There was no time to sort them out.

She rubbed her arms. "The others with you, are they all in the barn?"

Rio looked away before he answered. His sons were safe. Warm and dry, their hunger satisfied, they had fallen immediately asleep. It was then that he had left them for the second time to return to the house.

"Of course they are," Sarah answered herself. "Where else could they be." If she had run to the barn she would have blundered into them. She didn't even know how many there were. Lord, help her survive this night.

"You'll need dry clothes. There are some in the wardrobe in the spare bedroom. My cousin's husband is about your size. He left some things there."

Rio smiled grimly. Her voice was softer, less steady than it had been at first. She *was* frightened of him. That much he had accomplished.

Dry clothes. It sounded good. But what could he do with her while he changed? Those minutes in her room when he could not turn from the sight of her smooth, probably sweet smelling skin, were all the torment he would visit upon himself.

Part of him wished she were old and ugly. He did not want the problem of dealing with this strong-willed woman. He did not want any more regrets, or guilt, or the complication of being responsible for another's life. The odds of being followed here were in his favor. The rain wiped all tracks away. But those men were still out there, still waiting to kill him.

And Coyote was still up to his tricks. She brushed by him to get the lamp from her room, and left him with the scent of rain-washed hair and skin. Rio watched her enter the room across the hall. He did not immediately follow her.

He had to think of his sons. The very fact that he needed the reminder set his teeth on edge. Rio entered the room. As soon as he had cleared the door, he closed it behind him.

Sarah spun around. "What are you doing?"

"I'll accept your offer to make coffee after I have changed. You did not think I had forgotten your rifle is down there?"

The slight widening of her eyes, the tightening of her lips before she turned away told him he had guessed right. A sly little fox to be carefully watched. The thought of having to guard her, with the toll exhaustion had taken, was almost enough to make him think of quitting the house. He had brought out enough food to keep him and his sons for a few days. There were good horses to ride once the storm ended. She could not go anywhere.

But he did not leave. He took the shirt and pants she held out to him. He watched her walk to the window and stand with her back to him. The room held a bed stripped of linens and a dresser where the lamp rested.

Rio remained where he was and pulled off his shirt. He unwound the cloth belt, squeezing the water from it, then set it on the floor in front of him with his knife on top.

He knelt on one knee to untie his moccasin, all the while keeping his eyes on her back. It would not surprise him if she whirled around and attacked him. For her sake, he hoped she would not do anything so foolish.

Sarah stood as motionless as a statue, staring into the window's glass, where his every move was reflected. She knew she should close her eyes as he peeled his shirt off his shoulders and shrugged out of it. There was no hair on his chest. The brown skin was stretched tightly over curved muscles that looked incredibly hard. His nipples were small and dark. The skin of his belly was taut. His hair brushed his shoulders before he bent down and she lost sight of him. Then she closed her eyes, listening to the whisper of cloth falling to the floor. She was overcome by a wave of dizziness and gripped the windowsill to keep from swaying.

She should be insulted, outraged by his daring to undress in the same room as her. She thought she had been overcome by his masculine presence before, but this was an assault on every feminine sense she had.

She could no more stop herself from looking at his reflection than she could stop breathing. His limbs were long and leanly muscled. The smooth skin appeared almost bronze, but so alive, warm and touchable. She took several deep, steadying breaths.

"Does my nakedness offend you, *iszán?* Surely you have seen your husband? Or is it that I am Apache that upsets you?"

Sarah turned around to face him, stung by his mocking voice, but words failed her. She could not make a sound as he drew the cotton soft denim pants over his long legs, and calmly, as if she were not there, began to button the fly. He was of a height with Rafe McCade, Mary's husband, but Rio Santee stressed every well-worn seam of both the pants he wore and the shirt he put on.

"Stop putting words to my thoughts. You can't see into my mind. You don't know what I'm thinking."

"You are wrong, widow woman. A man has only to gaze into your eyes to know the thoughts behind them."

"Then look into my eyes and see that I am a woman who judges no man by the color of his skin or his beliefs. There are good and bad among all peoples. Even among men and women. I judge a person by their acts."

"And there I stand condemned in your eyes."

It wasn't a question, and Sarah did not try to answer him. "I am going down to the kitchen."

She issued both daring and defiance in the lift of her chin, in the way she pushed herself away from the window and started across the room toward him and the closed door.

His gaze rose from her bare feet washed as clean as her hair of mud due to his carrying her through the slashing rain. *And her body,* Coyote whispered in his mind.

Rio gave a rough shake and yanked the door open. He stood aside and followed her with the lamp.

Sarah reminded herself that she was not going to lose her life. She moved without hurry to stoke the fire in the woodstove, light the coal-oil fixture over the table and then make coffee. From pumping the water to measuring out the ground beans, she was aware of the way Rio Santee watched her every move.

Her nerves were drawn taut by the tension between them. She stopped counting the times she went to the window and stared outside to where the rain had slackened, but the wind still whipped the trees in gusts. She couldn't seem to get warm and wished she had taken the time to put on socks or her slippers.

The coffee began to perk. "Won't your friends want something hot to drink, too? My barn is dry and there is plenty of hay, but they must be cold."

"You forgot to remind me of the blankets I have stolen for them."

"I didn't forget."

"No. A woman like you would not forget."

"Stop saying things as if you know me. You don't." She went to the cupboard and took down two cups, then looked over her shoulder at him. He still held the now-empty single shot rifle, having grabbed it when she entered the kitchen. "I made the offer, what you do is your concern."

"You are generous to think of their comfort. I will fetch them." Rio started for the door.

"Take the slicker. It won't keep you completely dry, but it will help."

After he left, she glanced at the closed door, wondering why she had made the suggestion. Why should she care? She ran to the window, but could barely make out his staggering walk against the wind while the water still rushed through the open yard.

What had possessed her to think of the others? He

was going to bring them into the house. Wasn't one enough to deal with? And her without a weapon.

She rubbed her forehead. Think. There had to be something she could use to protect herself. Her gaze lit on the cupboard's drawer. She gave a last look at the window, then hurried across the kitchen.

How long had he been gone? She was wasting time. Yet she hesitated before she reached into the drawer and withdrew the thin-bladed boning knife.

Sarah stared at the knife. She held it tight, trying to think of where she could conceal it yet still be able to reach the weapon easily.

Would she have the courage to use it on him or one of the others if the need arose?

"Lord, I don't want to make such a decision."

She could not say what alerted her that Rio was back just a second before the door behind her opened. He came with the wind, sweeping a chilling dampness into the kitchen.

Sarah whipped her hand gripping the knife down to her side. The folds of her robe hid it from his sight as she turned around.

Rio pushed the door closed with his body. He carried a blanket and quilt-wrapped body. At least she thought it was a body. From the depths of the bundle came a frightened sound. She heard Rio's whisper in what she thought was Apache to his squirming burden. The blanket fell back.

Sarah gasped. A young child's face appeared between the covering folds. Both her hands rose to her chest. The child's eyes widened with fear, warning her that the child, as well as Rio, had seen the knife.

"A child?" she whispered. "You made me think..." The knife fell to the floor with a clatter.

# Chapter Five

Long moments stretched out before Sarah forced herself to look at Rio. His face was completely impassive, but not his eyes. She stared into them, reading too much, understanding too little. A promise of violence, a plea for compassion. A hundred questions clamored to be asked.

Sarah couldn't seem to summon the voice to ask even one. She couldn't utter a sound. The very last thing she wanted was for the child to be caught in the middle. Yet he was just that. And it was a boy she saw as he pushed the blanket down to his shoulders.

"I'm so sorry I frightened you. The storm made me nervous. Are you afraid of storms, too? You must be cold and hungry."

"Cold, yes. Not hungry. I ate ham and cheese and corn bread and a big piece of apple pie. I even drank the warm milk from your cow. Lucas would not eat the ham. He does not like it. He had the biggest piece of pie. He did not want to come and get warm. Father said he could stay with the horses. Lucas likes the horses."

"Father?" Sarah's question had a choked quality.

Rio placed one large hand on his small son's shoulder. "This is my youngest son, Gabriel. He is not shy with strangers."

"No, but he is cold." Sarah couldn't bite back the accusation in her tone. She was furious with Rio Santee. He broke into her house, threatened her, hunted her like prey, and made her aware of him as a man as no other had done since Judd died almost four years ago. Had he come seeking shelter for himself and his son, she didn't believe she would have denied him entry. But there was this other one...this Lucas.

"And Lucas? Who is he?"

The questions were directed at Gabriel, but Rio answered her.

"My oldest boy. He has little trust for me and less for white women."

"That alone would prove he is your son. Are there more?"

"No more. Just the three of us."

"Well, you can't leave him out in the barn. And you might as well return what is left from your raid on my pantry." She noted that her remark surprised him. It gave her little satisfaction. She might appear calm, but the questions were multiplying until her head ached. There was no time for them now.

"Come sit closer to the stove, Gabriel. You'll get warm in no time." As Sarah spoke she bent down to pick up the knife.

"Are you gonna scalp us while we sleep?"

"What!"

"Scalp us with your knife," the boy said.

Sarah recoiled. She looked at the knife in her hand, then at the boy. She shook her head, disbelieving what she knew she had heard. Rio's gaze offered her no comfort. She looked again at the boy.

"No, I won't scalp you or anyone. See, I'm putting the knife back into the drawer."

"The scalp hunters can get you if they find you alone. Sometimes there are lots of them, and they take many to kill. They sell the scalps for money. The…the Mexicans pay bounty. They don't care if it's a little boy. The mission lady said that's why they cut our hair. Lucas said she lied. They do it so we will all forget what band the boys are from." Gabriel looked at Sarah with large, dark, solemn eyes. "Are you like the mission women?"

"I should hope not, Gabriel. I wouldn't want to be like them. They don't sound like women I even want to know."

"But you do know women like them," Rio said.

Sarah didn't answer him.

"Lucas said they cannot help themselves. He said they learn these things with their mother's milk."

"Gabriel, enough."

Sarah was less bothered by the boy's frank talk. After Catherine had married last summer, Sarah had kept little Ramon working around the place. The boy often spoke frankly to her of things he heard and saw around town.

The child tilted his head back to look up at his scowling father. "But Father, I want to know how it can be. I asked Lucas. He said it is true. He did not know how it happens. Sometimes Lucas tells me things I do not understand. He said I will if I ever grew up."

"You will grow up to manhood, Gabriel. Your brother still has many years of his own to see himself fully grown. I will speak to him about these things he teaches you. For now we will speak no more of it."

Gabriel's smile and the softening of Rio's lips that made his face vitally warm and alive as he shared this private moment with his son shut her out. She envied him. She would never know such moments.

But Sarah puzzled over the child's remarks. All were about what Lucas told him. Where had Rio been that his sons were at a mission school?

*"The territory jail does not offer much comfort for the likes of me."*

How could she have forgotten Rio's words? Why didn't she question why he'd been in jail?

*Because you lost every smidgen of sense and only reacted to the man.*

She closed her eyes and once more experienced the feel of his fingers sliding on her throat, his mocking taunt filling her ears. A shiver coursed through her, and she saw the parting of her robe as he had bent his head nearer. She could almost feel the brush of his wet hair against her cheek, almost taste the sweet rain, his breath intimately warming her skin, the alarm of the button opening beneath his touch.

She hoped now, as she had not then, that he'd been unaware of her tightly drawn nipples pushing against the soft wool shirt.

She excused the physical reaction because of the cold, and the very real, dangerous threat of the man. It had nothing to do with being alone, and lonely. She refused to admit to any hunger for the passion she had once tasted.

She was a survivor. She only needed that to remind herself that she had lived through a marriage to Judd Westfall until his drinking, gambling and cruelty left her unable to feel. There was no guilt over his death. Not for him. Never for him.

She could live through this, too.

Rio looked up at the broken breath she drew and saw the distant look in her eyes as she opened them.

He knew with a primitive certainty that she was reliving those moments when he had imprisoned her in the upstairs hall.

He wished to all the gods of his people that he could wipe away the memory.

He never should have touched her.

But he had. And he remembered. Too well. The unwanted heat that licked over his body when he touched the smooth, bare skin of her throat. The feel beneath his fingers of her racing blood and hard-beating pulse.

His own pulse had quickened, and heat surged in his blood.

The woman scent of her stayed with him. Sweet

rain, and the faint spice of sage rising from her clothing.

He thought of the Appaloosa stallion and the blooded mares filling the stalls in the barn. Once the Appaloosa was bred and traded only by the Nez Percé tribe, a horse worthy of a war chief. Yet this woman, facing him with a passionate defiance, had gentled the wildness of the horse without breaking his spirit.

That wildness and strength of hers called to him on a primitive level he could not and would not deny.

But he fought against its lure.

He should have caught her mouth beneath his as he'd been tempted to do.

Then he would not look at her mouth and wonder what she tasted like.

Gabriel's noisy yawn and shift in the chair drew Rio's attention. He tightened his grip on his son's shoulder.

The move drew Sarah's gaze to Rio's skinned knuckles. The distraction helped turn her aside from probing her past. Unexpectedly her throat closed around a grief that she had never given way to. At first she could not bear it, then her grief became a habit.

"You've hurt yourself," she said.

Rio looked down. "It is nothing."

Gabriel sat up and turned to look, too. "That is when they shot—"

"Gabriel."

Sarah met the child's bewildered look. "Who are they?" Her hand tightened over the knot of her robe's sash. "More surprises?"

"None that need concern you."

"If I have to worry about being shot in my own home I'd say you're very much mistaken. But I won't argue with a man with such a stubborn chin. You'd better see to your other son. I'll stoke the fire in the parlor."

She started for the door, not caring if he agreed or not. Without turning around, she asked Gabriel if he wanted to help.

"No. My son will wait for me here."

"He is a child who needs a warm bed."

"What do you know of a child's needs?"

She swayed and grabbed hold of the door frame for support. Had he thrust a knife in her the wound would have been less painful. She stood there, unable to move and, for long minutes, unable to answer him. Where she found the strength to turn and face him, she didn't know.

"You're right. I know absolutely nothing about the needs of a child."

The emptiness in her voice brought an unexpected ache to Rio. He stifled the urge to call out to her, to whisper some meaningless word of comfort, because he was sure she would reject it.

He would have. He had.

She disappeared down the hall.

He spun around and went out in the rain.

It didn't matter what the widow thought. Or what she felt. She could not matter to him.

But she did.

* * *

Sarah awoke to an encompassing grayness. For a few moments she didn't realize that she was in her own room. There was no way to tell the time. All she remembered was stoking the fire in the parlor before exhaustion had swept over her.

Sleep brought merciful relief from her thoughts.

She snuggled deeper beneath the blankets, unwilling to think about last night.

But at some point Rio had carried her upstairs.

How could she have slept through it?

She watched the raindrops race down the window-pane. The steady drumming of the rain on the roof held less of the storm's fury. The howling winds of last night were reduced to an occasional gust that rattled the windowpane. It seemed to signal her to leave her warm bed, for chores awaited.

Sarah dressed hurriedly, drawers and camisole, a pair of black cotton hose, brown duck pants and a blue wool flannel overshirt. The shirt was new, a treat for herself at fifty cents since the Hudspeths started carrying more ready-made clothing.

She remembered leaving her boots down in the kitchen. Despite the scent of wood smoke drifting up from the parlor, the house was still damp and chill. She listened near the door but heard no noise. Likely they were still sleeping.

In the minutes she took to brush out the tangles in her hair and rebraid its thick, straight blackness into a single plait, Sarah made a decision. With her hair as tightly contained as her emotions, she resolved to treat the presence of Rio Santee and his sons as stranded

travelers. Unwanted houseguests, but guests neverthe-
less.

The mirror reflected the old haunting in her shadowed eyes. She had not cried over Rio's cruel words.
Nor would she. She rarely cried anymore. All that mattered was that her secret remain safe.

"Strong Sarah," she whispered. "You've been
there for Mary, Catherine and countless others since
Judd died. Now be strong for yourself."

And she would be, in spite of Rio's threats. The
taunting Apache half-breed had to know that the presence of his sons cost him a measure of her fear.

*But only a measure, Sarah. There is still the threat
of the man himself.*

# Chapter Six

The invading dampness made the wood stairs creak. Even the air Sarah breathed held a faint odor of mildew. The whole frame of the house was swollen from the continuous rains like an ancient crone with creaking joints.

She stepped into the parlor. The quilts and blankets that Rio and his sons used for their bedding had been folded and neatly piled on the settee. The fire blazed with warmth and cut wood had been stacked around the fireplace to dry off before it would be needed.

"A neat and thoughtful houseguest," she murmured.

Out in the hallway she felt the welcoming warmth from the stove along with the aroma of freshly brewed coffee.

"A guest who certainly made himself at home."

She paused in the doorway, half-expecting to confront Rio, but to her surprise she faced the man in the guise of a boy. Older than Gabriel, but the strong facial resemblance to the father was undeniable.

"You're Lucas," she said. "I'm Sarah Westfall."

He was seated at the table, facing her while he idly toyed with a spoon. An empty coffee cup was set to one side. The coal-oil fixture was lit against the pervading gloom of the overcast sky. The boy nodded at her but did not speak.

Sarah helped herself to the coffee. She took a few sips, leaning back against the dry sink.

"Where is your father?"

"Outside."

"But it's still raining." She took another look at him. His short hair, darker than Rio's, was wet.

"What is he doing out there?"

"Digging a trench around the house to help the water drain off."

"A kind and thoughtful thing to do." She took a swallow of the rapidly cooling coffee, warning herself to have patience. Talkative he wasn't.

"And your brother? Where is he?"

"Hunting eggs in your barn."

Sarah eyed the boy's muddy shoes near the door. Her slicker, the one she had offered last night to Rio, hung on its hook. Water still dripped to the rag rug below. She judged from the tired slump of Lucas's shoulders that he'd been out there digging with his father.

"I'd bet you could do with a hot meal."

The spoon he had been playing with hit the table.

"Don't want no charity from you."

"I'm not offering charity, Lucas. You've worked hard. And I could do with a hot meal myself."

Sarah glanced out the window. *Lord, give me lots of patience. This boy has a barrelful of chips on his thin shoulders.* She saw how the water ran in the shallow gullies in the yard. Mud was churned from the house to the barn. She couldn't see the wood slabs she had laid down as a path. A light rain still fell.

"Maybe the rain will slack off or stop altogether," she said.

"Not likely. Over to the north there's thunderheads piled high. 'Less a wind blows them off, it will rain for days."

Sarah finished her coffee and set the cup in the sink. "I'll see to my stock then I'll make you the biggest breakfast you ever had."

"Stock's fed."

"Well then, thank you, Lucas. Gabriel mentioned that you like horses. I do, too."

"Wasn't me. He took care of them."

"Busy man, your father." The remark was made more to herself, but Lucas heard her.

"He had a ranchero. Real fine place, too. Saddle-broke wild stock. He knows what he's about. Don't worry."

Sarah heard the words of reassurance, but she was forced to listen to the underlying resentment in his voice. This time she sensed the resentment was directed at his father.

"I wasn't worried. But you said he had a place— what happened to it?"

He looked up at her then as she moved closer to the table. He stared at her with intense, dark brown eyes.

"What do you think happens when an Apache half-breed claims to own land that whites want?"

"I don't know, Lucas. That's why I asked you."

Sarah sensed he wasn't going to answer her. He shrugged his shoulders, his mouth, so like the shape of his father's, tightened into a flat line. He looked away from her.

"They wanted the water and the land. They took it. They take everything."

"You're awfully young to condemn all whites by the despicable acts of a few, Lucas."

"I don't know what that word means. Sounds like something ugly. As ugly as the men that took me and my brother away to the mission school and those do-gooder mission ladies."

"I can't apologize for something I haven't done. But I have learned that you can't judge—"

"Don't preach to me. I had enough of that."

"And I won't. But this is my house, and you will not raise your voice to me while you're a guest here."

"I don't want to be here. I don't want to be with him."

"By him I assume you mean your father?"

"Yes."

Sarah decided to back off. She was learning more than she wanted to about Rio's problems with his son. She wasn't about to get emotionally involved with them.

She moved quickly from pantry to table assembling bowls and ingredients for making biscuits, flapjacks and corn bread. With a smooth economy of motion, she filled the kettle with water, added dried beans, then set the kettle on the back burner. An onion and a few dried chili peppers went into the same pot.

Sarah measured out flour into two bowls. She smiled at Lucas. "I know you like corn bread. I'll make that next."

"Who told you that?"

"Gabriel. From the amount he claimed to eat, I guess you traveled a far piece before the storm drove you to seek shelter here."

"You asking or telling?"

Sarah took a deep breath and once more prayed for additional patience. "I'm asking, Lucas."

"We came a piece."

"I hope you gave your horses some grain. It had to be hard riding through the storm."

"Didn't have any."

"Oh?" Sarah added buttermilk to the biscuit mix. "What happened? Did they steal them or shoot them?"

"They?" Lucas asked with all the wariness of a cornered wolf.

"Gabriel mentioned that they—whoever they are— shot at your father."

"My little brother talks too much."

"A trait you don't share. If you're in trouble I could help."

*Sarah!* The warning came too late. What had happened to her resolve not to get involved?

Sarah gave up using the spoon on the thickened biscuit mix. She plunged her hands into the bowl to work the dough. Not once did she look at Lucas while he appeared to mull over her offer.

"I'm wise to your tricks. They tried to get me to say things at the mission school. I wouldn't do it."

"Lucas, I really meant my offer to help."

His chair scraped back, and he mumbled something about work.

Sarah watched him stomp into his muddy shoes, ignore the slicker and slip out the back door.

The thin shirt he wore was no protection against the rawness of the day. Just those few seconds when the door was opened chilled the kitchen.

She didn't know if she should go after him or leave him be.

The thought of hearing Rio repeat his cruel words was enough to set her to work with a vengeance.

The kitchen had been Mary's province while she lived there. But now that Sarah was alone, she rarely cooked large quantities of anything.

She tried not to take out her frustration on the dough. Overworked biscuit dough made for hard biscuits. Once they were rolled out and shaped, she set the tray in the oven to bake. Minutes later, the corn bread pans followed.

She wasn't much for baking fancy cakes or pies, but she knew from Ramon that he loved cookies. Weren't all little boys the same when it came to having sweets?

There were slim pickings in the pantry.

"Oatmeal, dried applies and raisins. And honey." The honey was a hoarded treat, as was the small supply of sugarloaf. Without Mary's sewing and herbs to trade, or Catherine's eggs, Sarah had to watch how she spent her money. She had almost half of the five thousand dollars that Rafe had given her against the debt he felt he had owed Judd. Two Tennessee-bred mares and the prize Appaloosa stallion, as well as repairs to the roof, had taken the other half.

But she had known that building a herd of good breeding stock would take time and money.

During her trips back and forth to the pantry, she noticed that the wood box was filled to overflowing. Another reason to thank the thoughtful Mr. Santee. But it served as a reminder to check on the fire in the parlor.

Once there, Sarah heard the rain coming down harder. She took three of the fire-warmed blankets back to the kitchen with her. The three of them would be wet and cold when they came in.

She worked faster, trying to keep at bay the questions crowding her mind. But the conversation with Lucas—if she could call it that—left too many gaps.

Rio had had a ranch where he saddle-broke wild horses. It went a long way toward explaining how he had heard of her. She had been buying green-broke stock for almost two years and schooling them for either cutting or riding horses. With the town's population swelling, there was a growing demand for good horses.

And if he knew about her, his ranchero couldn't have been located too far away.

Sarah laughed softly. "How far is too far in the

territories? He could have settled up in Colorado, or south in Texas, even farther west than the Arizona territory.''

The biscuits came out of the oven, and the cookies went in. The dry ingredients for flapjacks waited for the small pitcher of buttermilk to be added.

Every few minutes she checked the window but there was no sign of Rio or his sons.

Sarah knew she should be the one out there. They were her horses. It was her land.

She poured out another cup of coffee for herself.

She sipped the black brew. The mere thought of getting into an argument with that square-jawed man was enough to keep her inside and away from him.

If he had been alone, she'd be tempted to lock him out. Not that locking the doors had kept him out of the house last night.

What was it that Catherine had said to her? Something about both she and Mary opening the door to strangers and finding love?

"Foolish notion. Thought so then, and even more so now."

The questions started coming again. She knew he'd been in jail. His son claimed that white men took his ranch. Had he killed one of them? Who had taken the boys to a mission school?

And who were *they* that shot at them?

Were men after him? Was she harboring a wanted killer? There were moments last night when she could swear he was capable of violence. And yet she had to temper those thoughts with the thoughtful things he'd done today.

The very least she could do was feed them. And hot soup was the best thing she could think of. He had returned both the half-wheel of cheese and the remains of the smoked ham. She sliced off all the meat she could from the bone, fetched potatoes, dried peas, onions and rice from the pantry. Two jars of canned tomatoes and dried herbs—a few of the many gifts Mary and Rafe had given her for Christmas—were all she needed for the soup.

"Now for the kettle."

Sarah dragged a chair into the pantry. She wedged it tight against the shelves. The kettle was stored on the top shelf since she had no need of the large kettle when cooking for herself.

She climbed up and reached for the heavy cast-iron pot. Rio grabbed the kettle with his left hand. His right arm snaked around Sarah's hips as she wobbled on the chair. One of her hands grabbed hold of the shelf and the other clamped on his shoulder to keep herself from falling.

"What did you think—"

"What I thought doesn't matter, Mr. Santee. You almost made me fall, yanking the kettle out of my hands like that."

Sarah glared down at him. If she moved an inch to the left his face would be flush with her breast.

His shoulder-length hair was plastered to his head. Water dripped from the cloth tied around his forehead. His mud-strewn clothing was soddenly molded to his muscular body. His boots were caked with mud. An earthy, masculine scent filled the small pantry.

Sarah told herself there wasn't one reason his appearance should make her stomach react with a funny little flip-flop.

She snatched her hand from his shoulder and clung to the shelf. She was uncomfortable with his ease in cutting through her guard. Not only did he make her totally aware of his dominating male presence, but he made her aware that she was smaller and female.

It was a primitive feeling that rose from deep inside her. She knew it for what it was, something lost within the first year of her marriage. A feeling she had denied, buried and refused to acknowledge.

Feminine need.

She met his gaze, stunned by the blast of guilt that swept through her. Here she was, safe and dry, while he had been out battling the elements on her behalf.

And from the sound of the rolling thunder and rising wind, they were in for another night's battering.

The fact that she had never asked him to do it was beside the point. The fact that he never asked for permission was pushed aside, too.

"You confuse me," she said, clearing her throat of its huskiness. "Last night you came into my home, threatened my life and made me afraid. Today you're taking over my chores, making free with my home, digging a trench. You're acting like a...like a neighbor, friend, hired hand, what? I don't understand you."

"You are a plain-speaking woman."

"Lies never served anyone. I can't abide a liar. You know what I said was the truth."

"Would you have given me shelter if I had knocked on your door?"

"You alone? I would have offered the barn, but with your sons, my home."

"My sons make you feel safe?"

"Yes."

"And I do not."

# Chapter Seven

His steady, probing gaze holding her own, even with the evidence of fatigue in those cinnamon-colored eyes, robbed her of the will to lie, the will to fight.

"No."

It was a breathless, soft admission that Sarah wished to recall the moment she spoke.

The skin over his high cheekbones seemed to be stretched so tight she thought it might split. His eyes moved over her. Intense. Heated. Weighing and judging, while she held her breath.

He looked at her for an agonizingly long time. Sarah couldn't bear watching his eyes move over her, so she closed her own. Heat banded her where his arm curved over her hips. A heat that spread inside despite the cool damp coming from his wet shirt.

Her breathing was shallow. She feared taking a deeper breath. His nostrils flared slightly as if he scented her fear.

"Your hair has a beauty all its own. Black and cool and sleek as a horse's mane, but more like silk."

She braced herself for his touch. It never came. But her nerves were strung tight being confined in this small space with him.

"No need for you to keep holding me. I'm steady now."

"Perhaps I am holding on to steady myself." He held her gaze with his for a few seconds more. "Stay here. I'll come back and help you down."

He left with the kettle. Sarah sagged against the wooden shelves. He might be out of her sight, but she still felt the imprint of his hand on her hip. She climbed down from the chair, only then becoming aware of the murmuring voices in the kitchen. His sons had been there the whole time.

She gripped the back of the chair, then roused herself to get out of there before he came back.

The boys' blanket-wrapped bodies were disappearing down the hall into the parlor when she looked.

Rio was filling the kettle with water. By the door lay a pile of the boys' muddy clothing and shoes. Outside, the dark wind howled, bringing a gloom stealing over the land as rain lashed the house.

One deep breath sent Sarah scurrying to the stove. She grabbed the oven's handle and yanked the door open.

She cried out both from the heat beneath her hand and from the sight of crisp, golden brown corn bread and cookies.

Rio caught hold of her arm and lifted her hand from the oven's door. "You burned—"

"Never mind me. Get the pans and trays out before they are burned."

Sarah pulled away. She went to the sink and tried pumping water with her left hand. Her palm was red and stinging as a few dribbles of water touched her skin.

Once more he came to her aid. He pulled her hand away from the pump. "No water. The cold is the worse thing to do."

He bent his head, breathing deeply and blowing his breath over her palm. "If you were frostbitten you would not want to warm too quickly. You cause more pain that way. It is the same for a burn that is cooled too fast."

A trembling warmth coursed up her spine as he continued blowing softly for a few minutes. She seemed to be on the verge of some discovery, but Sarah, being Sarah, backed away from it. She blamed it on the upheaval he had brought into her life.

The gentleness with which he held her hand was at odds with the hard look of the man. He worked the pump, then held her hand beneath the water. There was hardly any sting.

Sarah tried to draw her hand from him, but he wouldn't let go. She barely managed to stand still as he dried her hand then studied her palm.

"Do you have something to put on this?"

"There's no need. It feels fine. Thank you for what you did." Once more she attempted to pull away. Once more he held on to her.

"Do you have something?"

"Back shelf in the pantry. A small brown crock. It's a healing salve my cousin Mary makes. But really, I don't need it."

The last was said to his back. Sarah looked at her hand. So much fuss. When was the last time…she couldn't remember the last act of kindness from a man. A stranger, that is. Rafe no longer qualified. And if it had been Judd… Inwardly Sarah laughed with bitterness. Judd would not have noticed, or if he did, he would have ignored her.

She did not want reminders of Judd. Not here. This was her home. Never his.

Rio's return to her side was as silent as his leaving. She focused on his square, firm jaw. A very stubborn man.

She shivered, one of those chilling ones that raised goose bumps. Catherine always said someone walked on your grave when it happened. If Judd were alive he'd take great pleasure walking over hers.

Rio turned her hand palm up. With a sure, deft touch he spread a thin layer of the salve on her palm. The faint scent of pine rose between them.

Sarah thought of his remark about her hair being silky. She could say the same about his lashes. They were long, the same light brown as his hair, but with lighter tips that curled upward. She felt foolish noticing such a thing about him. She stepped back, physically and emotionally. Her boots grated on the gritty floor.

"Leave it unwrapped. Your hand will heal faster. And I'll clean the floor."

"I...I talked to Lucas," she blurted out, stopping him in his tracks. He did not turn around, did not make a sound, but she saw the rigid set of his shoulders.

"He told me about your ranch. How you lost it. Are those the men who followed you? Did they shoot at you? I need to know. We have the law now in Hillsboro."

The words burst forth like a dam giving way. "I have a right to know if they'll come here. I have a right to know why you were in jail. I want to know why they'd even try to kill you if they already have your land."

When she finished she sucked in a deep breath, but felt as if all the air were gone. There was such a dangerous stillness to him that she backed away although he had not moved.

"I have a right to know," she whispered.

The ensuing minutes of silence were rife with hostility. Sarah decided she would ask nothing more, not wanting to give him the satisfaction of hearing her plead with him for answers.

"Something's burning in here," Lucas said from the doorway. "Gabriel's hungry. He wanted another biscuit."

Sarah looked from the boy to his father. Rio had not moved. She practically shoved a handful of biscuits at Lucas. Now she smelled the scorched beans, but one look at Lucas's eyes and she knew he hadn't been talking about them.

"Take these. I'll make flapjacks and call when they're ready."

The boy stood in the doorway. He clutched the blanket wrapped around him along with the biscuits. His eyes bored into his father's back as if he willed him to turn around. As suddenly as he had come, he left them.

Rio got to the stove and removed the pot of beans before Sarah did.

"I'll scrape these out and start another pot," she said without looking at him.

"No. I will do this. You have done enough."

"It's my kitchen."

"And your food. But you labor to feed me and my sons."

"Next you'll accuse me of giving you charity just like Lucas."

"He had no right to speak to you so. But it is true. You said you went to the reservations—"

"This isn't the same at all," she protested.

"No. This time we have come to you."

"You harbor as much resentment as your son."

Sarah moved to the table. She poured the milk into the bowl and, one-handed, started to mix it in.

Rio came near and put his hands on the rim of the bowl, holding it steady for her. Sarah looked up at him, but his gaze was cast downward.

"Those questions I asked you, I want them answered. Why can't you tell me what brought you here?"

"It is trouble that will not touch you."

"Oh yes, it will." She dropped the spoon and covered his hands with hers. "I have the right to know if

I'll be murdered in my bed because someone is after you.''

Rio's hands tensed beneath hers. "You will not be harmed.''

He spoke through gritted teeth. Sarah wasn't going to back down again. "That's not what you said last night.''

"I never threatened to—''

"You threatened me. The what and how or why doesn't matter.''

He looked up then, straight into her eyes. In some ways Rio reminded Sarah of a wild horse—strong, solitary, self-sufficient. Until man and his greed to possess destroyed what he could not tame.

"Tell me. Please," she whispered.

"You cannot change what is past.''

"I know that, but I can listen. Maybe even help.''

"There is no help for this.'' He threw his head back, eyes closed, his throat working. He felt the strength of her hands holding on to his.

Rio opened his eyes and stared at the flickering shadows cast by the coal-oil fixture as the darkness of the storm made the light appear brighter in the warmth of the kitchen.

He looked down into eyes lit with a black fire, intensely passionate eyes that pleaded with him.

"They wanted the land. My grandfather's land. My white, half-Irish grandfather. He knew he was dying. He had made out his will, but he wished to file the deed in my name.

"The law, the white man's law did not allow for

half-breeds to own land. He said he would fight to have the law changed.

"There was no fight. He died before he had one letter answered. They waited until I was from home with my sons. Then they came. To burn our house, our barn and fences. They drove off my horses, they slaughtered my stock. They skinned my stallion.

"And they murdered..." Rio yanked his hands from under hers and turned away. He stood, spine rigid with tension, his hands clenched at his sides.

Sarah moved without thought to come up behind him. Her hands hovered for a few seconds then came to rest on his back. She didn't say anything. She couldn't think of anything to say. All the words of comfort would be meaningless.

"I killed two of them."

"Is...is that why you were in jail?"

"No. The killing came after. There are three left. I had to get my sons back. Once they are safe I shall hunt them down."

She sensed there was more that he wasn't telling her. She couldn't press him. His voice was tight, she almost felt the tension vibrating in his big body.

"Rio, I—"

He spun around so quickly that Sarah had no chance to evade the hands that grasped her shoulders. Her head rocked from the way he shook her.

"So now you know. Tell me how you will help me escape the justice that waits for me? Tell me any white person will believe I had a right to their lives after what they did to me and my sons? Tell me, *iszán*. I wish to hear the sweet, lying words that will ease my spirit and bring peace to those who have gone.''

Sarah's eyes filled with tears. She blinked rapidly to stop them from falling. At that moment, if he demanded to know who the tears were for, she could not have answered him.

She knew the look in his eyes. Grief without end. Agony that burned all the way to the soul.

He released her suddenly with a small push away from him. Before she could utter a sound, he was gone.

She ran to the door and peered out, but already the storm's darkness had swallowed him up. She pressed against the door frame, one hand gripping the metal door latch, the other clutched around her middle, her head pressed tightly against the wood.

From out of the rain-swept gloom came a primitive howl of grief. Raw. Powerful. Filled with pain. A rage against heaven.

Lightning struck close to the corral fence. The cry came again, and the sound ripped through Sarah's carefully built wall.

She was tossed from this time and place to where bitter winter snow hurled its fury on a lone figure. She could hear the screams coming from her throat, the cries of pain that went on and on until no sound came at all.

Grief without end. Sounds from the past. The cries beseeching mercy. The rage that she still lived.

Her body shook from an inward chill. She forced herself to close the door, then turned so that her back pressed against the latch. She hated him at that moment. Hated hearing his grief when she could not give vent to hers. Hated him for raking up the past where all she knew was pain.

*Strong, strong Sarah. You survived then, you will survive now.*

"But I never wanted to," she whispered to the empty room.

Silence was all the answer she ever heard.

But not this time.

"I am very hungry. Lucas said you were cooking. Will you feed me soon?"

Gabriel, dragging most of the blanket wrapped around him, stepped into the kitchen. He sniffed, then wrinkled his nose.

"Something burned," he said.

Sarah ducked her head and wiped her eyes. She stood away from the door. "Yesterday's ashes burned. Tell me, Gabriel, how old are you?"

"I have seven summers. Soon eight."

*Too old. Stop, Sarah. Stop now, before the past destroys you.*

It was wisdom she could not argue against, or fight.

"Will you feed me now? I liked your biscuits," he said, coming a little farther into the kitchen. A shy smile was offered up to her. "They were not hard like those at the mission school."

"And I promise you the flapjacks won't be, either."

She knew how work helped keep the dark thoughts at bay. Work had become her salvation.

She set to work in the kitchen with a vengeance that

would have impressed Mrs. Horace Pettigrew, the town's most notorious busybody. Not that the woman did a lick of work herself. She'd even hired several boys to walk her spoiled little dog, Posie, after someone remarked that the animal was so fat from the bonbons she fed him it was a wonder he hadn't died.

Sarah rarely was a target of the woman's wagging tongue, but Catherine had come in for her share until she married Greg Mayfield, a prize Mrs. Pettigrew had earmarked for her youngest and only unmarried daughter.

The heavy cast-iron skillet sizzled when she tested it with a few drops of water.

"Tell me, Gabriel, how would you like yours? Big ones or little?"

He chose small ones, as she knew he would, for she had at the same age when her grandmother offered the choice. She also was rewarded with another smile.

"I will stay with you," he said with a glance toward the window. It was black as night out there now, except where the faint bluish light of lightning showed.

"Lucas said the Thunder People sent the storm to show how angry they are with the white men that take gold from the earth. You are white. But I am half-Apache and will protect you."

"You are gallant and brave, Gabriel, just like the knights of old."

"I wish to be like my father. But what is a night of old? Night is when the ghost people come. I do not wish to be a ghost."

"No, nothing like that." She spelled the word for

him. "When I was a little girl my grandmother used to tell me tales of a great king. His name was Arthur and he had many brave soldiers. They called them the Knights of the Round Table."

She finished a stack of flapjacks for him, then made another larger one for Lucas when he was drawn into the kitchen.

At Gabriel's urging, she told them stories as she remembered her grandmother telling them, dragging from memory all the drama and pageantry that accompanied the knights' feats of daring.

A year ago, she wouldn't have been capable of sharing these hoarded precious moments. Her great-grandfather had been a schoolmaster, and he instilled a love of reading and history into his daughter. Sarah knew her mother had shared in that love, but she died when Sarah was born.

Only a slight redness remained on her palm, but no pain. She got the soup started, then salvaged what she could of the beans as the boys enjoyed the cookies she had made.

Water to wash their muddy clothes was heating on the stove. A few minutes later they returned to the warmth of the parlor.

Sarah almost called them back. She had no desire to be alone. She found it strange that neither boy asked where their father was. Not that she wanted him back inside. Not now.

She had directed all her energies during the past four years to rebuilding a new life for herself. It had not been easy. She had had to quell all needs in herself beyond the need to live on. She had friends, a home she loved, her precious horses, and family.

Her cousin Mary, and Rafe, Beth, his daughter from his first marriage, and now their infant son who she had helped bring into the world. There'd been no pain for her then, she was too caught up in Mary's joy at giving birth after years of being barren.

And there was Catherine, the dearest of friends who always made her laugh, married to a wonderful man who couldn't seem to give her enough. Her frequent letters were a cause for laughter, filled as they were with her coping with a socialite's life that Greg's sister Suzanne had introduced her to. Then there were the women's causes Catherine rallied to fight, and the farmhouse she and Greg were building on New York's Hudson River.

Sarah had found her own peace. There were a few men in town who had attempted to court her, but she discouraged most of them. Buck Purcell was the most persistent, but even his offer of marriage couldn't tempt her. She allowed him to escort her to church socials, danced with him, and even flirted a little, but the banker seemed to be resigned to the fact that he was not going to marry one of the merry widows of Sierra County as the townspeople of Hillsboro named them.

She had no desire for marriage. No *need* for it. Passion belonged buried with a young, innocent girl's romantic dreams.

And no man was going to change her mind.

Not even one whose grief touched a matching chord in her soul.

# Chapter Eight

Sarah left the soup simmering on the stove. She washed the boys' clothes. She hung them on twine strung from the two armless parlor chairs in front of the fire. Lucas had replenished the fire before he had fallen asleep, his brother tucked close by his side. She covered them with another quilt.

She returned to the kitchen where she filled two metal canteens with hot water. The rain had settled to a light fall. She intended to go out to the barn and see for herself that her horses were all right.

The hot water was to make a warm bran mash, for the storm showed no true sign of ending, and she worried over getting outside again.

She tied her floppy-brimmed felt hat on with a scarf and slipped into her slicker. Slinging the canteen straps over her head so they rested across her chest, she flipped the latch. The door required all her strength to open it. The wood had swollen from the rain pounding against it.

She struggled to close the door after her. Her footing was solid, thanks to Rio widening the board path she had laid when the rains first came. There was plenty of cut lumber from the two henhouses that Catherine and Greg had built as a result of a building contest between them.

"Some contest," she muttered, ducking her head as she made her way across the yard. "They both came out winners."

She couldn't help smiling. As indulgent as Greg was to Catherine's desires, he had drawn the line in attempting to transport his building effort all the way back to New York. Sarah had the houses torn down after Catherine sold off most of her flock, all but Miss Lily and her chick. They traveled with them and the worst tomcat of all, Lord Romeo.

But there were plenty of half-grown cats left. Six at last count.

Sarah saw the light shining through the small cracks in the barn doors. She knew Rio must be inside. She gave no thought to that being part of the reason she had come out there.

Two lanterns pooled light on the center aisle where fresh sawdust sprinkled the floor.

She breathed in the steamy warmth mixed with the earthy scents of horses and hay, the damp wood. From the faint odor of soiled bedding that remained she knew that Rio had mucked out the stalls. It was an onerous chore at best. She wasn't sure though if she was grateful for him having seen to it, or annoyed that he had taken over her domain.

One of the barn cats, a brown tabby, entwined its

supple body around her feet in a bid for attention. She bent to scratch beneath its chin, holding the canteens aside.

On her right she noted the fresh hay in the cow's manger. The stanchion rattled as the animal turned to look at Sarah. Placidly chewing her cud, her tail swished back and forth in a whiplike move that revealed her annoyance with Sarah's unscheduled visit.

"Don't worry, girl, I know it's not time for milking."

The four mares poked their noses over the doors to their stalls. At the far end of the barn, in the largest box stall, the stallion snorted, ears pricked forward as he caught Sarah's scent.

At each stall she stopped, rubbing the offered velvet nose, or scratching the hard-to-reach place between the ears. She stroked the proudly arched necks and noted that every horse had fresh hay and water. Even the bedding was as thick with the mix of hay and sawdust she preferred as if she herself had mucked the stalls and changed the bedding. Their manes and coats gleamed, showing the care of curry brush and comb.

If Lucas had never told her that his father had cared for horses, more, loved them, she could see the evidence here for herself.

From the loft came a meow, and she looked up to see one of the half-grown kittens perched on the loft's overhang like a watchful guard. Sarah made her way to where the warm glow of light spilled from the open door to the tack room.

From within came a muttered curse, then the sound

of hammering. The cat streaked back toward the front of the barn.

The loft, with its stacked hay, had softened the drumming rain on the roof. The tack room had no such protection. It was aptly named, not only for holding saddles, feed buckets, brushes and combs, horse blankets and halters, bridles and ropes, but for having been an afterthought of the previous owner. The ceiling barely cleared seven feet. A long, rectangle-shaped room, it ran the full length of the back of the barn, and was half as wide.

The single lantern hung from a hook on the roof post, spilling its light on the far corner where Rio was hammering. The old cluttered worktable blocked her view of him, but she noticed the corner had new boards, ones only partially weathered nailed over the old rough siding.

Sarah felt reluctant to call attention to herself. She turned to her right, away from him, toward the shelving that lined the short wall. There she straightened the various tins and bottles of Wittemore's leather dressing, Arabian Night harness oil, Chicago hoof remedy, Mill's harness soap and Hoppins horse liniment. The shelf below required no fixing, but she made sure that he had put back in order the currycomb, the thick-tooth mane comb, the Mexican rice root brushes and hoof picks. Below this shelf were stored the various hair clippers, shears, horse rasp, file and assorted bits and hobbles.

She bent over to pick up the awl that had fallen and set it back near the harness needles and trace splicer.

An old rusted plow leaned in the corner along with a sickle and scythe.

Sarah frowned. She had never gotten rid of the old miner's pick and gold pans. Like the hickory-neck yoke she had no use for, they cluttered up the space behind where the manure hook, hay fork, scuffle hoe, rake and shovel leaned against the wall.

Bridles, including the new hand-braided leather one she paid J. P. Crabtree five dollars for, hung from nails in the wall. There was a larger assortment of nickel-plated bits, too.

The hammering suddenly stopped. Although there was no sound, Sarah knew Rio was aware of her presence. She felt the intensity of his gaze on her back.

She turned but didn't look toward him. A few steps took her to the table. She lifted the cribbing muzzle that she had used on one of the mares who tended to gnaw on the wood side of her stall. The habit was finally broken. Spurs and washbasins, strap hinges for the stall doors, all lay in disarray.

Her hand fluttered over objects, not touching any, just a small indication of how nervous she was. He could say something. But then, so could she. It was hard, after that scene in the kitchen, to know what to say.

"The boys ate. They're sleeping in the parlor."

The canteens she still carried bumped against the table. Sarah seized upon the reason she had come out here.

"I intend to make a warm bran mash for the horses.

It's chilly enough in here and with the rain continuing I don't know—"

"This is your place. They are your horses. You need not explain anything that you do."

"Well, no. I know that. I was just being polite. Just making conversation. Talking. You've done a lot of work out here."

"I need to keep busy. When there is time on a man's hands he thinks too much."

"Or remembers too much," she added in a soft voice.

"Yes, that, too. When one is helpless to stop the things happening around him, work is the only ease for the mind and body."

"That's just as true of women."

She could hear him stacking the lumber he didn't use. The rain dripped heavily from the eaves, and the world seemed to shrink down to this space. The faint, restless stampings of the horses came to her ears, but beyond that it was quiet.

She began clearing a space in front of her. Rio set the large basin down. Sarah looked up at him.

"I...I'm sorry that I made you rake up painful memories. I hated it when others did that to me."

Rio felt it again. Her strength coming up against him. Her eyes, black as her hair, sharp and measuring at the same time, but warm with compassion.

"Yes, you know. You have lost your husband. You do understand what it is to grieve for the loss of one's love."

Sarah averted her head. She did nothing to dispel

his notion that she still mourned Judd's loss. Yet grief was in her throat with a taste all its own. Swallowing only lodged it deeper, so it lay cold and heavy where no warmth ever touched.

"It is not the Apache way to speak of the one who is gone. But then, I was not raised to only follow my mother and grandmother's ways. No one left behind is ever free of the memories," he said in a husky voice. He found himself strangely compelled to offer her comfort, even more, to confess the reason for his anger with her.

She stood still, with all the wariness of a wild creature set to flee. He lifted one hand, turning it so that the backs of his fingers brushed against her cheek. He didn't miss her slight flinch, even as she stood her ground while he repeated the gentle stroke.

"I was wrong to return your kindness with anger, *iszán.*"

She held his gaze, unable to look away. His touch was only an offer to comfort, but she didn't feel comforted.

His touch heightened her senses to a startling degree. The pounding rain echoed the beat of her heart. The heat of his body seemed to envelop her into a tightly drawn space where there was room for none but the two of them. Even his features appeared tightly drawn with an intensity that mirrored her feelings.

Sarah wasn't aware of breathing deeply, but she had taken his scent inside her. Sweat, horses, the damp of his clothing. Scents that warmed, then heated sharply to a sexual maleness releasing a primitive call to her.

Every moment whispered a warning that he was dangerous to her. But she didn't heed it, she could not.

Her whole being filled with waiting. Her pulse pounded. Her gaze slid down to his mouth, then lower to his throat.

It was harder to breathe. The air was heavy, like that of summer when heat lightning danced and thunder rumbled in the far-off hills. Hot and sticky, flicker and fire, but without bringing the needed relief.

She felt a shiver course down her spine and was drawn to look up at his eyes. The intensity was still there, waiting, it seemed, for her to decide. What? she wanted to cry out, but speech was beyond her, for his gaze was suddenly hot.

His hands came to rest on her shoulders, and they were strong, heavy male hands. She knew he was going to pull her closer, close enough for bodies to touch, close enough for lips to meet.

*Run, Sarah.*

And she didn't heed this warning, either. She stood, waiting, knowing she'd open her mouth to his willingly. Hunger too long denied was a powerful force. More powerful than Sarah could fight at that moment.

Then his mouth covered hers.

She'd expected something more harsh, forceful, with a need to master. She knew his strength and his violence, could have tasted, taken what she wanted from that.

But Rio surprised her. His lips touched hers for a moment, feathered across her cheekbones, then moved on to brush gently against her brow before returning to her mouth.

He tasted her softly, teasingly.

Sarah sensed his holding back. She moaned deep in her throat, half longing for the hunger she had waited for, half hoping for a fierce, savage demand she could resist.

But this gentleness, this coaxing, left her aching for more.

And Rio left her aching, pulling back, then he stepped away from her.

One look at his hard-set features silenced her need to know why he stopped. She could ask, she thought she could even plead to know—shocking as it seemed that the reason was important—but she knew he wasn't going to answer her.

Her hand curled around the edge of the table. Her breath shuddered out of her. "Why? Why did you—" She broke off, shaking her head. She wasn't going to ask, yet she couldn't stop herself.

"Did your elders teach you nothing? It is not for a woman to ask a man."

Only the lingering taste of the gentle kiss quieted her temper. "Maybe that's true among your mother's people, but it isn't among mine."

"You lie."

He said it calmly, looking so directly at her with a dare to deny him in his gaze that her breath hissed out from between clenched teeth.

A cold and very cynical smile that never reached

his eyes curled the corner of his mobile mouth. The mouth that moments ago had teased and tantalized her.

"My grandfather was an educated man. He wanted me to see and learn all I could about both worlds, Apache and white. I traveled with him to St. Louis, and then to New Orleans. I was very much in the company of charming and very curious white women.

"Hungry women who did not shrink from bedding a half-breed. As my grandfather wished, I added to my education. I learned about deceit, and the lies they whispered with no more thought than you used when you wielded your rifle to protect your home from me.

"They live with their lies, as tightly bound with them as they are in their bone corsets and layers of clothing. They never asked why. To ask is to show a willingness to hear the truth. I learned well from them."

Resentment, hot and flaring, added an edge to her voice. "But you never let me finish my question. I only wanted to know why you kissed me, not why you stopped." Pride made her lie. She lifted her chin, pouring a challenge into her gaze, a challenge that dared him this time to answer her with the truth.

His hand pressed tightly along his thigh. "How long since your husband died?"

Confusion clouded her gaze. "Four years," she answered.

"In that time did you take a man to your bed?"

Sarah dug her fingertips into the wood of the table.

"No. There has been no man. But if you think I intended—"

"What I think, widow woman, is that you better go back to your house. It is safer for you there."

"Safer? Perhaps. But only for a little while. Then you'll be there, too."

"With my sons," he reminded her.

"Yes, with your sons." Humiliation beat aside all other feelings. She went around the table, heading for the door. There she stopped and looked back at him.

"I answered your questions. Truthfully, too. Now, you answer mine. How long since your wife died? Have you taken a woman to your bed?"

"I have had no bed since she died. And no need to bury myself in a woman's heated softness."

Sarah wanted to push, just a little bit further. She prided herself on a lack of fear, of being able to cope with just about anything. He stood watching her, much the way he had the night before in the hallway. There was enough distance between them that should have made her feel safe. But safe wasn't what she felt.

She thought he could spring across to her in moments.

But even that didn't stop her.

"And now, Rio Santee? Have you a need now?"

"Are you hungry enough to hear the answer?" he whispered, his voice low and insinuating. "The truth or a lie. It is your choice."

Sarah stared at him. She felt as if some wild stranger had taken over her body. Then common sense reasserted itself. She could feel shocked color flood her face. She jerked around and ran to escape him.

# *Chapter Nine*

For Sarah there was no real escape from Rio. Not later when he joined his sons for supper, or while he sat in the kitchen as she cleaned up.

Not even after she helped settle the boys for sleep in the parlor and retreated upstairs to her bedroom.

She wasted no more time thinking about it, for she couldn't order him from the house. She wouldn't be able to live with herself if anything happened to him or his sons. The weather was enough threat to make that possible, but there were men hunting them. Men who had killed, and likely would try to kill again.

The hot water she had brought up earlier had cooled to a comfortable warmth for washing. She might be alone, but she couldn't chase Rio Santee from her thoughts. Couldn't rid herself of the taste of his warm mouth against her own.

What was wrong with her?

The man still grieved for his dead wife. *One's love.* That's what he called her. She was supposed to be mourning her husband.

Damn him!

He had driven her to lie to him.

And taunt him.

Where had that come from?

Sarah looked up then, the washcloth pressed against her belly. She bared her thoughts as her body was bared.

With a cry she threw the cloth into the washbowl and turned away from her reflection. She slipped into a flannel nightgown, then her robe.

She had not wanted him to stop kissing her, she thought with dismay.

Why? Why this man? Why now when everything was falling into place for her? Contentment, if not happiness, was hers.

She paced the small confine of her room, her arms wrapped around her waist.

It was need. Loneliness and need. She was no better than Mary or Catherine. She had lied to them. Lied every time she told them she had no desire, no need to have a man share her bed, her body and her thoughts, and her dreams.

*Oh, Lord.*

But nothing really happened. Just a kiss.

He'd wanted to prove she was no better than those other curious women....

No! She could not lie to herself.

Maybe at the end his words had been calculated to make her believe that, but not at first. Not when he had stroked her cheek, not when he feathered his lips over her face, not when his lips covered her own.

Gentleness. So unexpected from a man like Rio.

Hunger. So unexpected from herself.

She was so alone. All she could do was to avoid temptation. She was good at that. She had made herself be. Strong. Guarded. Protective of herself in order to survive.

The cold forced an end to her restless pacing. She climbed into bed and snuggled deep beneath the covers. She closed her eyes, tired of thinking.

Rain dripped from the eaves, wind whistled through the cottonwoods near the house.

"Let the storm continue," she prayed. "Let every track they left be wiped clean. Let them be safe."

And she drifted into sleep, wondering why her prayer was for them to stay and not go. What had happened to the need to protect herself?

Rio lay with his head cradled on his folded arms, staring up at the ceiling. He'd counted to thirty, then heard the floorboard creak above him.

Her room.

It appeared the widow could no more find her way to sleep than he could.

The fire was banked for the night. He had refused her offer to sleep upstairs, and so had his sons.

Gabriel had abandoned his favorite sprawling position to sleep cuddled at his side. He could not seem to get close enough, for he stirred in his sleep, his small body pushing against his father's.

Lucas couldn't make his bed any farther and still

have the warmth of the fire. The boy blamed him still. It showed in every sullen word, every damning look.

He wrestled for a moment with the temptation to get up, but he realized almost as soon as the thought occurred to him that he couldn't do that.

She might hear him moving around.

She might even come down those stairs.

They'd be alone again.

*Only you, trickster Coyote, could have directed my steps here.*

*Only you could put such temptation in my path.*

"But I cannot blame you for the lies I spoke to her."

He lay there listening to the rain, and the wind and the occasional snap of green sap licked by fire.

And Rio listened for the whisper of ghosts.

*She* came to him in the night, giving him no peace while her death lay unrevenged.

She, who had brought peace to his soul and joy to his heart.

A quiet sigh escaped his lips. He missed her so. She had left behind an empty place inside him that would never be filled.

He closed his eyes, willing himself to sleep. The floorboard had ceased its creaking. Perhaps the widow, too, had given up her restless thoughts.

Would that he could.

But he was too filled with sorrow. It was a living thing, this empty darkness that never left him.

And then the image of Sarah's face swam against his eyelids.

And he knew he lied to himself.

There had been no sorrow when he gazed at her. None when he reached out and touched the softness of her skin. None when desire to taste her mouth won over his promise not to touch her.

How long, she had asked.

Too long. Much too long since he'd lost himself in an eagle's soaring flight, in the heat and the hunger to become one.

From tormented memory came his beloved wife's face. A forbidden thing to think of, to speak of, to wish to see. But he heard again the words of their marriage blessing.

*Now you will feel no rain, for each of you will be shelter for the other.*

Two made into one.

*Now you will feel no cold, for each of you will be warmth to the other.*

Hands clasped, holding tight.

*Now there will be no more loneliness, for each of you will be companion to the other.*

Eyes locked, gazing deep into hearts, into souls.

*Now you are two bodies, but there is only one life before you.*

There was need, and promises, and love...waiting...just waiting...

*Go now to your dwelling place to enter into the days of your togetherness.*

And the waiting was over. Passion waited yet, and joy. Such incredible joy to join as one.

*And may your days be good and long upon the earth.*

But his good days had ended. Too soon. Much too soon night had come.

And if he continued to walk this path, his days would not long be on this earth.

*And what of your sons? Who will guide the path they are to walk? Who will teach them the ways of the People? Who will teach them to survive where white men rule?*

*And the widow? What is to become of Sarah?*

She is strong.

*But what if they come here looking for you?*

*Would you see her beaten? Bleeding? Broken? Cast down like that ravening pack's leavings?*

She is a white woman! They would not dare to touch her!

*And who will stop them? You have brought this trouble to her home. You will be less than a man to leave her.*

And if I stay and they come here? How much of a man will I be if I cannot protect her?

*Will you leave her rifle? Will you take it to save yourself and your sons? There is no other weapon. You have searched twice now and found no other.*

Leave me! Leave me be!

He arose in a controlled rush, snatched hold of his shirt and almost ran through the darkened hall into the kitchen and out into the night.

Upstairs, Sarah sat up. She heard him leave the house. There was no doubt it had been Rio.

What demons refused him sleep and drove him from the house?

She thought about going after him. Thought about it, then decided against it.

She wasn't sure she wanted to know. There was too much at risk.

Heartache, for one.

But she dreamed the warning had come too late.

Sullen-eyed clouds hung over most of the morning and by afternoon released torrential rains on a land drowning in water.

Rio worked all morning widening the trench he had begun around the house. Now he worked to dig one around the barn. The board path lay under inches of muddy water.

Sarah too had put restless energy to work. The horses couldn't be let out. No, she had refused to let them out, but they also showed signs of temper from their enforced confinement. She had walked each one up and down the center aisle of the barn until her legs threatened to give way. Two of the mares were in foal, and she worried about them.

Both Gabriel and Lucas had helped her muck out the stalls. Getting rid of the soiled bedding proved to tax whatever patience she had left. The wheelbarrow became mired in the mud. After the second time she had given up using it, and hauled it out shovelful by shovelful.

She worried about her few head of cattle, wishing she could saddle up and ride out. A futile wish.

Since clothing was a problem the boys complied with her request that they stay inside. But the dreary day and lack of something to do left them bored and restless.

She had no toys or games, but there was the trunkful of books that Greg had left behind. Sarah joined them in the parlor.

Lucas stood by the front window. One finger repetitiously followed the track of raindrops on the glass. Gabriel lay on his stomach before the fire, arms bent at the elbow, hands scrunched beneath his jaw to prop his head. Every now and then he released a sigh, and Sarah felt for him.

"I know it's hard having nothing to do," she said. "I'm sure at the mission school you had lessons and play time to keep busy."

Lucas gave her a sullen look over his shoulder and went back to watching the raindrops. Gabriel rolled over, hands now cradling his head.

"I can add."

"Would you like to do sums?" she asked with forced cheerfulness.

"Will you yell if I do it wrong?"

"No, Gabriel. I—"

"If you had paper and charcoal, Lucas could draw for us."

Sarah didn't know why the notion that Lucas liked to sketch struck her as odd. She glanced at him just in time to catch the brief longing visible at his brother's request, then he turned away.

"Paper?" she murmured more to herself. All she

had was the small record book used to keep track of chore lists and expenses.

"You should not ask," Lucas said to Gabriel.

"No. No, it's all right. I don't have any white paper, but I do have..." Sarah broke off as she hurried from the room.

"She'll find something. You'll see. Then you will be happy, Lucas."

"And what will you do, little brother?"

"I will ask her to tell me stories. I like her stories. Better than the ones the mission ladies told us. I don't want to be a good Christian. It is too hard to give up all the things I like. Mostly," he added in a whisper, "I didn't like giving up being with Father."

Sarah paused just before the doorway. She heard the last. She wondered who would tell her why the boys had been taken away from him. But questions could wait.

She went directly to Lucas. "We cut open these Union Paper Company bags. They're something new our shopkeepers in town have begun using. We can get charcoal from the fire. Or you can use my pencil."

She practically shoved the things into the boy's hands when he made no move to take them. With a bright smile, she turned to Gabriel.

"While Lucas draws, would you like me to read you a story?"

"Tell me one."

Sarah joined him on the floor. "I think I told you most of the ones that I know."

"Tell me again."

She couldn't resist his smile. This youngest child of Rio's had a sunny nature. And when he smiled, his eyes reflected its warmth. She sat with her back resting against the leg of the settee and within minutes Gabriel cuddled by her side. She resisted the urge to see what Lucas was doing and went on with her storytelling.

One story led to two, and by the time she finished the third, Gabriel was restless. She was about to suggest milk and cookies in the kitchen when he jumped up.

"I want to see, Lucas."

Sarah added her own plea. Gabriel reached him first, snatching the brown paper from his hand.

"Give it back, little brother."

Gabriel shoved it behind his back, skipping out of his brother's reach. Lucas started after him.

"Gabriel, if Lucas doesn't want to share his drawing that's his choice. Give it back to him, please."

"He never shares them. I want to see it." Gabriel walked closer to Sarah and the fire.

Sarah's curiosity got the better of her. She leaned toward the younger boy to see the drawing. Whatever she expected, it wasn't to see a rendering of herself.

"Lucas," she whispered as Gabriel handed over the rough-feeling paper. "You flatter me."

"You do not like it."

"No. No, that's not true. I've never had anyone sketch me. I don't even have a tintype. But this, oh, Lucas, you are a talented artist. You should be studying. I never did well with the lessons I had, but my friend Catherine was very good."

She looked over at Lucas. "As good as she was, you're better. Much better."

"I draw what I see," he said with a defiant air.

"Then you saw me with very kind eyes, Lucas," Sarah replied softly. She traced the image of her face with one finger. He had captured strength in the bone structure, but there was a soft loveliness in the eyes. Was this truly as she appeared? She could not ask him. His pride was as prickly as a barrel cactus.

"May I keep this?" she asked.

"Keep what?" Rio demanded, entering the room with an armload of firewood.

Gabriel gave no one time to answer. Once more he snatched the drawing and ran with it to his father.

"Look! Look at what Lucas made. He's mad at me again. Mad because I showed it to the lady."

Rio dumped the wood by the fire. He wiped his hand down the side of his pants before he looked at the drawing.

He studied for so long that Sarah grew breathless waiting to hear his praise. She noted that she didn't wait alone. His oldest son watched him with a look of raw hunger for approval. She had to fight to keep still. She wanted to stand by the boy with her arm around him and reaffirm her pleasure in his work.

Some dark, swirling emotion filled Rio's gaze. His eyes went from the drawing to his son, then settled on Sarah.

She tried a silent plea, willing with all her being that he read it in her gaze and give his son what he needed.

To her shocking dismay, he let the drawing fall from his hand.

"Father?" Gabriel started to say.

Rio's long stride took him out of the room before Sarah could move.

"Stay here!" She didn't look to see if the boys obeyed her order, but she did pause long enough to close the parlor doors.

She went after Rio. On some deep, inner level she knew what she would find when she reached the kitchen.

He didn't disappoint her.

# Chapter Ten

No, that was wrong. He didn't disappoint her. He confirmed her thought.

Rio stood framed in the pantry's doorway holding a whiskey bottle. Sarah had never allowed any liquor in the house, but there were a few bottles left from Catherine's wedding, then a few more added when Rafe visited over the holidays.

She should have destroyed every one of them, but her own growing need to finally put her past behind her made her keep them. That, and seeing for herself that men like Rafe and Greg could drink without turning into animals.

Now she wished she had gotten rid of them.

Even as she watched, he ripped the cork free and tilted the bottle to his lips. She could only stare, overwhelmed by images from the past. It wasn't Rio she saw leaning against the door frame, but Judd raising the bottle for another drink while she pleaded with him to stop.

Sarah wasn't about to plead. She was no longer that weak, begging woman.

"You miserable bastard! How could you crush your son's pride like that? How dare you call yourself a father?"

Rio's answer was to raise the bottle again and drink deeply enough to feel the liquor's burning heat seep inside him where cold twisted and squeezed like an enormous snake. His eyes burned from the sleepless night and all the other nights that preceded it. For a few minutes back there he had been tempted to rip the drawing to shreds.

The knowledge sickened him.

How could he think of destroying something that Lucas had made?

And now, his own demons weren't enough, he had to face the widow as a warrior, ripping him apart with her words.

*How dare he?*

He swiped the back of his hand across his mouth.

"You forget yourself. I am his father, *iszán.*"

*"I am your husband, Sarah. Don't ever, ever forget that."*

As if she had. The words from the past sent Sarah staggering back until she felt the wall behind her.

"No. No," she whispered, shaking her head from side to side.

"It is not for you to say. They are my sons."

"They need someone to speak for them."

He slouched in the pantry's opening and took another long pull from the bottle.

"Don't you understand? You hurt your son. Do you believe whiskey will help you forget it? It won't. There isn't enough liquor to make what you did to him go away. And what of Lucas? What will he do to forget? Or were you planning on sharing that bottle with him?"

For an instant everything in Rio's world, including the blood in his veins, stilled. He stared at her.

There was something more than her attacking him over Lucas and his drawing. He sensed it, but the thought was vague, too much for him to reach for now.

Sarah had closed her eyes briefly. It hadn't been Rio that she saw, and the words weren't for him alone. Ghosts. Hated, haunting ghosts.

It was the paleness of her face that forced him to speak. "I asked you before and ask again. Where does the wisdom of a child's needs come from?"

Unable to answer him, Sarah tilted her head back against the wall and stared at the ceiling. That dark, disturbing voice of his seemed to demand the secrets of her soul.

"What the hell good is this gift of his hands and his eyes? Where will my son use it? When will he be given the chance?"

"Only you know," she said in a dull tone.

"In the mountains of Mexico where the renegades have their hidden camps? You know nothing of us. Less of the path we are forced to take."

She glanced at him, then away. He was drinking again and with every drop of liquor that he swallowed, more demons were loosed into the room.

"You keep your thoughts and tongue to yourself. My son has no time for foolishness. He'll need sharp eyes to keep watch, to find game for hungry bellies. His hands are useful as tools to gather wood, to wield a skinning knife, not a damn pencil, with skill."

She pounced on the last. "At least you admit that he can draw with skill. Pity you didn't tell him. He needed to hear that from you."

"Silence your tongue!"

Rio lurched from the doorway to the table. He set the bottle down and ripped the wet headband off his head and tossed it onto the table. He tunneled his hands through the damp length of his hair. His temples pounded like ceremonial drums. No amount of rubbing would ease the pain. No amount of liquor would drown the truth of the widow's flaying tongue.

He didn't know himself anymore. He didn't like what he was thinking, didn't like what he'd done or said.

A rendering sorrow twisted inside him. He had not known that Lucas could draw so well.

Another thing stolen from him. Stolen from his son, as well.

He caught the edge of the table, shoulders hunched forward as he struggled to contain his temper.

Unfortunately, his grandfather's passionate blood ran in his veins. The Irish inheritance, he'd named it years ago. A cauldron of temper, and love of horses and music, and deep family devotion, and inevitably, the lusts of the flesh.

He looked up then and glared at Sarah. What the hell did she know of lust?

Sarah had been staring at the bottle, then his large hands splayed on the edge of the table. They appeared strong enough to rend the wood. She switched her gaze back to Rio's face. He was watching her intently. Their eyes locked and she could not summon the will to look away.

The world grew very still around her. She felt the hair stir on the back of her neck. A prickling sensation coursed down her spine. It was happening again.

Every sense she possessed was poised on the edge of acute awareness of this time, this place and this one man.

The feeling was just a hairsbreadth shy of being painful.

His hand moved to the bottle. Her gaze tracked the move. She saw his fingers curl around the amber glass and followed the bottle's rise to his lips only to find that he still watched her. He tipped the bottle and she watched him swallow, wondering why she stayed, why she couldn't find the words to condemn him to hell and order him from her house.

She shivered. The small whispers of awareness continued to make her uneasy. Rio, with his dark, dangerous look, made her uneasy. She'd never experienced a reaction like this around any man.

Then again, she reminded herself, she had never been in a situation like this.

"I wonder what secrets you hide, *iszán*. At times you seem fierce as the she-bear protecting her cub. At others, the wary fawn. Which, I ask myself, is the woman.''

Sarah blinked and took a step to the side. Her chin came up. "I can be both. There is no shame in my being wary of you.''

"Yes. I threatened you.''

"Seeing where you get your courage,'' she said, making a gesture toward the bottle, "I have a right to be wary. Men who drink can't control themselves. They become animals.''

A mocking smile creased his mobile mouth, but there was no mockery in his eyes. He studied her as if he were silently repeating her words to himself, and she was sorry she had spoken.

He shoved himself away from the table and walked around to block her escape.

"You flayed me over my son. Shall I do the same? Drink with me, *iszán*.''

Sarah eyed the bottle with something akin to horror. Her lower lip trembled. There was a dangerous, challenging air about him that set her already raw nerves on edge. She badly wanted to run. Emotions clogged her throat. She could barely shake her head in refusal.

He leaned close, whispering. "No secrets to hide? No voices to drown?''

His chest sawed in and out with every angry breath he took. Her gaze went to his corded throat, then to his face that could have been carved from stone. She was forced to breathe the scent of him, damp, musky and all male.

His free hand rose and she cringed, wishing the wall behind her would open. But he only touched her hair.

"Don't." She turned her head.

"Was he an animal, Sarah?"

She was distracted, hearing her name for the first time from his lips. Soft. So whisper soft it sounded like a caress.

"Drink with me."

If he'd shouted a demand with anger, she might have shoved him away. But the words escaped his lips quietly, the way a snake slithered after prey. She couldn't focus. And it wasn't her home she stood in, not her kitchen, as the outside sound of the storm receded to be replaced by the tinny sound of an out-of-tune piano, and laughter. God, the laughter, seeping through the floor, the walls, filling the very air she breathed. And Judd, pinning her against the wall, forcing the bottle to her lips. And the fear that made her open her mouth, fear that choked her as she swallowed, fear of what would happen if she didn't do what he wanted. That cold, hard constant knot of fear that no amount of whiskey could warm.

The drunken slur of his voice, cajoling, then angry. Silken whisperings. And then the rage.

She wasn't fully aware that she crossed her arms protectively over her chest, that she hunched her shoulders, ducked her head. And trembled with fear.

This time he would make good his threat.

This time he would kill her.

"Have you tried to outrun the voices calling out to you? Have you climbed until your hands are raw and bleeding and found yourself on the highest point of a towering pinnacle of stone only to have your pleas for mercy turn to ashes in your mouth? Have you not found the blackness that waits in emptying the bottle? The blackness that steals all feeling, even the pain? Speak to me, *iszán*. Let me hear your soft woman's words now."

She could barely swallow, much less find the moisture needed to speak. But her focus came back. She wasn't with Judd in some nameless town surrounded by strangers who wouldn't stop him.

This was her home. Her kitchen. The man who leaned close was whispering of her heart beating like a captive bird beneath his hand cupping her breast.

"Have you found the path to forgiveness, Sarah? Do you know the way?" he asked, nuzzling the sensitive skin beneath her ear. "Will you share the path with me?"

His face was buried in her hair, his hand sliding over her shoulder in a circular, caressing motion.

Sarah's eyes cleared. She ground her teeth together in an effort not to scream at him to take his hands off her, to leave her be, she had no peace to offer him when she still searched for it herself.

His lips nibbled delicately at her throat. Her insides somersaulted, and she softly moaned. He took hold of her hand, lifting it to slip inside his shirt, holding it palm down against his skin. Sarah made an attempt to withdraw her hand, but Rio wouldn't let her. The heat of his body drew her to curl her fingertips into his hard flesh.

He sucked in his breath sharply.

Sarah snatched her hand back. She took a half step that molded his body from knee to chest against hers. Her gaze went to his. His lips hovered scant inches above her mouth. There was nothing she could do about her nipples beading in response, or the warmth that trembled through her body.

Sarah was afraid to move. He was perfectly still. Raw hunger made his eyes appear bleak as his gaze became fixed on hers. She fought the almost irresistible urge to thread her fingers up through his hair and draw his head down to her.

Rio swallowed. There was color in her cheeks, and he thought it better than the sad, lost look she had a few minutes ago. He should leave her be. He had no right to touch her. But his body howled in protest and he strained toward her.

"Sarah?"

A forbidden and unaccountable feeling of tenderness swept through her. It was like nothing she had ever experienced before. She knew what he wanted, and she wished she could grant him his desire.

And her own. She should hate him for the memories he forced her to recall. Hate him for all he had done to shatter her peace.

His mouth captured hers. It was not an expected kiss. Hunger. Possessiveness. A kiss that demanded complete surrender. For a moment she resisted. Her mind was set against him. But her body had other needs that overruled. Heat. She heard herself moan.

There was something almost savage in the way he

kissed her. No gentle coaxing. No practiced art. This was raw, needy, seeking her response, and then demanding more.

Sarah gave.

There was no choice when measured against her own needs.

He ravaged. He possessed. Something she wasn't willing to give threatened to break free. She wanted to push him away. Her arms curled over his shoulders.

She wanted more.

More than pleasure. More than passion. She had tasted those before. The feelings churning inside her made her ache and yet frightened her, too.

Then, suddenly, he released her. She stared up at him. Thoughts and emotions shuddered through her. She still felt the wanting. Still tasted him on her mouth.

Wearily Rio scrubbed a hand over his face. He tried to push back the sudden rush of anger, the memories, too. Whiskey. How could he forget? The sleeping bear he must never let loose again.

He took a deep breath. The fault was his. Not the widow's. Never the lovely, giving Sarah's.

She couldn't know what he dealt with, nor did he want her to. Noting that his hand holding the bottle trembled with tension, he bit back an oath. His blood felt hot and heavy running through him. He could have taken her, could have buried himself in all that woman's softness and for a little while found peace.

Lightning slashed through the torrent and thunder,

but all he heard was the raspy sounds of their mingled breathing.

He couldn't look at her. Didn't want to step away.

Sarah sagged against the wall. She was shaking. Her hand lifted as if to touch him, then fell to her side. She had her own demons. She didn't want his.

But his needs called to her and she found that she could not, would not, walk away from him.

She eyed the bottle he still held. He'd been in jail but not for killing those two men. Those boys admitted they hated being taken from him and sent to the mission school.

"Rio," she began softly, finding the courage to speak. "Drinking won't help. But I think you already know that. Don't let your sons see you like this. They've suffered, too."

"My drinking, it frightened you."

It wasn't meant as a question, but Sarah thought of it as one. Judd always accused her of caring too much for people. Strangers. He'd laugh at her concerns, or stop her whenever he was around. She had met Rafe McCade over such an incident. But Rafe was a good and decent man. He'd acted to stop a brutal beating on a woman and a horse.

And Judd was dead. He could no longer stop her. And she couldn't stop herself from trying to help this one man.

"Yes. It makes me afraid."

She pressed her hands flat against the wall, hoping she could keep her voice steady. He couldn't know the cost of her admitting that.

"Your husband drank."

"Yes."

He held the bottle out and stared at it. "This is the only solace I found for her death."

"But you had your sons!"

She didn't think. She rushed at him, snatching the bottle from his hand and threw it across to the dry sink. The sound of shattering glass and the fumes of whiskey filled the room.

Horrified at what she had done, Sarah could only stare at the shards of glass glittering beneath the light. Suddenly she rounded on him, and saw Lucas hovering near the doorway.

"Stay in the parlor with your brother," she ordered. "This isn't for you to hear." With a sharp look at Rio, she added, "Or to see."

"Are you a coward?" Anger laced her low voice. "Is that the man you'll show your sons? You can't hide in that bottle. You won't find anything you're looking for there. You asked if I knew of a way to forgive myself. I don't know." Her voice fell with pleading. "Rio, you're alive. You have two beautiful sons who love you. Don't you understand the gift she left you? How can you think to harm them? And yourself?

"Don't you dare throw that away! You loved her? Then how can you let yourself wallow in self-pity? Is that how you keep her memory? How dare you? How dare you?" Her voice rose on the last in a shrill, shaken note. She shook beneath the force of the emotions let loose.

"If he drank and you hated it, why do you mourn him?"

Her head jerked back as if he had slapped her.

"This isn't about me, damn you!" She caught herself before she backed away from him.

With a defiant lift of her chin she searched his bleak features for a few tense moments.

"You told me I know nothing of the path you're forced to walk. Maybe that's true in your eyes. But I do know how your sons are feeling right now. I know what it is to see someone you love destroy themselves before your eyes. I know how helpless they feel that they can't stop you, can't give enough love or caring to make you see what you're doing.

"Go to your son, Rio. Tell Lucas what you told me. Tell him his work is skilled. That you're proud of him. Go now," she whispered, motioning toward the doorway. "If you don't do it now, you'll end up mourning the loss of more than you realize."

Silence hung in the room when she finished.

Rio knew she was right. What was it about her that made him believe every word she spoke?

In a move that surprised him as much as it did Sarah, he held out his hand.

"Come with me."

## Chapter Eleven

Rio thought about the passion in her voice. It was nothing sexual. Nor was there anger. She merely pleaded with him to see his sons as she saw them. He doubted that she was aware of the intensity of her gaze or her stance. Her thoughts were all for Lucas. Only for him. The depth of her compassion moved him.

She reached for his hand. His fingers closed tightly around hers.

"You do understand, don't you, Rio? He needs you now more than ever. Gabriel does, too. The love of those boys...oh, there's nothing..." Her voice broke, then she rallied. "There's nothing to compare to the love of a child. They are so giving."

Rio looked down at their joined hands. "And you, do you give your love without condition?"

Sarah thought of things in her life that she loved. Her home, the horses, her small family. But they weren't really hers. Mary had Rafe and the children. Catherine and Greg and his sister with her large family. They weren't here with her. There was no special someone in her life to love.

Her gaze was drawn to their joined hands. He probed too deeply with his questions.

"I know the answer," he said after a few moments. He studied her face when she looked up at him. A slight frown creased his brow. "Why did I not see their need?"

Confused, Sarah stared at him. "Are you asking me, or yourself?"

"Both, it seems."

Sarah lifted her other hand to his cheek. "If you care enough to change, that is all that will matter to your sons."

He drew her hand to his lips. "You are a wise woman, and a most forgiving one, Sarah."

There was that feeling again. He'd have every secret she harbored if she allowed him any closer. He'd leave, and he could easily take her heart with him. She had to protect herself. But her gentle tug wouldn't move him to release her.

"Don't say anymore. Please," she added.

He lowered his mouth to hers. A gentle taking. Sarah could have pulled back. She didn't. And the warnings were ignored as his lips roamed over her face.

"You taste of the goodness in your heart," he murmured. "I desire you." His voice grew dark and husky. "I taste the wanting inside you, too. You no more wish to feel this than I do."

His mouth settled on hers with a touch of anger.

Sarah tasted his and her own. His tongue probed deep as he pulled her closer. She offered no resistance. Strong, practical Sarah would return soon enough. She stole what she wanted, what she needed from him.

Her fingers combed through the long length of his hair, then wandered down to the muscles of his shoulders and back. She wanted his strength.

He slipped both hands upward to cup her breasts. He wished there was no cloth between them. Not that he needed to touch her skin to know it was soft and warm, like her kiss. He heard her moan as his thumbs brushed her nipples. This was a madness he could not stop. He wanted nothing else but to have her. Passion drove him as it never had before.

He fought the temptation to pull her to the floor and take her. Swift and fierce. Hot and deep. Then this gnawing desire would leave him. His blood would cool, his thoughts become his own again. That was what he needed. Not her.

He pulled away abruptly and stared down at her. Her breathing was as quick as his own. Passion clouded her lovely dark eyes. He gripped her shoulders.

"I will not lie to you. This wanting…no, this need for you is a feeling I do not like."

"I'm not innocent, Rio. I tasted the anger of your kiss. You're not alone. I don't want you."

"No lies, *iszán*."

This time there was no harshness attached to the Apache word. If anything, his voice caressed it.

Sarah held her gaze steady. "No lies. I am what

you called me, a woman. Not a girl. I know what it is
to want and not have. You're in no danger from me.
I won't provoke you.''

''And if I came to your room?''

Sarah stepped away from him, thankful that he let
her go. ''I don't know what I would do. I hope you
will not force me to make that choice.''

''Will there be force, Sarah? Will there be a
choice?''

He looked away from her. Outside, the lightning
flared nearby. Rumbles of thunder followed. He
wanted to be outside in the storm. It could not be
worse than the one that raged through him.

''You should know I would not be a gentle lover
with you.''

There was no reply she could make. She already
knew that. Did she want him? Sarah left the kitchen.
She was afraid her choice had been taken from her.

Hours later Sarah carried Gabriel's smile and Lucas's drawing up to her room. She had stood by
through the awkward meeting between Rio and his
sons, but at least Lucas was reassured that his father
found value in his skill.

He'd told the boy he had the sharp eyes of an eagle
to see so clearly and so deeply and capture her face.
She had requested the drawing, and before Lucas answered, Rio offered it as a gift. Sarah knew she walked
a delicate line between them, but she wanted the boy
to answer. When he did, she was sorry she insisted.

*''Keep it. It is as he says. A gift.''*

Sarah instantly looked at Rio's face. She couldn't miss the hurt in his eyes. *He says*…not my father.

She fretted over the terrible thing that stood between them. How much more could she pry? Should she even try? She felt saddened to know how much alike they were and how far apart they stood with their guarded emotions. Thankfully Gabriel acted as a loving bridge between them.

With her door closed and the lamp lit, she stood for a few moments, searching for a place to put the drawing. She rejected hiding it in a drawer.

Vanity had nothing to do with her final decision. She wedged the edges into the corner of the mirror's frame.

She needed the reminder that she was still young, still a woman, one with needs. She traced the suggestion of a single braid lying over the line of her shoulder, then touched Lucas's drawing of her lips.

Was this the woman Rio saw? Was she the one he had kissed. Did the loneliness show in her gaze?

And the hunger?

*"You should know I would not be a gentle lover with you."*

"Who asked you to be?" she whispered.

Annoyed with herself, she rubbed her hands over her face.

Too many questions. She needed a long stretch of time when she could forget the dreams of the past.

Rio would not be a gentle lover. He would not be a patient one, either.

And what did she truly want?

"To be whole again," she murmured, then turned her back on the drawing.

Through a restless night's sleep, questions nagged her.

What had Rio seen when he looked at her?

Were her secrets safe?

For the next two days there was an uneasy, tense truce in the house. It lasted that long because she made every effort not to be alone with Rio.

Gabriel helped her. Unwittingly, true. He attached himself to her from the moment she set her foot on the last stair.

Theirs was an isolated world. Water stood knee-deep from the front yard to the road.

Sarah worried about her friends in town. But they had the advantage of being near other neighbors.

As much as she was beginning to hate the continuous deluge of rain for the confinement to house and barn, she prayed that it would keep on, for Rio and his sons were safe here.

She knew he worried, as she did, that those three men were out there...waiting.

But where? How close had they followed Rio before they lost him in the storm?

But Sarah couldn't dwell on this threat. She had other problems to deal with. The boys, busy while doing chores, were showing signs of restlessness as only boys can. They squabbled, and they fought. Due to their lack of clothes to change, going outside was limited to necessity.

Sarah improvised a game of marbles using dried peas. Most didn't roll smoothly, but that provided balance between Gabriel's enthusiastic shooting and Lucas's uncanny skill once she had taught them the game. Broken twigs from the kindling pile gave them a supply for the game of jackstraws.

Once more Lucas, with his quick eye and hand, excelled.

Sarah found a way to separate them. They were running low on foodstuffs. She had been lavish in her meals and most of the smoked meat was gone. She asked Gabriel if he would like to help her take stock of what was left in the pantry.

Sarah thought having him count the canned goods and the jars of the garden's bounty would help him feel important, and work on his addition.

He insisted on climbing up onto the chair while she held the lantern. But after one shelf was inventoried, Gabriel stopped and looked down at her.

"Are you old?" he asked, his eyes intense.

Sarah's mouth opened, but no sound came out.

"I should not ask?"

"No. I mean, it's all right to ask me."

"Are you old?"

"I imagine I'm old to you."

"Are you old enough to be a mother?"

Sarah almost dropped the lantern. She started to shake. She stared straight ahead but couldn't focus on one thing.

*Not this. Dear Lord, have mercy. Not this.*

"I made you angry with me."

"Oh, no, Gabriel. I couldn't be angry with you." She forced a smile to wooden lips. She found a way to work around the pain. Like his father, and Lucas, this little boy's need touched her heart. And this, despite all her warnings to herself.

"I guess I am old enough." Sarah raised her free hand to his arm. Touching him like this wasn't enough. She could see he was crying out to be loved, to be hugged. She set the lantern aside.

"You miss your mother very much, don't you?"

"Sometimes," he whispered, placing his hand over his heart, "I hurt in here."

Sarah cupped his face. "I know. I lost my mother when I was a little girl. The pain will go away, Gabriel. I can promise you that. But not the good memories you have of her."

"Did...did someone bad kill your mother, too?"

"No. It doesn't matter how she died. She was gone and I thought I was alone, but I still had my father. Just like you do. And my cousin Mary. She and I were very close. Just like you have Lucas."

He bent his head so that his forehead touched hers. "Sometimes Lucas does not like me. But he is my brother. I still wish I had a mother. I did not want to be like the other boys in the mission school. They did not believe me that I had a father. They told me if I had a father I would not be there."

Sarah lowered her hands until she could hug him. After a few moments, Gabriel pulled back. His small hand brushed across her cheek.

"Do your tears fall for me?"

"And for me," she answered as honestly as she could. "Sometimes it's good to cry. And you must not remember what anyone said about your father. You're all together now. That's what is important."

"But I still wish—"

"No, Gabriel. Don't. Please. You do understand that I can't be your mother. No one can take her special place. I will be your friend."

"A special friend? *Varlebena?*"

"A very special one," she whispered. "What does the word mean?"

"It is an Apache word that means *forever.*"

Sarah swallowed hard. She forced herself to smile.

"Yes. *Varlebena* friends."

Gabriel's hug was hard and tight, and her own no less. She blinked rapidly to stop the tears as the ache inside her lessened. There was, just as she told Rio, something healing about a child's love. She wouldn't think about the coming day when he could be gone with his father and his brother. She would only take each day's sharing and treasure it.

Later, after Sarah had set the kitchen to rights, she was surprised by Lucas's request that she join them in the parlor.

"In a few minutes, Lucas. I was just about to make a cup of tea."

Sarah turned as the boy left. She had tried to give Rio some privacy with his sons at night. This was the first time they had asked for her company.

She didn't want to speculate why.

She couldn't push aside the reason that came to mind.

Rio was leaving.

Before the thought settled she left the room.

Both doors to the parlor were open. The room was cozily warm with the fire blazing. Lucas lay on his stomach, legs swinging back and forth, his chin propped on his hands. Her gaze went to Rio, who sat to the side with Gabriel on his lap. She didn't miss her rifle leaning against the wall, near the wood box and within Rio's reach.

The firelight cast its burnished glow over one side of Rio's face, and left the other side in shadow. But she could make out the deepened lines of tension.

"Sarah, come sit with us," Gabriel said. "We left room for you on the quilt. Father is going to tell us a story about the Mountain People. They have spirits that can heal."

"I'll look forward to hearing it." Her fingers curled over the edge of the door frame. "I was making tea. Would anyone like a cup?"

The boys refused. Rio watched her. Had the quaver in her voice given away her unspoken fear? From the way Rio looked at her, she had to wonder if her thoughts were evident.

"I'll just be a few minutes," she called out, and hastily retreated to the kitchen.

The wind and rain had died down, but she felt the cold drafts of the night seeping through the door and window.

Sarah impatiently paced, waiting for the water to

boil. She saw that the wood box needed replenishing. Two more passes in front of the stove and still the kettle wasn't steaming.

She hadn't been outside all day. Before she thought about it, she snatched her slicker from the hook and slipped it on. The moment she opened the back door, the cold air made her shiver. But she did not have far to go.

The light from the coal-oil fixture streamed from the doorway and the window. It was enough to guide her steps to the woodshed where the light ended abruptly. She bent over, one hand extended as she felt for the kindling pile.

She had four or five pieces of wood cradled in her arm when she was overcome with a gooseflesh-raising chill. The hair on her nape rose. Sarah spun around.

"Who's there?"

She searched the area at the edge of the light, sensing something out of place. There was no movement, no shadows that didn't belong.

But her every instinct denied what her eyes were seeing. She looked around again. There to the left…was that…

Sarah never completed the thought.

# Chapter Twelve

Rio glanced toward the parlor doorway. He had to
wonder if Sarah had changed her mind. She'd been
gone far longer than the few minutes needed to make
a cup of tea.

Gabriel squirmed on his lap, giving voice to his
thoughts about what was keeping her.

A burst of green sap threw a shower of sparks upward in the fireplace, then it was quiet again.

And in that quiet they all heard the whistling of the
kettle.

Rio released a mounting tension he hadn't been
aware of. She would be coming soon. For the past two
days he had maintained his distance from her, but not
without a cost to himself. Even when she was out of
sight, she remained constant in his mind.

The hair on his nape rose as the noise from the
kitchen continued without break. Surely she heard it.
Surely she had poured the water for her tea.

Rio lifted Gabriel from his lap and rose in a controlled rush. He didn't want to alarm his sons. Not

when he had no true cause for alarm. Being hunted had finely honed his instincts. He wasn't about to question them. Something was wrong.

"Stay with your brother," he whispered. He glanced at the loaded rifle within his easy reach.

"Don't either one of you leave here." His hand caught hold of the rifle's barrel, and he started for the door.

Behind him, Gabriel made a garbled sound. He looked over his shoulder to see that Lucas had his hand over his brother's mouth, while he pulled him toward the darker corner of the room. Rio nodded to see that the fireplace's poker was in Lucas's hand.

He stood in the parlor's doorway. The water in the kettle hit a violent boil. The metal pot rocked with a clatter, and the whistling sent out its hurried call. He knew then that Sarah was not in the kitchen. She had not passed the doorway. He had been watching too closely for her to have slipped upstairs.

Outside then.

But why? What could have drawn her to leave the house?

Rio could not stop himself from looking back into the parlor. He did not see either of his sons. And their safety was the most important thing in his life.

He was torn. His sons. Sarah.

She needed him.

He knew it on a deep, gut-wrenching level as if she had called his name.

And that could only mean one thing.

Somehow, despite the storm that had washed out any tracks, *they* had found him.

He tensed, muscles tightening as he started toward the lighted kitchen. So much warmth, so much truth, and such new, fierce desire had been found within those walls.

He sensed the room was empty. No sound reached him but for the rattle of the almost-dry kettle.

And that in itself was a cry for help.

*Sarah!*

His gaze swept over the darkened area near the front door, and then tried probing the darkness beyond it.

If those three men had discovered him here, they had Sarah.

With every screaming nerve ending he wanted to reject his own logical conclusion.

But enough time had passed for her to return from every reason that would have drawn her from the house in the first place.

She had not cried out.

He was certain he would have heard her. Or maybe he told himself that, because he wanted—no, needed—to believe it.

Rio inched his way toward the front door, his back pressed against the wall, his grip knuckle-white on the rifle.

He called upon every Apache god to be merciful. Nothing must happen to Sarah. Not like…

He had to shut out thoughts of the violence these men not only were capable of, but relished.

Rio slid back the latch. Holding the rifle with one

hand, he turned the knob to ease the door open just enough for him to slip outside.

Fear walked out with him. The fear he had lived with for so long. The chilling air left him with hair-roughened skin.

He made no sound and kept his back to the wall of the house as he worked his way across the front porch. At the corner he paused and listened.

Water dripped from the eaves, but the rain had lessened to a drizzle. As his vision accustomed itself to the night, he began to make out the darker shadows of the trees.

Making his way around the side of the house, Rio felt the pull of the mud and stepped with a gliding motion. Water ran in the trench he had dug, but the night held a strange silence. A waiting one.

He was about to skirt the woodshed near the back corner when a faint noise arrested his forward step. Slowly, almost afraid to breathe deeply, he stepped back. What exactly had he heard? Was it the scrape of someone brushing against the wood? He closed off thought. He sent his senses to probe the night.

Not too long ago he had watched and waited with infinite patience before he made his move. He had been one with the shadows that night, oblivious to the cold and wet. But that night, both fear and excitement had pricked his senses alert.

He could only account for the fear tonight. Fear for Sarah.

Rage over the transgressions of the past raised his bloodlust. He would be too late to keep Sarah safe from those animals. He was not going to relive the nightmare of the past.

His senses quested the darkness. He shut out the faint rattle coming from the kitchen, the scent of wood smoke drifting, the dank odor of wet wood and the smell of the earth swollen with life-giving rain.

He had to cross the small trench. No danger from the few inches of water that ran in it, but he had to beware of the treacherous mud. His feet sank deeper with every minute that he delayed moving.

With his long legs, a few steps brought him around the back of the woodshed. Now he could see the spill of light from the kitchen window. There was no sign of anyone moving about in the room.

He started toward the barn and the corral, probing the night-shrouded corners where someone could hide. He strained to hear alarm from the horses, but he could hear nothing that alerted them to the presence of strangers.

Rio stilled as he heard the same small noise as before. It *was* from the woodshed. He fingered the gaps in the rough planking, knowing even before he tried that he couldn't see anything within.

*Find Sarah!*

Like the two-beat chant of the circle dance, timed by drum and rattling gourd, the urgent order replayed in his mind.

Rio eyed the shed's roof. He thought about the diminished woodpile. There was more than enough room within the darkened interior for a man to stand.

And wait.

The bait was snared.

The trap set.

It only awaited him playing his part.

But he had no wish to die. He would not leave Sarah and his sons defenseless.

Rio lifted the rifle above his head and slid it onto the shed's roof. They would expect him to cross the open ground and search the barn. He had no intent of following that path.

He withdrew his knife, setting it between his teeth. He searched the edge of the roof, stretching his arms above his head to find the space between the boards. Good food and rest had given him back his strength. He needed it now as he grabbed hold and hoisted himself up and over the roof.

He heard the scrape of his clothing, wet now as the intermittent drizzle turned steady. He held his breath, praying that a wrong move from him wouldn't end Sarah's life.

He glanced toward the barn. Was a bullet waiting for him to move?

He had no choice. Prone, he inched his way to the front edge of the shed.

Rio's gaze roamed the spill of light from both the window and glass in the back door. The slices of light were muted at the edges where night swallowed them up.

His teeth clenched over the cold blade, leaving his hands free to curl over the edge. He used that hold to gain a few inches. Now he could peer over the roof.

The deep pocket below revealed nothing the first

time he probed it. The roof's slant—higher in the front than the rear—limited his vision to whatever was directly below him.

Rio no longer questioned if someone waited.

He could smell him.

The odor of fear, the strong stink of tobacco, the reek of rancid sweat and food like the rotten stench of spoiled meat.

A foul, breathing thing that Rio refused to call a man.

He'd been so long in the dark that the sight of a glint of metal below didn't surprise him. He heard the scuffle of a boot scraping against the debris on the shed's floor.

*That's it. Come forward. Come to me.*

Rio slowed his breathing. The pounding beat of his heart slowed, too. The heat of rage receded and was replaced by an icy determination that this one was breathing his last.

Impossible to demand that he wait. Yet, that's just what he did. He knew the delay of his presence worked on the other's nerves. There was another small noise. Then another.

He refused to think of the other two.

If fate and gods decreed that he meet his death this night he could only insure that he did not die alone.

But not Sarah. Innocent Sarah must never pay with her life for her kindness.

Rio was staring so hard at the spot below that he took moments to register what he was seeing. The glint of metal came from a handgun's barrel.

Rio felt his patience was paying off.

An icy wind sprang up as if anxious to catch the increased tempo of the rain.

He was chilled, and clearly felt the cramp of his muscles as the strain of maintaining his position became almost unbearable.

Rio turned his thoughts away from the man.

Away from Sarah, too.

The Apache believed that if you kept your thoughts concentrated on a living thing, your thoughts would reach out and touch the mind of the other. The same held true for staring.

These were things he employed without thought when hunting. How could he have forgotten them tonight?

He thought instead of the horse that carried the piece of filth here.

Somewhere out in the blackness that horse was tied. Between the rain and the wind the animal was restive. The horse longed for the warmth of a sheltered place, grain, a bait of corn, sweet hay. All deserved, for the animal had come a far piece.

Rio closed his eyes for a few moments. He had to imagine the horse. He had to see the front hoof pawing the muddy earth. See the head that tossed, the neck that bunched with muscle as the animal jerked his head to pull free of the rein that held him.

Again, and then again, he envisioned the horse, until he could see the sidling motion of the animal's body. Could almost sense the tugs on the reins getting stronger.

*There is power in your mind, grandson. Use it. Listen to your senses. They never lie. Will them to be your obedient servants. They have gifts to give.*

Rio felt a tearing within his mind as he cast aside thoughts of those he loved, the ones he had sworn to protect and allowed the flow of his thoughts to find the animal. Shelter. Food. The nostrils flared as it caught the scent of these things and more—the company of others of its kind.

And from out of the rain-swept blackness came the whinny of a horse. Faint, to be sure. But there it was again.

Rio almost sagged with relief. The whinny told him things he needed to know. If there were three, one would have been left to guard the horses.

But he heard only one horse whinny. One animal? One killer?

Would the gods be so merciful?

For Sarah, and for his sons, they had to be.

Now, being greedy, he wanted the torrential male rains of the Thunder People, not this soft female downpour. He wanted the rumble of thunder to conceal noise.

And he wanted the killer below him to step out into the open.

Rio gathered his body. All doubt that what he wanted wouldn't come to pass had left him. He took the knife within his hand, coming up to a crouch, knowing that his quarry would emerge into the night.

Then, a darker, stinking mass separated from the shed's interior.

The horse's distressful whinny pierced the night again. Rio could almost taste the surge of fear from the killer below him.

Wait, Rio whispered to himself. *Wait.*

From stillness came motion.

The man stepped out, his gun swinging from side to side as if he sensed his prey close and would have the first shot.

"Where are ya? I can smell ya, breed. Nothin's savin' ya this time. I got ya. This time I got ya all."

*One more step. Take one more step.*

His quarry did more. He took several steps to the right where he searched the side of the shed. It was that move that Rio had waited for.

He landed on the balls of his feet, rising up to lock his arm around the killer's throat. The choking hold cut off a cry.

For an instant rage blinded Rio. He wanted, needed, to plunge the knife into the heart of his wife's murderer.

He longed to be the true warrior of his mother's and his wife's people. No mercy to an enemy.

The staying hand of reason whispered he needed information first.

"Where are the others?" Rio demanded in a harsh whisper. He brought the point of the knife up and flicked the tip across the man's cheek.

Rio had felt the strength of his enemy gathered for a struggle. The small cut ended it.

The man was half a head shorter than Rio. As Rio assessed the man's broad shoulders and the powerful upper body, he jerked his head back, the move tightening his hold.

The killer gagged, and as he did, he sagged forward so that his weight forced Rio to bend with him or lose his grip. But Rio had wrestled with the Apache as a boy, and they were lessons not to be forgotten. Not if a boy had the stigma of white blood to overcome.

Rio slammed his knee into the small of the man's back. His fisted hand over the handle of his knife jabbed downward on the man's gun hand. It was a silent struggle, but no less deadly as Rio hit the hand repeatedly in an effort to get rid of the weapon. His biggest fear wasn't for himself taking a stray bullet, but of one hitting Sarah.

If she was there...

He couldn't spare a moment to look for her.

His side took a beating from the elbow slams and still he hung on, tightening his choke hold.

The rain granted his earlier wish as the storm released a heavy driving rain along with talons of icy wind.

Rio grappled with the man, struggling to retain his footing in the treacherous mud. He barely managed to jerk his head aside as the killer reached back, fingers groping for his eyes, his hair, any part of him that he could grab onto.

Still Rio wouldn't release him, even as he felt himself slip sideways. Quick to take advantage, the shorter but heavier man slammed his boot heel and heard Rio grunt when the heel connected with his shin.

The man's fingers ripped at Rio's arm. The gun

went off, the bullet falling harmlessly into the mud. Rio used his strength, the force of his rage, and even his fear to bring the man down to his knees. But he went down too quickly and Rio slipped, loosing his choke hold.

The slashing rain blinded Rio. He could only use his other senses, but he was concentrating on the gun and never saw the man's elbow come smashing into his temple. Rio was knocked clear.

He heard the shot, felt the spattering of wood bits and mud hit his cheek. He rolled over several times, rising just enough to throw his knife.

The gun was emptied in rapid fire accompanied by a gurgling sound. For a few moments Rio lay stunned, until the pounding rain forced him to move.

He had to find Sarah.

# Chapter Thirteen

The woodshed was empty. Rio spared a glance for the body sprawled in the mud. If anything had happened to Sarah, he'd want to kill him all over again.

He retrieved his rifle, fighting the urge to call out her name. He trusted the instinct that told him this one was here alone. Yet, there still remained that fragment of fear for what they had done to his wife, to his home. Not finding any sign of Sarah nourished that fear. Had the others been here before? Did one or both of them have Sarah?

Soaked to the skin, he slogged his way through the muddy ground and searched the corral, behind the overflowing water trough, the nearest woods.

Rio had to caution himself to enter the barn alert for trouble. The wood bar across the doors was not in place. His doing. The rains had swollen the wood to where he had had to hammer it free. A rope with a simple slipknot over the wooden hooks where the bar rested was what held the doors closed.

He set the rifle against the wall, his fingers, stiff and

cold, fumbling to free the rope. He could hear the stallion's challenge, a penetrating cry in the night. For all the trouble he was having, he should dismiss the idea of Sarah being inside, but he had to be sure.

No one had been in the barn. He saw that with the sheltered lantern light. He was the one who had tracked in fresh mud and water. There was no time to calm the horses. He left quickly.

The cold wind and slashing rain stole his breath as he searched the brush behind the barn, then fought his way to the pasture where the rising waters slowed his progress.

*Think. Think,* he ordered himself, forcing a halt beneath one of the towering cottonwoods.

If Sarah had managed to break free but was injured, she couldn't have gone far. He refused to allow the image of her stumbling into the flooding waters, unable to get up.

Rio might refuse to acknowledge the image, but it was there in his mind. The image drove him out to search for her closer to home.

Her name, born of panicked desperation, clawed its way free from his lips. The wind distorted the sound, but another, then another followed until Rio was back at the woodshed.

He stood there, his hair plastered to his head, rain running down his face, blinding him, and he screamed her name.

A warning whispered through his mind. He spun around, bringing the cocked rifle to bear only to see the blanket-shrouded face of his son Lucas revealed by the lantern he shielded close to his body.

"We heard the shots. I had to come. Gabriel was afraid. I found the body. I could not find you."

Rio said nothing. He opened his arms, stepping toward his son. He clasped the boy's slim body to him. One thin arm wrapped around Rio's waist. He felt the racking shivers from his son's body and held him tighter.

"I'm safe. Maybe we all are, Lucas. But I've got to find Sarah. She came out. I don't know what he did to her. Here, take the rifle and go inside."

He set the boy away from him, hating that his son had to see more violence. He had had enough in his young life. Rio had had enough, too.

Yet, in a strange way, he was grateful for these few moments. Lucas clung to him. Loving concern had broken through the boy's bitterness.

"Go," Rio shouted, urging Lucas toward the house as he took the lantern from him.

"Is he one of them?" Lucas yelled, pointing to the body.

*Is he?* Rio didn't know where the question or the hesitation had come from. He had to be sure. He had killed the man.

"Go, Lucas!" he repeated. "I must find Sarah."

"Let me help you."

Rio clasped his son's shoulder. "I need you to be with Gabriel. You said he was frightened. And if Sarah comes back, I need you to be there for her." Rio's grip tightened for a second, then he let his son go.

"This is the first time you said you needed me."

"I've always needed you, Lucas. Always."

He watched his son reach the safety of the kitchen door and disappear inside.

Rio walked out, counting about fifty feet, then quartered the area, returning to begin again. Some minutes later, as his search grew frantic, he noted that the rain had slackened to a dreary drizzle. He worked over the backyard, then the side, and the front. Everywhere he hunted for a sign of Sarah.

Chilled to the bone, he dragged his weary body around to the other side.

Where could she be?

His throat was raw from shouting her name. He stumbled his way to the cottonwood trees, lifting the lantern to the lower limbs on the chance she had managed to climb to safety.

Nothing.

He started his count away from the house, slogging through the ankle-high water. He couldn't feel his feet. When he tripped, he barely managed to hold the lantern high as he went down on one knee. His hand dug down through the mud until he touched the corner of a flat rock. He pushed his body, staggering until he could stand.

His fingers were numb, curled around the handle of the lantern. He swung the light back and forth, refusing to give up. She was out there. Somewhere. And he had to find her.

Rio made his way back to the house, sagging

against the wall. He drew ragged breaths, pushing off to start again.

He was stumbling around blindly, feeling the pull of the past. He fought the images coming to mind. The smoking timbers, the carnage of what had been his home. The sickness working its way up to gag him, and still he searched, and then, falling to his knees.

The scene replayed itself in his mind, but he suddenly found himself on his knees in the mud, the lantern gone to land at a crazy angle, the soft earth cushioning its fall so that its light glowed brightly.

He threw back his head, howling his grief to the heavens. Only when the rain threatened to choke him did he lower his head, and there at the corner he saw the overturned rain barrel.

Rio crawled through the mud. Every thought wiped clean but his need to get there. His hand touched the boot first.

"Sarah?" The whispered demand tore from his lips. He shoved at the heavy oak barrel with one hand, pulling her legs free. He cursed the mud that held the barrel fast, dragging out her limp body.

"Sarah?" he cried, cradling her close. He needed light to see where she was hurt. She wasn't dead. The faint warmth of her shallow breaths touched his lips.

Rio struggled to his feet with her limp body, unable to speak the words of thanksgiving that came from his heart. He carried her slicker-clad body around to the back door, showing no surprise that Lucas was there to open it.

"Hot water," he whispered to his son, heading

straight for the parlor. He knelt on the quilt, carefully removed the slicker and tossed it aside.

It was then that her injury was discovered. Rio didn't find it. Gabriel did.

"She is bleeding, Father."

Rio's gaze followed the boy's shaking finger that pointed to the lump of broken skin on the back of Sarah's head.

"Father, is she…she…"

The note of terror in his child's voice snatched Rio's attention from Sarah. "Sarah's alive. I'll show you." He took hold of the boy's trembling hand and set it palm down over Sarah's lips.

"They have come again. They want to hurt her like they did to Mother."

He gathered his son to him. "No, Gabriel. I won't let them hurt any of you ever again." He closed his eyes for a moment, hugging his son. Silently Rio cursed the animals that still hunted them, still brought nightmares and fear into their lives.

"I need your help, Gabriel. Sarah needs all of us to take care of her." He pulled back, his hands coming to rest on the boy's small shoulders. "Can you do this for me?"

The boy nodded, but his eyes darted to the still form of Sarah. He bit his lower lip and blinked rapidly, ashamed to feel tears.

"Go to Sarah's room. Bring her nightgown and robe. Socks, too, if you can find them. We must get her warm."

Gabriel nodded again, but this time he moved off to do his father's bidding.

Rio gently turned Sarah's head to the side so there was no pressure on the wound. It was then that he saw how filthy his hands were. The heat of the fire became painful as it penetrated his cold body. He forced himself to his feet, unwilling to taint Sarah with the blood on his hands.

He grabbed the clean borrowed shirt and pants and headed for the kitchen.

Lucas sat at the table, the rifle before him. He turned when he heard his father. "Sarah?"

"She will be all right. Go stay with her. I need to clean up."

Within minutes, Rio had stripped and, using the harsh lye soap and cold well water, he washed the grime from himself. Once dressed he checked on the water Lucas had heating. It was barely warm. He searched the pantry, gathering what he needed. All the while he kept his thoughts from the body outside.

Sarah came first.

Rio had just set his clothing to soak when Gabriel summoned him. Sarah was moaning.

Carrying a basin of warm water, the salve and linens he'd found, Rio entered the parlor. He sent his sons from the room to wait for him in the kitchen.

"I will keep watch," Lucas said, then took his brother by the hand.

And Rio, remembering what his son had said about needing him, looked up. "I depend upon you, Lucas."

"And me, Father? Me, too?"

"And you. Go on."

"Sarah," he whispered when they were gone. "Can you hear me?" He didn't wait for a reply that might be a long time coming. He washed her face, noting that his hands were trembling. There was no avoiding what had to be done. His sons could not do it.

Her flesh was so cold to his touch. She was soaked to the skin. Wounded.

All valid reasons for him to strip her quickly.

But Rio could not rid himself of the thought that the very private Sarah would hate him undressing her.

He tugged off her boots, rubbing her chilled feet between his hands. His thoughts turned back to the first night he had broken into her home.

He had ignored his own chilled flesh after chasing her through the storm. He saw himself once more standing in her room, denying her the right to wear the very pants he was sliding down the long, shapely length of her legs.

He fumbled with the tie of her drawers, feeling again the way her pride and strength seemed to come against him.

And the hot flare of desire that had made him so angry. With her. Although he had known she had done nothing to provoke it.

He hurried now to remove her shirt and camisole.

And for a moment he once more feasted on the slim, wild beauty of Sarah, before he covered her with a warmed blanket.

He had threatened her. Mocked her. All the while he had fought the heat of his blood, the betraying body that forcefully reminded him how long he had been without a woman.

He had finally turned away from her. Away from his own needs.

But then he had not tasted the passion of Sarah's kiss. Had not really cared what happened to her.

And now...

With a ruthless shove, Rio closed that mental door. He wasn't ready to think about what she meant to him now, or to his sons.

A slow fever rose inside him at the allure of firelight and shadows shifting over her pale golden body. The breath caught in his throat as he gathered the folds of her nightgown and gently slipped it over her head. He smoothed the cloth over her arms, breathing in the sweet and spicy scent that touched all her clothing. A scent very much like Sarah herself.

He caught hold of the faded blue ribbon ties that would draw the cotton together over the shadowed valley of her breasts. The whisper of his name jerked him from his thoughts.

"Hush, Sarah. You are safe." He avoided looking at her face. In his effort to hurry, his fingers were made clumsy by her every breath that lifted her breasts to touch his hands.

"Tell me." It was all she could say. She moistened her lips. The firelight picked out the tight set of his mouth, his still-damp hair. The shadows licked at his face, proud features of a man not easy to know. A sea of nausea lapped her insides. She could not focus any longer with the pounding in her head growing stronger.

She couldn't see him, but she could feel his hands on her body. The slide of the blanket that covered her. His gentle tugs to pull her nightgown down. His gentle handling brought moisture to her eyes, and she blinked it away. There was no way to deny the warmth that stole into her from every place his hands touched. Through the wave of pain in her head she realized she didn't want to try.

What had happened? She remembered going to the woodshed. Had she fallen?

"Please?" Her voice held a pitiful sound. She groped for and found his hand as he resettled the blanket over her. Sarah held him tight, entwining her fingers with his. His hand was a comforting anchor while the room spun around her.

"Tell…me. Now." She struggled to convey her overpowering need to know. Something had happened. Every sense attuned to this one man, every sense that she trusted told her so. Something terrible. She did not question it. She *knew*.

"First a sip of tea." He cradled the back of her neck in one hand and with the other brought the cup of cooled liquid to her lips. "Good thing you have all those little crocks labeled. You must have the grandfather of all headaches." Her eyes were closed, but he could feel her looking at him, judging him. He kept his tone soft as she drained the cup in steady sips and, when she was done, he carefully lowered her head.

He replaced the soiled pad of cloth with a fresh one

dipped and wrung of cold water. "You have a bump and a cut, but the bleeding's stopped." Fingers shaking with the barely controlled rage that she had been caught up in the violence of his life brushed back her hair.

"Rio."

He backed away until he knelt beside her. She wouldn't release his hand. And he told her.

Sarah heard his stark sketch of events told in a deadened voice. She squeezed his hand tighter.

In the silence that followed, she opened her eyes. It was an effort to focus on him. He knelt beside her, his head bent, the length of his hair obscuring his face. His shoulders curved inward as if he were beaten.

A bright flare of fury obliterated pain and the nausea for Sarah. And with it came the realization that Rio was ashamed of telling her. No shame for what he had done to protect them all, but just for telling her.

Once more she found herself unable to question the rightness of knowing it to be true.

"How do I thank you for my life?"

"Your life? If I was not here there'd be no threat to you."

"Rio, you did what you had to. I can't thank you enough. Lucas? Gabriel? Are they—"

"In the kitchen. Worried about you."

Without raising his head, he lifted their joined hands to his lips.

"Sarah, I—"

"Would you hold me?" Head pounding, body aching from her ordeal, she managed a half turn and braced her body on one elbow.

## Chapter Fourteen

She would swear that she saw him flinch. His head came up slowly. Sarah held her gaze steady on him.

He stared at her as if he had not heard her, or he could not believe what she had asked of him.

But there was something else in his own searching gaze that seemed to touch upon each feature of her face. She didn't know what he was looking for. She only knew the need to feel his strong arms around her.

And then, from their joined hands, Sarah felt his pain race up her arm into her heart.

"You did not hear me? I told you I killed a man," he said in a rigidly controlled voice. He held up his hand and then lifted their joined ones. "With these."

She knew what he wanted from her, and she was just as determined not to give it to him. There was pain in her head, but it had not clouded her thinking. She could not condemn him for taking the life of a man who had destroyed his life. He really didn't need her to do it. He was punishing himself.

"I heard you," she whispered. "Now, would you hold me?"

Touching her at all was a mistake. She was warm, slender and supple, seemingly lit with the same fire that burned in his veins.

Her fingers tangled in his hair. He felt her thigh trembling against his own as he drew her up and held her closer. She turned her face to his, her black eyes and her parted lips invited more.

She knew what had killed the joy in him. But she found herself wanting to give it back. She longed to take his grief and rage, and yes, even the dark despair akin to her own. She knew what he felt—alone, stunned from having love torn away.

"Sarah."

The intensity in his voice matched the intensity of his eyes. Those eyes that darkened as his lashes swept down, hiding them. His kiss had a bittersweet taste. She wondered briefly if he felt he was betraying the memory of the wife he still grieved. Because she leaned into his body, she felt the tension vibrating through muscle and bone. Almost, she thought, like the rope holding a green-broke horse, too tightly drawn, fairly humming with the strain.

Against this was the very gentle way his lips touched hers, the feeling of safety and of tenderness as his hand stroked her cheek, turning her face, tilting it up and taking more of what she could offer him now.

But Sarah took comfort from him, too. She couldn't remember a time when she had not had to be the strong one. Hunger was tempered by tenderness with every deepening moment of being held, of kissing him.

Rio caught his breath and shuddered. It nearly killed him to let her go. He had tasted her passion, but the past few minutes he knew another Sarah, one who kissed with a gentle giving that was a balm of peace spreading inside him.

He looked into her eyes and discovered within this woman a heart flame that could burn away the coldest winter night, the darkest corner of despair in a man's soul.

But with the tender concern in her eyes, he felt some deeper, unnamed emotion reaching out from her to wrap around him.

Rio used a great deal of care to nestle her cheek against his chest and wrap his arms around her. Without hesitation, without a word spoken, she accepted what he could give of himself.

Sarah closed her eyes. She felt soothed by the stroke of his hand up and down her back. And inside her, there was an easing of the small, empty ache that had been so much a part of her. She did not understand why it should be so, why this man could bring some warm balm to that empty place, but silently whispered a prayer of thanks that it had happened.

The strength of his hand was like the strength of the man himself—tempered with gentleness. She found her thoughts drifting to things both Mary and Catherine had confided about their husbands. Both

Rafe and Greg were strong men, but they also had a gentle side.

Catherine's wish came back to her, that she too would find love with a stranger who entered this house. She sighed and snuggled closer as she inhaled the clean, fresh scent of rain and the maleness that was Rio's alone. She couldn't remember ever cuddling like this with Judd. Not even when he courted her. She had thought herself wise not to spend too much time alone with him. Hindsight showed she'd been as foolish as a man who judged a horse by its harness.

She waited for the anger to come whenever thoughts of Judd entered her mind. But it wasn't there. For the first time that she could remember, at most she felt a mild annoyance that she thought of him at all.

The herbal tea Rio had made of Mary's sleeping mix was beginning to work. The warmth of the fire, the heat of Rio's body and the tea combined to lull her. And that unnamed emotion that stirred shadowlike in her mind? She couldn't put a name to it, couldn't bring it forth to examine.

With another deeper sigh issuing forth, Sarah laid this flight of fancy directly on the blow she had received. It could be nothing else.

Their quiet calm was broken by a whisper of concern from the doorway. Lucas wanted to know if she was all right.

There was no hurried breaking apart. "Come and see," Rio invited, then slowly withdrew his arms.

As he nudged Sarah to lie down again, he heard Lucas call out to his brother. For the last few moments of privacy, he found himself clenching his fingers around a loose fistful of her hair. He didn't want to release the silky mass but had to.

Rio leaned closer to her. Without knowing why he did it, he brushed his lips over her temple.

"Sarah, I need to go."

Her fingertips touched his lips. "I know what you need to do." Her vision was blurry again, then cleared. Something akin to pain passed over his features. With the tip of one finger she shaped his lips. "Stay safe," she murmured.

He didn't know what waited out there for him, even as she understood he had no choice but to go. Once she had stood armed with holstered gun and rifle and declared to Rafe McCade that she was ready to protect her home and the women who lived there against any man who dared think he'd found easy pickings.

Now she had to depend on Rio. She didn't have the strength to toss a teacup.

He moved to stand when Sarah's eyes flared wide. She grabbed his arm. "The gun. I forgot."

"What?"

"I can't wear the gun belt when I work with the horses. In the barn near the front. I left it hanging beneath an old jacket." She shook her head. "I can't believe I forgot. You get it. If you leave the rifle for Lucas you'll have nothing else."

"All right. Just calm down. Come on, Sarah, you need rest."

She whispered something, lost to both of them, and then he was gone.

\* \* \*

Hours later Sarah woke from a fretful doze. For a few minutes she did not know where she was, then it all came rushing back. She gingerly turned her head to the side and saw that Gabriel slept beside her. Lucas was on the settee with his head flung back, the rifle cradled in his arms, but he too was soundly asleep.

She winced as she turned her head. Her fingers probed the wound, sticky with salve, and then the lump above it. The hard pounding had dulled to an ache, but she was relieved that the nausea was gone. Silently she blessed Mary and her potions.

Darting her gaze toward Lucas and the rifle he held, she remembered that Rio had left him to guard them. She ought to take the weapon from him so he could rest more comfortably but quickly decided against it. Touching him might waken him and if Lucas was frightened, he could fire the rifle.

But where was Rio?

The question was no sooner thought than faint sounds from the kitchen trickled into her consciousness.

She waited a few moments. But this night there was no sense of alarm that a stranger was in her house.

Rio was back. A glance showed only darkness beyond the lace curtains. If he was back, it meant he hadn't found the other two killers.

Sarah found getting up an effort. She felt weak and a little dizzy. More so when she managed to add a few small logs to the fire without waking up the boys. The licking flames brightened the room, and she saw her robe tossed over one of the side chairs. She slipped it on, grateful for the added warmth as she left the parlor.

There was grit beneath her bare feet despite all the efforts to keep the floor clean. Cool drafts snaked through the hallway and chilled her.

The coal-oil fixture shed only a feeble light in the kitchen. As she came to the doorway and stopped, the light above caught the sheen of Rio's knife on the table. He stood off to the side.

He was drenched. His hair was plastered to his head, beads of water dripped off the ends. Heavy with rain, his clothes clung to his body.

"Something dry, Sarah."

It wasn't a request. She spun around too fast and had to cling to the doorway a moment before she hurried back to get his clothes and a blanket. He had to be chilled to the bone.

She was back in minutes, and forced herself not to utter a sound.

Rio had stripped off his shirt, his moccasins, and had unbuttoned the front of his pants. He stood near the dry sink pumping water. His olive skin shimmered from wetness, his back and shoulders bunched and knotted as he forced his soaked pants down.

Sarah was assaulted with such a sharp bite of desire that white knuckles showed where she held the cloth. And as the longing rose hot, she felt vulnerable.

She must have made some sound, for he glanced over his shoulder at her. His gaze held hers for what seemed long minutes. Those eyes, dark and penetrating, probed for all her secrets.

She swallowed, and then forced herself to take a few steps closer to him. She handed over his borrowed shirt and pants. The blanket fell from her fingers.

"I—" She couldn't speak. He reached for her, and she fled.

Sarah wasn't sure how long she stood at the parlor window watching the raindrops rolling down the glass. Closing her eyes didn't help wipe away the sight of his smooth-skinned chest or the muscled curve of flank and thigh. He'd been fully aroused. She had not been consciously aware of seeing his rampant sex, but that sight, too, was impressed on her mind.

Even with her arms wrapped around her middle, she couldn't stop the flare of heat in her blood.

But why him? Why Rio?

It had nothing to do with his being part Apache. She simply didn't care. It was more that he was running, would always be running and she had had enough running to last a lifetime. She pressed her forehead against the cool glass. She wanted him. Wanted him now, had wanted him, if she was being honest with herself.

And Catherine's words came back to haunt her. *"Just promise that if a man not old enough to be your father walks through the door, you'll give him every chance."*

And Rio, like Rafe and Greg, had come through the door looking for aid, but in the first two cases they had found love, as well.

But Rio wasn't looking for a woman to complicate his life. As for herself... Sarah sighed deeply. What did she want? She expended her passions on her home and her horses. She thought it was enough. She knew herself content.

Or had she been lying to herself?

She wanted him gone. She needed her peace back. *You don't want to live, to be fully alive, you only want to hide.*

Her hands flew up to cover her ears as if to still the inner voice. Still the truth. But Sarah was not about to lie to herself.

She wasn't fully alive. She was hiding.

How many times had Catherine asked if she hadn't missed being held at night? How many times had she denied any need, sexual or otherwise to be had from her husband? The last was only part lie. Judd had never held her without demanding his rights. She could never have asked him, as she earlier had asked Rio, to just hold her.

Rio. Just saying his name to herself conjured strength in her mind. Oh, Lord, how he had suffered.

But she had suffered, too.

What harm would there be if, for the little while he remained, she stole a bit of happiness for herself?

And maybe, just maybe, Rio would find his own pain eased.

She turned away from the window. What if she was wrong? What if he didn't want her?

Sarah started forward, her arms once more wrapped around her waist. Asking herself questions wasn't the way to find the answer. Only Rio could do that.

# *Chapter Fifteen*

She smelled the aroma of fresh coffee as she made her way back to the kitchen. Rio poured a cup for himself before he sat at the table with a weary sigh.

She paused again in the shadowed doorway when he added whiskey to the cup. Her fingers bit into her sides. Old fears died hard. She had to remind herself that Rio was not Judd. Rio was cold and tired, the liquor would help warm him, no more than that.

"I did not think you would come back here, Sarah. But come join me. You have no reason to spy. This is your home."

There was hesitancy in her steps into the room. She didn't sit down. The absence of emotion in his voice was something new. That deadened tone bothered her. She saw the way he stared at the bottle. She wasn't sure he remembered she was there at all until he spoke.

"I never learned to like the *tiswin* the Apache drink. Grandfather called it gray water. A weak beer made from corn. But I pleased him by liking good whiskey.

He never knew just how much I came to love this sweet amber poison.''

"Rio, don't do this to yourself."

"Why? There is no one else to do it for me, Sarah. I need to remember it all. I especially need to remember the deep shame that I turned from my young sons when they needed me more than at any other time in their lives. And all I could do was to lose myself in bottle after bottle until I fell into that waiting black pit."

"Stop it! You're not helping yourself. All you're doing is punishing yourself over what passed."

"Do you know," he went on as if she had not interrupted him, "how many hours I stared at a bottle, swearing that I would stop? That I could resist the temptation. But the bottle and the forgetfulness of the whiskey was always so close. Waiting, just waiting, a mere handspan away to remove all the rage and the grief and pain of being less than a man.

"I cannot remember how many nights I shuddered on my blanket, closing my eyes…hating the whiskey and craving the blessed darkness it would bring. And then later, knowing its poison for a lie, I'd curse it and my weakness until I had nothing left."

She was on the verge of snapping at him for daring to indulge in self-pity, but she swallowed the words. She had not turned to liquor, but hate had served her as well until she learned it would only destroy her.

"Rio, that was awhile ago. You have your sons with you now." Without realizing it, she had come closer to him. Close enough to see the despair in his eyes.

"Everyone lives with regrets of things they should have done or said or the opposite. You are not alone, Rio."

She wasn't aware that he pulled her nearer. She hesitated, then stepped behind him. Her hands cradled the sides of his head as he leaned back. There was nothing sexual about his head resting against her breasts. She was only offering the kind of comfort that he had shared earlier with her. At least that's what Sarah tried to convince herself it was.

A belief that lasted a minute or two. She could not deny that every nerve end shimmered awake. Her breasts swelled and the nipples peaked tight, pressing against the soft cotton cloth of her nightgown. She felt a heated surge inside herself, and with it, a feeling of tension that coiled hard and tight. She shifted her weight, squeezing her thighs together, all the while hoping Rio was unaware.

To distract herself from the rising tide of sexual feelings that threatened to take control of her, she started to question him.

"What did you find?"

"His horse. Your stud led me to him. That stallion does not shy at the scent of blood. I had no choice but to use him to carry the body."

She didn't want to hear this. But what choice did she have? She was not going to run away from him again.

"I bought the stallion from an army major after they closed the smaller forts around here. He told me the animal had seen him through a few battles."

"I could never sell…no, I would sell him to begin anew."

"The major had no choice, Rio. He lost an eye and a hand in a skirmish with Victorio's band. The man couldn't ride again."

Sarah began a gentle massage at his temples. She worried her lower lip with the edge of her teeth. "Did you…find any sign of the other two?"

The utter stillness of his body sent an arrow of fear plunging through her.

"Rio?"

"No. But it is impossible to search out there. They could be so close."

"Maybe not." She refused to let fear dispel hope. "They could have split up. It would be easy for them to become separated during these days of the storm."

"True. It seems my grandfather did not leave me his legendary luck. I have a feeling, here," he said, rubbing his belly with one hand, "that I have not seen the last of those men. Sarah, I—" he stopped, his hands now holding the enamel cup.

"I want to take my sons and leave here before another one finds me." Her fingertips stilled, and no matter how he strained, he could not hear her breathing.

"I am afraid for you."

Rio grabbed hold of her wrists with lightning speed before she could pull away.

"Listen. If they come you tell them I went south. Or say nothing. But you go nowhere without your gun."

South? What was south? She struggled to remember

something she had heard or read before the rains started. It nagged at her.

Then she knew. The halfhearted tug against his hold did not release her.

"You're going to join Geronimo and his renegades in Mexico," she said in a flat voice.

"It is better you do not know where I go."

"You'll die there. And so will your sons. There are rumors that General Crook will be appointed to bring in Geronimo and his bands. Crook wants to use other Indians to track them. Some say he's looking for Apache scouts. How long will you be able to hide from them?"

He let her go. His eyes closed. He could feel the desire thick in the room. The longing in her pierced him like a sharpened quill. What he felt for her was so intense it was painful. He did not want to care about her. She was more dangerous to him than facing those two remaining killers unarmed. She forced him to look at what he had done, and what he planned to do. She made him see that without the dreams, there was nothing of life to look toward.

His continued silence was a depth of tearing hurt that surprised her. She had not known until this moment how very deeply Rio had touched her.

But she knew that he didn't want her. No, that wasn't true. He would take her body, but not the love and strength that made her the woman she was today.

"It's late. You need to sleep. There's no sense in running now."

"I did not want to hurt you, Sarah."

"You haven't," she said with faint anger in her voice. He didn't know what she was feeling. He knew nothing of what she needed or was willing to offer him. And maybe that was for the best.

She found herself backing away from him until the sink stopped her backward flight.

"Rio, you're not the first man that crossed the doorstep in need. They left when those needs were met. So stop worrying about me." *But they had found love, too. You forgot to tell him that.*

"Where does all this kindness come from, Sarah? How can you continue to offer your home and comfort to a man who brought violence into your life? You were almost killed out there."

"It may surprise you to know that is not the first time. Likely, it won't be the last." She stared at the back of his head. Desire rose in her to be close to him, to touch and to hold and be held. But desire for this one man was dangerous to her.

"I know what you offer, widow woman. There is within you a healing. All a man need do is reach out."

"But you won't."

He winced at the bitter tone and fought the urge to turn around and look at her.

But he didn't answer.

Sarah didn't repeat it.

"I hate knowing that anyone hurt you. I hate this helpless feeling that robs me of clear thought. Who hurt you, Sarah? And who taught you this endless well of forgiveness?"

"It's not endless. And I taught myself. By forgiving

myself. I…'' *Tell him!* She wrapped her arms around her waist, biting hard on her lower lip until she felt a burning pain.

He looked over his shoulder at her. For the space of several heartbeats Sarah couldn't look away from his intense gaze. His warm brown eyes both demanded more and yet held a haunting quality that forced her to look away.

"Sarah?"

"I lived with violence as daily bread. Not here. I didn't have a home. But I know what it's like to rage and be helpless. I know what it's like to lose a piece of yourself that will always remain empty. If those lessons allow me to be forgiving or compassionate, well…'' She stopped and shrugged.

But she couldn't look at him.

Not even when she heard the scrape of the chair as he rose and then moved toward her.

"Can a man be thankful for your forgiveness and your compassion, but sorrow over the way you learned it?" He reached out and stroked her hair. "But there is more to this. I can feel it here." This time he laid his hand over his heart.

His nearness and his touch drew her to look at him. Her gaze went again to his eyes. This close the warm shades of brown mixed with deep almost-black flecks. She shuddered inwardly.

This was not the first time Rio had left her feeling that he could see more than she ever wanted to reveal to another soul.

He said there was more to it without making it a

question. Even if he had asked, she could ignore him. There was yet time to escape him, to run from the tension that coiled around the two of them.

But there was a small voice that clamored for her to tell him. Rio would understand. She could let the wound that had festered all this time out in the open. And it had festered, despite the lies and denials.

The gentle, undemanding way he stroked her hair had a calming effect on her. Endless patience. Rio had it in abundance.

She had told Mary and Catherine very little about the details of her marriage. They knew she and Judd had moved around a great deal. They knew Judd gambled. Both women had learned more after Rafe McCade had come here seeking help for his wounded child.

Rafe. She had been shocked to see a face from her past, something she knew would eventually happen, but nothing had prepared her for the reality.

For Rafe had been there when she tried to help a woman being beaten by her husband, only to be stopped by her own. It wasn't that Judd was a coward. He believed the man was within his rights. Rafe had put an end to the beating, but then killed the man to save his own life. And she had always had the feeling that he knew more about her and Judd than he'd let on.

She owed Rafe a debt of gratitude. Mary would never understand why she had not told her the truth. Not before Rafe came, and not after he married Mary.

Looking inward, seeing the livery stable that hot

day and what happened there, made Sarah admit that she was the coward.

*"Iszán,"* Rio whispered in a caressing voice. "I have let you inside me." He lifted her hand to press against his cheek, then drew her palm to his lips. His gaze held steady on hers. "You did not judge me as harshly as you judge yourself. Can you not share the darkness that takes the smile from your lips, the light from your eyes?"

Each time he saw her, an arrow of shuddering awareness sliced through him. The feeling was nothing as simple as lust to take her woman's body to his blankets. He could deal with that, one way or another. No, what he felt for Sarah was a sharp indescribable hunger that poured through him like hot sun in the middle of the desert. Sexual desire, but more powerful, more complex, and so he knew it was much more dangerous.

"Why? Why is knowing about my past important to you? You're leaving, remember. Or—" and here her voice took a sharp edge "—is it pity that makes you ask?"

"No pity," he snapped. "Pity is for the weak. You are a strong woman. A soft one, too. I care, Sarah. I care the way you have cared for a stranger's pain."

He placed her hand on his shoulder, then lifted both of his to her head. He enjoyed the cool, sliding pressure of her hair caught between his fingers. It was the only way he dared allow himself to touch her. And touch her he must, as he must breathe. This gentle hold, that nonetheless held her before him.

And he waited with infinite patience to learn what haunted her dark eyes.

Outside, the lightning leaped repeatedly in a brilliant display. Thunder rumbled, too distant to be more than a warning. Soon the storm would once more expand to fill the sky with its might against everything that stood helpless before it.

As he stood helpless with the need to steal her secrets as effortlessly as she had stolen his.

"You could try telling me," he urged.

"Some things are too painful for words."

"Yet I shared my shame and my grief with you."

Sarah lowered her head. She realized she had to accept responsibility for what she was now, not what she had been. This was where she stood, in truth, a house of her own making.

The acknowledgment released something inside her. She looked up to see his eyes, glittering strangely in the feeble light, but she could not read the emotions behind them.

"Sarah, were I a shaman of the Apache, I would build a fire and blow the smoke and sacred pollen to the four winds to heal you. Were I full-blood Irish, I would seek all the magic of their beliefs and implore healing for you.

"I stand before you a man who offers you a heart and mind to listen to your sorrow and arms to hold you.

"Will this be enough, Sarah?"

# Chapter Sixteen

"I'm not sure where to begin," she said in a halting voice. "I thought I loved Judd. I have no excuse. I knew he gambled. But he always seemed to win. When he talked of moving on, seeing new places, he made it sound exciting. I was young enough, and foolish enough, to be lured by the rich promises he made of what it would be like.

"For a while it was just that. The best hotels, the prettiest gowns and always Judd's promises that one big score would have him settle down.

"I'm not sure exactly when things began to change. He came in one night and said we had to leave. It wasn't until later that I learned he had killed a man after he'd been accused of cheating."

Sarah looked to the side, distancing herself the only way she could.

"Judd started drinking heavily after that. He no longer went to towns but to the mining camps. Every time I begged him to leave me behind, he'd rant and rave, then threaten me. He never hit me, not then, but when I'd tell him I had to leave, that I couldn't go on living like that, he'd hold me and cry and swear he couldn't get along without me.

"I married him for better or worse. I kept hoping the worst was past."

Despite Rio's closeness, she wrapped her arms around her waist, her upper body swaying back and forth as she drew forth memory after memory. Some she discarded and others she told him.

"There were winters when the only way we survived was my cooking and doing laundry for miners in camp. Judd was drinking so much that he couldn't hold a deck of cards. And all the time he'd swear he'd stop, that things would be better and go back to the way they were."

Rio's hands slipped from her hair to her shoulders, then around her to draw her to him. She rested against him for long minutes, and he did not press her to continue.

But as the silence grew, so did his worry. He could feel there was more, much more that she had not told him. He hugged her tight, feeling the chill of her body measured against the heat of his.

"Sarah, was there no one you could ask for help?"

"No. No one. I was too ashamed. And then he found color on a claim he was working. I'm not sure how he got the money to buy the miner out. The man was disgusted that he hadn't gotten rich as quickly as he was promised and was only too glad to pull out with a stake.

"It wasn't a rich strike, but there was enough to get

us to Denver. Judd felt his luck had finally changed. He swore this time the gambling was to one end. We'd buy a place and settle down.''

She tried to pull away from Rio as the anger grew and was revealed in her voice, but he held her tight.

"You'd think I'd have learned my lesson not to believe him. I hadn't. But I learned to be a thief. When he'd come in so falling-down drunk that he wasn't sure who I was, I'd get him to bed and go through his pockets or money belt and steal as much as I dared.

"It was uncanny how drunk that man could get and still remember how much he'd won or lost. But he didn't think I had any reason to lie to him.''

She managed to lift her head and look at Rio's face. "Do you really want to hear this?"

"Do you want to tell me?"

Her eyes glittered with the meld of turbulent emotions that seethed in her. "I've never told a soul what I'm saying to you."

"Do you think I would use this against you, Sarah?''

She studied his features, absorbed his calm, and the warmth of his body. Slowly then she shook her head and resumed her place where she could lean on him.

But her voice was no longer strong, just a soft, trembling whisper, her words dragged forth from battle-stained memories.

"He found the money I had hidden away. I think he knew then that I'd leave him. He was insane. The fighting…''

"I am here for you, Sarah. He is not. He cannot hurt you again. No one can."

"You can't understand what it means to a woman to think herself strong with purpose and find that she cannot stand against a man's violence." The words tumbled out in a rush, mumbled, broken with sobs, as if saying them would rid herself forever of nightmares.

"I hated him. There were times I couldn't be in the same room with him without wanting to kill him. I hated breathing the same air as he did. I despaired of ever being free of him."

The last was a whisper as if she had lost all will to fight.

And the silence came again, leaving Rio to wonder what more had happened. The man was dead. She had gotten free. He found himself saying those words to her, over and over as he rubbed her back.

"You don't know," she moaned, pressing her cheek against his chest.

"Tell me, Sarah. If a wound festers long enough, it will poison and kill. You are a strong woman, too strong to allow that."

"Strong?" She pulled back to look up at him. She shook her head. "No, I'm not strong. I was never that strong. If I had been, I...I..." She swallowed and couldn't go on. She averted her eyes from his.

Rio drew her against him. Her body was cold, his on fire. She was totally unaware that they were joined from breast to knee without space for a feather. He reined in his body's unruly response to her nearness.

"He's dead, Sarah. He cannot hurt you again. How did he die? Can you tell me?"

"He died."

Her flat tone told him there was more to it. He stroked her neck, then began to knead her back to help relieve the tension. Sarah was strong, just as he had told her, but there was also a lush femininity to counter that physical strength.

Into his mind entered the idle thought of lifting her up, featherweight and vulnerable, and carrying her to bed to still her cries. The silence from the parlor told him his sons slept soundly. Sarah would be spared their knowing. The painful desire he felt for her allowed the image, but the sane part of his mind held him back from acting on it.

Making love to Sarah—and he was struck by the thought that he would make love to her, not satisfy lust—would not help her now. And he wanted to help her as much as she had helped rid him of so much poison.

It took him a few minutes to fight the heat and the tension in his groin. He held her close until the sobs had ceased and her breathing became calm.

She surprised him by pushing against his chest, wanting to be free. He let her go. With her arms wrapped around her waist, she paced away from him.

"Tell me how he died, Sarah."

"I'm…I'm not sure."

"Not sure? Were you not with him?"

She shook her head.

Rio watched as she retreated from him. Not only in

the physical sense, but emotionally, too. And once more he called for patience and waited until she was ready to talk.

And he was rewarded.

"I wasn't with him when he died."

The words were whisper soft but held a chilling edge of guilt. Rio held his silence, afraid now to speak, to ask the hundred questions that prowled his thoughts.

"You thought I grieved for him, but I didn't. I couldn't. Whatever we had, Rio, was long gone over the years. There wasn't one overwhelming tragedy. At least not until the end. It was all a series of small deaths. Love and respect, friendship and caring, pride and dreams. And maybe it never ended. I somehow survived," she said, keeping her back toward him.

"Somehow I went on, at times feeling less than half alive. I had the house and then news came that my cousin Mary was widowed and destitute. She needed me, and then our friend Catherine, widowed too, came to live with us. I really believe we gave each other strength. I know I learned to smile and laugh again."

She rubbed her arms. "And we sang, every night. Songs from our childhood, others we had learned. That's what began the townspeople calling us the merry widows. If only people knew what I've told you."

She stood near the doorway. Rio thought her poised to flee. He had listened. And now he mulled over what he had heard. She had been married to a man who had no right to call himself one. He was no husband to

Sarah. He had not cared for her as was a man and husband's duty to do for the woman he took to wife.

Sarah had made him see that even had he been with his own wife on that fateful day, he could never have prevented her death. If anything, he would have added his own and those of his sons.

But the more he thought, the more he realized that Sarah had never really answered his question about her husband's death. And it seemed there was more, much more that she had not told him.

*"Not one overwhelming tragedy. At least not until the end."*

"Sarah?"

"Now you know," she answered, without turning to look at him.

"Sarah, who is it that you grieve for?"

Rio started toward her, then changed his mind. He refilled his coffee cup, and found one for her.

"Come have something hot to drink. You must be cold." He pulled out a chair for her and stood there waiting.

"Was there someone else, Sarah? Some man who learned to care for you? Is he the one you grieve for? Was he killed? Did he fight your husband? Is that how they died?"

His hands gripped the back of the chair. He listened to the demands he made on her, and knew where they came from, even as he wanted to deny it. Jealous. He was that and more. What confused him was the lack of betrayal he felt to his own dead wife. He had loved her, loved every moment of their shared time, but he was not left alone and lonely. He had their sons, and she lived on in them.

But Sarah had no one.

"Why are you punishing me by asking for more?"

"Is that how you feel? I wish to…I…" He abandoned his place to go to her. He drew her back against his chest and held her. Rubbing his cheek against her hair, careful of her wound, he absorbed her silent sobs.

"Nothing happens without a reason," he murmured against her hair. "More of Grandfather's wisdom. I believe it now. I do not know which spirit led me here. I thought it was the trickster Coyote. But now I wonder. You eased my heart's pain. I only want to ease yours.

"I would wound my own flesh before I hurt you, Sarah. I can feel your pain. Holding you like this makes me feel it. Let me care for you."

As he spoke, he felt the tension leave her. She leaned back against him, until he was taking almost all her weight. He drew her back toward the chair he had abandoned and sat down. She offered no resistance when he coaxed her to sit on his lap.

Her arms were still wrapped around her waist, but she rested her head on his shoulder and he once more held her.

"There was no other man," she said softly after a few minutes. "I don't remember much about that last winter. We moved around a great deal. But spring was late coming to the mountains. I do recall the cold."

Silence again. Then she shook with sobs, her eyes closed, her body rigid even as he rocked her.

Finally she blurted, "I can't. Can't talk about this. Not to you. Not to anyone."

"Then do not. Let me hold you. No more than that."

The room grew colder, but Rio was afraid to move to add kindling to the stove. He listened to the wicked hiss of rain and wind beating against the house and sat in the gloom while she cried. He had no sense of time, and knew the fragile woman he held in his arms did not care of its passing.

"I wish," she said suddenly in a broken voice, "that I had told someone. It wasn't until spring or early summer that I knew I carried his child."

He held his breath as she paused, totally caught off guard by her admission. A child? He had no thought, no suspicion there had been a child. He smoothed the hair from her face and kept her tucked close to his body.

"I begged him to find a house for us. Begged him on my knees. He yelled and he left me. He didn't want a child. And he finally admitted that he didn't want me. But he found a place. An old cabin far enough from town that there would be no help for me. When he remembered, he came with food.

"Most of the time he was drunk and would pass out. I'd steal what I could from his money belt. Then I'd take his horse and ride in to buy supplies. He never knew, never caught on. No one knew I was his wife.

No one asked. And I was so...ashamed I never told anyone.

"He must have hit a winning streak. I didn't see him for weeks. I often wondered what made him come to see me.

"I found out. He was waiting for me to die. He didn't have the guts to kill me. Not so blame could be laid on him. But he was waiting for me to die."

"Sarah, oh, Sarah—"

"No. Please. Let me finish," she said in that same flat voice.

"The weather grew colder. I had to go farther and farther to find wood. I had hidden most of the food I bought. I was so afraid that he would find it and take it from me. At night I would dream of my baby. I knew I had to get away from him. I had money that I'd stolen. I used to think of my grandmother watching, disappointed that I'd become a thief. But I had no choice.

"Sometimes I prayed that someone would find me and take me away. But there was no one. My baby had only me to depend on."

She turned her head, pressing against his shoulder, burrowing, almost as if she would crawl inside him and hide.

The rocking motion of his body and her own drew her back to the times she would sit and rock herself. Her hands over her swollen belly, cradling, soothing the tiny life within. She didn't want to remember the first time she felt life and dropped a load of wood only to stand there, waiting, expectant of feeling it again.

And each time the flutter came, it renewed her strength to see a way clear. And when the kicks became stronger, how she felt less alone.

No, these were not the things she wanted to remember.

"What happened, Sarah? If he were not dead, I swear to you I would kill him for what he did to you."

"No. It was for no one but me to do. And in a way, I had my chance. I went into labor. I knew it was too soon. But I prayed. Prayed so much and I was so afraid of being alone. I don't remember all of it. I know I was weak. I tried to…I tried… Oh, God, how I tried," she cried out.

Her hand clawed its way to his shoulder where her fingers grabbed hold. Her body shook with the renewed pain of remembering, of speaking of a time that she had held secret.

She wasn't hearing Rio's words, only the soft murmur of his voice. And she was cold, a cold that came from inside as she struggled to get the words out.

"I lost track of time. My baby…my little girl was gone. I couldn't protect her. I couldn't save her. And all I wanted to do was die. But the Lord was cruel. He wouldn't let me. He wouldn't give me the peace I craved. And he brought that bastard back into my life.

"I remember dragging myself from the shack. I crawled to a little tree and used a rock to dig a grave. And that's when Judd came. When I was burying our baby.

"He was hurt. Someone had shot him. Too bad they missed his black heart. He wanted me to take care of him. There's a blank space there. What I recall is being in the shack and it was night. Judd was drunk. I stole his money belt, and his horse and I left him there. Weeks later I heard he had been caught cheating. That's how he got wounded. I'm not sure how he died, or even where. I only heard he was dead.'' It seemed to take what was left of her strength to lift her head and look at him.

''So now you know. I've never told this to another person.''

He kissed her forehead. ''Now I know what makes Sarah a woman rich in forgiveness and in compassion. I know her as a woman whose strength is measured beyond that of a man's. I know she is beautiful in her heart, even more than the loveliness my eyes behold.''

Rio brushed his lips over hers for a fleeting moment.

''No tears?''

She thought about that. She shook her head. ''I cried so much and it hurt for so long that it became a part of me.''

''It is time to let go of the past, Sarah.''

She closed her eyes, her sigh deep and heartfelt.

''You regret telling me?''

''No. No, Rio, I don't have any regrets. Like you, I punished myself for a long time.'' She opened her eyes. ''I recall reading something about burdens being shared becoming halved or lighter or some such thing. I'm not really sure what I feel now.''

His fingertips trailed over her cheek. He tried to smile. ''You honor me with your trust, lovely woman. Now, no more talk. You need to rest.''

Rio rose with her still in his arms. He hushed her protest as he carried her through the hallway and up the stairs to her room.

She didn't ask for the lamp to be lit, and he had no wish for her to see what he was sure was in his eyes.

But when he set her on the bed, she surprised him.

"Would it be terrible of me to tell you that I don't want to be alone."

"Sarah—"

"I'm not…I mean, I just need to be held. Like you did before. I don't know if I can explain, Rio, but I don't want to be alone and in the dark, left with memories that are more like nightmares to me."

"You do not know what you ask," he managed to say.

"Do the Apache have some taboo against being a friend? That's what I need, Rio. A man who has proven himself to be trustworthy, a man who listens with an open mind and heart."

*A man first, Sarah. A man who wants you as a man wants to claim a woman.*

The words remained unspoken.

"You held me before when I needed you."

"Yes." The word was torn from his lips. But she didn't know what he had been feeling for her. She did not know of the hunger that prowled now, or the need that arose in him to change nightmares into sweeter and more powerful memories. Sarah knew nothing of his longing to hear her cry out his name in the heat of passion. If she did, she would never ask him to stay.

"Will you stay with me?"

## Chapter Seventeen

Rio did not know where the strength to resist her softly uttered plea came from. She offered him a chance to hold her. She asked for nothing more, made no promises, asked for none from him.

Why then was he still hesitating?

The moments in the dark bedroom stretched into minutes. Her hand reached out to touch him. She said nothing more.

Rio listened to the deepening cadence of their mingled breathing and wondered why she was not aware that the very air in her room sizzled with tension.

"Rio?"

A whisper. But it came from Sarah. And he discovered he had very little defense against it.

The bed creaked as she turned away from him.

His own words about not hurting her came back like a fierce, rushing blow. She trusted him, and he was turning away, shutting her out.

"Sarah, I—"

"No. It's all right. I understand. Really, I do. I was wrong to ask…just wrong."

He put his hand on her shoulder, felt her stiffen at his touch but left it there. He could no longer stop himself from gently rubbing, then he stroked back and forth from the curve of her neck to her upper arm until he felt her body relax.

"You were not wrong to tell me. I am not standing here and judging you, Sarah. It is me. Not you. Never you."

He heard the stifled sob. Touching her, he could not miss the slight tremble of her body. Before he thought, he gathered her close, turning to once more hold her as he sat down. He cradled her against him.

"It is ever so. A woman says she has no more tears and from some deep well, she finds them. Cry, Sarah. Cry till there truly are no more tears. Mourn your little girl, grieve as you have not and I will hold you safe."

"And who…who will hold you?"

"You are, right now." Rio called himself eight kinds of fool. Sarah was not the woman for him. He knew it. All he had to do was get his body to believe it, too. She had only to touch him, to smile and he wanted her with a hunger he had never known. But he would never act on it. She needed a man who could give her her dreams. He had nothing.

Sarah locked her arms around him. She sensed the loneliness in him, the darkness, too. She knew he could be harsh and tender by turns. She moved her head and her hair flowed over his arms. His hand came up to cradle her cheek. His thumb brushed at the silent tears she couldn't seem to control. He tilted her face upward. Not that either of them could see the other in the dark, but Sarah suddenly became aware of a new tension there in the room with them.

With one hand she traced his features. "Perhaps what you said about the spirits bringing you here is true. With you holding me I'm beginning to feel a peace I can't remember ever having. Thank you, Rio," she whispered, and then kissed the edge of his jaw.

"You give gifts of healing, too." Her head rested on his broad shoulder, absorbing his strength and his heat. His arms were a haven she could steal for a little while. She had to stifle the flare of sensual awareness that made its presence known. Rio didn't want any ties. And who could blame him. After what she had told him about herself, what man would want her.

Rio would have to be made of stone not to feel the fine trembling in her fingers as she stroked the back of his neck. He schooled himself not to react. The darkness helped. He kept telling himself that she was upset, that she did not know what she was doing.

But he could not find the words to tell her to stop.

Her touch was both torment and pleasure. So equally divided that he did not know if he could stand more, or die if she ceased her caress.

He did not want her to tell him to go. Holding her near, breathing in the scent that was hers alone did little to ease the building hunger, but it was all he had, all he allowed himself.

"Rio?"

He closed his eyes and steeled himself. She was going to say it now.

But Sarah nestled her head closer so that her breath blew against his neck.

"I...I want you to know I've never felt so safe with a man." Shy and hesitant, she struggled to tell him what she was feeling, what he made her feel. "I told you that you had gifts of your own. I've never trusted another man. Not enough to tell him about my past. I was always afraid that I would be judged. But you didn't judge me. You're so special, I despair of finding the words to tell you how very special you are."

"Sarah, this is a mistake. Let me lay you down. You need rest. This has not been easy for you."

She raised her head from his shoulder, wishing now the lamp had been lit. She wanted to see him, see his eyes.

"Am I asking too much to ask you to stay with me? I don't want to be alone. I've been alone so long."

He couldn't know what that admission cost her. It was as close to begging as she could come. It was also the truth. She did not want to be alone. They had both revealed secrets of the heart to each other. But it was more. There was something about Rio that had taken down every wall she had hidden behind. She felt both shattered and vulnerable, and tempering both was a renewal of spirit that he had given her. She had found a new life for herself, but Rio was still searching for his. She had no one hunting her, endangering children, ready to steal their lives and his.

And she wanted so desperately to give something

back to this man. Sarah shied from naming what more she felt.

Now she was glad it was dark, glad that he could not look into her eyes. Her emotions roiled so close to the surface that she knew she would never be able to hide them from him.

"Sarah," he whispered, raising his hands to her shoulders. "I am going to leave before we are both sorry. I have nothing to offer you. And you, *iszán*, have too much to give to a man."

"One man. You. But I won't stop you or plead."

He swung her aside and rose, a darker shadow in the room, but so close she had only to reach out to touch him.

There was no censure in her voice. She understood that he was protecting her in the only way he knew. But then she felt the brush of his hand as he reached out to her.

"Sarah, they would hang me for what I am thinking."

"Who?"

"White men. You know that. I can't wish away what I am."

"There's no one here but me. And your sons. They're still sleeping. I want...no, I'm not asking for promises, or anything more than what you want to share."

"Ah, Sarah, truly the spirits of my ancestors smile down on me."

He touched her as if she were a small, frightened little bird he was afraid of hurting. The fierce desire he had for her, and her alone, was there, but held at bay. There was about her a softness that she had not revealed to him before this moment. She invoked the strong male drive to protect, and an even stronger drive to claim. No longer was she the widow who had faced him with rifle in hand, fleeing and then, when caught, the woman who had used her feminine strengths against him.

And still he hesitated, protecting himself and this woman the only way he could short of walking away from her. He knew he could not leave her now. She had bared her heart to him. There was no way he would add to the cruelty she had suffered.

"Sarah, would you understand if I said that I did not want this to happen and yet have hungered to feel your arms around me, your lips against mine? That I dreamed of you, and denied need?"

Sarah came to her knees in the middle of the bed. Her fingers trembled as she reached up and began to unbutton Rio's shirt. Her hands explored his body, hard and heated, his skin stretched tight over muscles. She parted the cloth, palms flat against his rib cage and pressed her cheek against his chest. Her own desire stirred as she absorbed the warmth of his body into her own.

He lifted one knee to the bed. The shift in his stance spread his thighs. She moved to fill the space he'd made.

She inhaled the rain-washed scent of him, the animal heat, dark and potent. A strange, frightening excitement knotted her stomach. She thought of all the times she had watched him. Her hands skimmed the long, hard shape of his thighs. Her lips parted with a breathless sigh as his fingers slid through her hair and cupped the back of her neck to lift her face up toward his.

She braced herself against his chest, her hands splayed wide over his smooth skin. She felt the beat of his heart, the pace quick like her own.

He was a looming dark shadow, lowering his head toward her until his breath fanned her lips. She wanted his kiss, wanted to taste again the hungry passion that left no room for lies.

Desire for him rose so powerful within her that she shook from its force. She closed her eyes. It had been so long, too long since she had been held. And never like this, as if she were something precious, fragile almost. Or was he afraid that she truly did not know what she wanted.

She heard his low, hungry sound before his mouth covered hers. The kiss was a wild, exploding assault on her senses.

Sarah clung to him, trembling. The edge of his teeth held her lower lip captive. Soft moans escaped her. His arm swept down, wrapped around her hips and drew her tight against him. She felt the pulsing heat of him spread to every nerve ending.

Sarah curled her fingers into his shoulders. He was so hard, the only giving softness found in his lips that gentled and savaged her mouth by turns until need, for him and only him, was the single thought allowed.

The night belonged to him. Dark, forbidding and

dangerous. And the storm was his, as well, like the passion he drew from her. Wild. Hot. Unknown.

The kiss suddenly gentled, the tip of his tongue cherishing the shape of her lips. She moaned and clung to him. His warmth and his tender kiss filled her senses. Her lips parted. She offered a helpless invitation for more. His groan was filled with pleasure, his mouth took hers with need.

"Sarah? Sarah," he said softly against her mouth, not lifting his head at all. "Tell me to stop."

"I can't."

Her breasts swelled, heavy with the need to be touched. The force of his kiss bent her head back. Her hands slid into the long, silky length of his hair until she held his head and drew it down.

His mouth gentled yet again. She cried out.

His tongue swept the inner softness of her mouth, desire threatening his control.

Sarah jerked her head back. "Don't," she pleaded in a broken voice. "You can't want me to use a whore's kiss with you."

"No, Sarah, no. Is that what *he* told you?" His breath sawed in and out, hard and fast.

"He said—"

"No. No words of his. Nothing of him. Only you and me. No more holding back. No more secrets, Sarah. I want you. All of you. Before this night is done you will forget every memory of him."

No chance to resist. To protest. To stop him.

Rio took her mouth with a gentle savagery that

swept aside memory and reason. He tasted her as if he couldn't get enough.

She shuddered against his hard, rocking body. She knew she had never measured, never felt this depth of hunger for a man.

Empty and aching. A violent trembling took hold of her. And she wanted what Rio did. All. Nothing held back.

His body told her more clearly than words what he wanted. He swelled against her. She took what his lips offered, long and hard and deep, and fought off shyness, buried any hesitations.

When at last he pulled away, his harsh breathing mingled with hers. She used the tip of her tongue slowly to sweep up the lingering taste of whiskey and coffee, and the heat Rio had left behind.

He quickly stepped away from the bed. From the darkness came the rustle of cloth. She moistened her lips again, wanting to say something, unable to think what to say.

Before he stepped closer, she removed her robe. She had just taken hold of the nightgown's hem when his hands covered hers. Her mouth was suddenly dry.

"Let me," he whispered, desperate to slow things down, to regain whatever control he could. She was burning him alive.

Sarah sat back on her heels in the middle of the bed. She used one hand to caress him from waist to thigh. His skin was damp, sleek and drawn tight. And hot. She hesitated, then touched the rigid evidence of his maleness. He shifted but made no move away from her tentative touch. His groan was one of pleasure as he clenched his hands.

She wondered at her boldness. Very gently, and shyly, she curled her fingers around him.

"Sarah!"

Her hand jerked back. "What did I do? Was it wrong? You're so strong and sleek and hot and I just wanted to...needed to touch you."

"*Enju, iszán.* It is well, Sarah. You are so good that I stand like a green boy before you, afraid to touch, afraid that I will hurt you."

"You couldn't, Rio. I know that." Even to her own ears her voice was shaken by the emotions she felt.

"Trust me, Sarah."

"I do. It's me that I don't trust. I have never wanted like this."

"I will not hurt you. I am not an animal, Sarah."

"I know that. I'm not afraid of you. I'm not afraid of what I'm feeling." In the dark, she tilted her head. "Are you waiting for me to change my mind?"

"Do you want to?" The words were wrenched from him. The fierce need to mate with her drove him wild. He shuddered, even as he forced himself to give her yet another chance to turn him away. Heated blood surged through his body until his skin stretched taut. He could barely stand as he waited in agony for her answer.

Waited for words.

Not the sudden move she made toward him. Not the feel of her hands shaping him from knee to thigh. Not the heated sweep of her breath over his aroused flesh.

She kissed his hip, the tip of her tongue tasting him. "No," she whispered against his skin. "I can't stop now, Rio. I'm aching. It almost hurts. Come to me. I—"

"Hush, Sarah, hush." He gathered her close and held her tight. "I wanted to be gentle with you. I need that." *Lies.* He did not feel gentle. He was battling the deepest of male urges to possess.

Sarah didn't argue. She couldn't remember a time when Judd had been gentle, not once they had been married. She scattered kisses over his taut belly, a move she made without thought, more from need and even instinct. She used the tip of her tongue to taste him again, then the edge of her teeth in a delicate bite. Once more she drew back, shocked at herself. His low, hungry sound filled her ears.

Rio curved his hands over her shoulders, then glided across the soft cotton covering to her even softer skin. His thumbs met and gently measured the pulse beating in her throat. She made a little moaning sound when he moved his caress down her arms to her wrists, where he found her pulse rapid and erratic.

Her arms were slender but strong. Like her long legs. He already knew what she felt like stretched out beneath him.

But she had been fighting him then and he had added to her fear with his threats.

Sarah was not fighting him now.

He leaned over and gathered the edge of her nightgown. He drew the cloth up slowly, his hands caressing her thighs. He felt the tremors, just as he inhaled the faint scent that rose from the cloth. More potent was the feminine scent of arousal that came from Sarah herself.

"Rio?"

He calmed himself, then raised the drift of bunched cloth over her breasts. He really did not trust himself not to fall on her and sheathe himself in passionate heat. Had it been anyone else...but it was not. This was Sarah. Sarah who had not been with a man in a long, long time. He knew that she wanted him. It was agony to prolong this. She had already loosened the ribbon tie. The nightgown easily slipped over her head. He tossed it aside.

Their lips met as Sarah shifted to make room for him on her bed. He followed her down on the mattress, covering her with his strong, hard body.

So long.

Rio struggled to remember if he had ever touched a woman as soft as Sarah. He felt no disloyalty to his wife's memory, for she was a maid and Apache. There were no thoughts of soft bodies when work had been all she knew.

The taste of passion on her lips was new, as potent as whiskey. She arched upward as his hand curved over her full breast. A wordless sound escaped from her lips as his thumb brushed the rapidly firming peak. He leaned to the side and slipped one arm beneath her as he lifted her to his mouth.

"Rio? Oh, please...I..." Her voice broke. His mouth, soft and heated, closed over her tightly drawn nipple. Blood rushed and swelled her breast, the feeling so exquisite that she cried out, arching her back, silently asking for more.

It wasn't enough. Sarah, at first afraid that he would hurt her, now found herself gripping his head and pulling him harder against her. She wanted him, needed him with a desperation that she could not begin to explain. Soft whimpers came from her lips. She twisted against him.

Her head fell back, offering him her bare throat. Rio tested the smooth curve with kisses and love bites that had her crying his name with husky sounds. He pressed her closer, then closer still, as if he wanted to draw her inside himself.

The warm, hungry kisses she scattered over his skin wherever she could reach nearly drove him over the edge.

Sarah tried to regain a sense of sanity. Then he touched her, parting her thighs, stroking, readying her. She bit back cries of surrender as she trembled and opened to him, yielding pleasure as he found softer, hotter flesh.

Her cries scored him to his soul. The hunger he had leashed flared up, shortening his breath, making his blood run heavily, hardening his body that was already rawhide taut. He caressed the sultry heat of her that he needed to touch as much as he needed water to live.

His groan was lost as her hands slid down to cup the hard, throbbing male flesh. She stroked and caressed him, murmuring wordless sounds against his lips when one fingertip caught the tiny drop of moisture that escaped him.

Rio rolled to his back and lifted her over him. Her plea of want and need was all he heard. Her long legs were pressed alongside his. He stroked from her shoulders down her back, cupping her slender hips, rubbing her softly against him.

Sarah braced her hands against his shoulders, her fingers digging deep as she gripped him. Within her, tiny explosions built to an unbearable tension that made her believe she would die if she could not have him.

A moan built to a cry. His hands guided her hips. She wanted him deep inside her, joined to where there was no Rio, no Sarah, but only one flesh. No matter how she twisted, or implored him, he took her gently, by tiny increments.

"Rio, please…"

A passionate cry that echoed the one in his mind. Bone-deep need demanded that he fully claim and possess this woman. But Rio stopped himself driving into her, knowing that once he did, once he was fully sheathed within her warmth, he would never withdraw.

Sarah. He had never felt so much the man as he listened to the pleasure cries of his lover. The trembling release that went through her was shared, and he could not stop from pressing deeper, ignoring the warning screaming in his mind. She lured him with her graceful abandon to go deeper still, for she was hot, sleek and making time cease. Once more her body tightened, and he held to the edge, just until the very last moment.

With a wrenching cry, his fingers bit into her hips, lifting her up and away as he spilled his seed in an endless release that he could never, ever share with her.

Sarah had felt him move through her like a storm, all raging lightning and thunderbolts, but her last cry of pleasure turned bittersweet.

"Why? Why, Rio?"

# Chapter Eighteen

Sarah wished she had the strength to move away from him. Tears stung her eyes, eyes that had already cried too much.

"Why?" she begged.

Rio could only hold her. He ignored her attempt to push away from him. He felt raw, exposed and almost vulnerable. How could she forget? How could she ask why?

He clenched his jaw until his teeth ground together. He was angry, cheated by his own act, and yet with the bit of sanity he clung to, knew he should be thankful that he had hung on to the last shred of control to protect her.

He held her, rocking gently. The storm of emotion still seethed like a coil of thunderheads ready to unleash its power on them again.

"Tell me. Please, Rio, tell me why."

"You forget what I am," he said in a ragged voice. "I cannot. I am an Apache half-breed, Sarah. You are a white woman. I will leave you this memory and no more. Do you understand now?''

"How could you think that matters to me? You're a man, Rio. I see you as nothing else. More man than I've known. You made love to me. And yes, this is a memory to savor and treasure. But keep your lies to yourself. Don't ever lie to me about this.''

"I speak no lies. Only the truth. You would be scorned if you ended carrying my child.''

She tried to rise, but he held her down against him. Her fingers bit into his arms.

"All you said. Nothing held back. I didn't hold anything back, Rio. I surrendered everything of myself to you. Damn you for cheating both of us. Damn you for being like every other male. Making up my mind for me. Making decisions. You have no right.''

"I took the right.'' He lifted his hands to cradle her face above him. Again he wished he had lit the lamp. Never had he wanted to see her as he did now.

"Think, Sarah. Think what you say. Think about what you ask of me.''

"I can't. I don't want to. I only know what I feel. You stole something from me, Rio. And it hurts every bit as much as Judd telling me I was worthless as a woman and a mother when my baby died.''

He felt the shining scars of tears on her cheeks. Tears he kissed with a wish that she be healed, but he could not let her words go unanswered.

"Sarah, his words were for wounding, mine to protect. But then, you could accuse me of being worthless as a man, unable to protect his home and family, unable to save—"

"Oh, don't, Rio. Don't. I'm sorry. I swear...I'm so sorry. Don't do this to yourself. To me. Just hold me. Hold me tight."

And she held him. She realized fully what she felt for Rio. She loved him. For the first time she understood the terrifying nature of love. Love never took for itself. Love gave with an open heart and mind where there was no place for any defense.

Her cheek pressed against his shoulder, all the fight gone out of her. She couldn't tell him. She could not, dared not whisper the words. He would see them as a trap. She knew that as surely as she knew she had to stop crying.

Rio stroked her slender back, her body as damp with passion's mist as his own. He absorbed the tremors that rippled over her body. He fought to bury his frustration and anger.

Nothing had felt as good and as right as being sheathed inside Sarah, feeling her come apart around him. His every pore drank her pleasure like the earth drank life-giving rain.

And he still wanted her. His flesh as hard and hurting as if he had not joined with her.

He covered her mouth with his.

Desperation. Something they both felt.

And need.

An outrageous, wild need to taste. To touch. To belong.

There was nothing between them. Flesh to flesh.

Heat to heat. Hard to soft. He felt her quivering response all the way down to his bones. Hunger prowled his body, and he trembled with its force.

She called his name in a voice raw with need.

Her body convulsed against him.

He gave her no time. Gave himself less. He was over her, pulling her legs around his hips, pressing against her. And she held him tight in response as he sank into her. Her imploring whisper sent him over the edge. He could not fight her and himself. Now, he did not want to.

"Give me your mouth," he demanded.

His tongue drove into her sweet mouth with the same driving rhythms he used to take her body.

Sarah's head thrashed back and forth. He was filling her until she cried out.

"I can't!"

"Yes. Yes, Sarah. You wanted everything. All of me."

Then heated sensation shimmered and burst inside her. She clutched at his shoulder, slippery with sweat as he pushed into her, slamming her against the mattress. There was no pain. No fear. She held on to Rio against the spinning world where ecstasy waited.

He buried himself so deep inside her that she felt every pulse beat, before her senses exploded without warning.

Sarah tore her mouth from his. She bit her lip to still her cry as the force of his seed spilled into her. A guttural sound came from his lips. She held him tight, knowing that she had all, nothing held back and that Rio was there to ride out the last of the storm.

Together.

Touching.

Belonging.

Slowly, very slowly, Sarah tumbled back to reality. She was back in her bed, in her room. They were bathed in sweat. His lips caressed her bare shoulder, and she barely managed to stroke back his damp hair. She buried her face against his salt-damp skin, and he cradled her close. Words, for the moment, appeared to be beyond them.

But not feelings. She felt rich, and warm, and blissfully sated. She had loved. And Rio, without words, had loved her.

He stirred, taking his weight from her, but instantly drawing her against him. Harsh breathing was the only sound in that room.

Rio recovered first. "Listen, Sarah. The rain has stopped."

She murmured some sound. Her ear was pressed to his chest and the only thing she listened to was the beat of his heart. She opened her eyes for a few moments, it was still dark.

She felt him pull the quilt up and over them, tucking it close behind her. She felt his hand as he gently brushed her tangled hair back from her face.

Every touch was tender. She felt herself drifting off to sleep and tried to fight it. Every moment was now precious. All to be savored and treasured against the time he would leave. But Rio's dark, murmuring voice lulled and soothed her to sleep.

Rio held her a little while longer, then, with reluctance, he eased away from her. These past few hours with Sarah had taken the edge off the tension that rode him so hard.

He knew it would not last. Just as he knew that loving Sarah, the forever kind of love, was not a choice offered to him.

He was going to leave her. He would finish his quest for revenge, then somehow he would find a substitute for the peace that pervaded his mind and body now.

Sarah. A gift of benevolent gods and spirits. Or was this loving, giving woman a messenger sent from she who was gone. For all his dual upbringing, he still respected the Apache way of not thinking or speaking the name of a departed one.

Sarah. He could not stop himself from leaning over her, his lips touching her forehead. There was no guile in her.

The thought of keeping her was not as selfish as it seemed. She was a woman for a man to love.

He reached down and very lightly touched his palm to the curve of her belly. She had shared her secret with him, he had shared her grief, and she had wanted and taken all of him without thought of tomorrows.

And he, with less thought than a boy of fifteen with his first woman, had spilled his seed.

What if Sarah carried his child?

Could he leave her?

Would he turn from his set path to stay with her, protect her, love her?

And what of his sons?

Tormented questions for a tormented man.

Rio eased his body away from Sarah. He gathered his clothing and, with a look of regret, left Sarah to her dreams.

Lucas barely stirred with a sleepy murmur when Rio took the rifle away and urged him to sleep. He covered the sprawled form of Gabriel, and stood silent as he watched his sons for a few minutes.

Was Sarah right? Did his plan of running with them into Mexico lead to doom?

Everything had been so clear. He was going to steal the horses, take supplies and leave. Why had he let this widow woman draw him into staying?

In the kitchen a sullen grayness speared into the room from the windows. The rain had indeed stopped. Outside was muddy ground. He added kindling, stirring the few coals until the wood caught fire. He reset the stove plate and heated the coffee left from last night.

With his fingers curled over the edge of the dry sink, he stared out at the muddy yard. His options were limited to staying or running again.

Rio did not spare himself. Running out on Sarah was a coward's answer. But staying would bring more pain to a woman who had had more than her share.

But how could he leave her with the threat of two more killers on his trail?

What if they came here looking for him and found Sarah alone?

He squeezed his eyes shut, but nothing would block out the sight burned into his mind of what he had come home to find.

And if he stayed, maybe, if Coyote was off doing his mischief to some other poor soul, he could protect Sarah and his sons long enough to have his revenge.

*And if they come and kill you?*

"Then Sarah and my sons would be at their mercy," he whispered in answer to the double-bladed question. "But those men have no mercy."

He had lingered here too long. His own need, the silent one that pleaded with him from Sarah's dark eyes, trapped him as surely as had the weather.

What the hell was he going to do?

And what made him think that Sarah wanted him to stay?

What did he have to offer any woman?

Nothing. He owned the clothes on his back.

Sarah deserved more.

He never heard her come up behind him. Her arms slipped around his waist. Her hands sent a jolt of heat through him when she pressed them against his belly. His fault. He never buttoned the shirt.

"Did you make coffee?" she asked in a soft voice, pressing her cheek against the warmth of his back.

"Last night's. It should be hot by now."

"Rio? Why did you leave me?"

"I made no promises. We both had needs. There is no more than that."

*Bastard! How you can lie to her? Is that what your grandfather taught you? Is this the honor of your mother's people?*

To his surprise, Sarah did not release her hold on him. He had to do something. Say something.

"It was a long, long time since I was with a white woman." *And never like you, Sarah.* "You said there had been no other man. Six years at least."

His knuckles showed white. She did not utter a sound. He gritted his teeth. He was hurting her. And he was going to go on until she ordered him out.

*Coward!*

No! he wanted to shout his denial. It was the only way he could protect her. With him gone, if those two left came here and questioned her, she had to hate him. It had to show how unwilling she'd been to have him there.

"Nothing to say, Sarah? I performed my good deed last night. One a day is all I allow."

Sarah froze. What had happened? Where had this cold, angry stranger come from?

"I know you're pushing me away, Rio. I just don't understand why." Her arms fell to her sides, and she stepped back and away from him.

"You're right. There were no promises. And no, I'm not in need of stud service this morning." She bit her lip, hating what she was saying, what she was making of what they shared. "That's what you wanted to hear, what you practically forced me to say." His silence, his hunched-over position, all grated on already-frayed nerves. She wanted to strike out at him.

How could he turn what had been so beautiful for her into something cheap and ugly?

Sarah stood for a few minutes more, hoping he would face her, hoping that he would take her into his arms. She desperately needed to hear him say he hadn't meant a word of what he had said. The man she had trusted could not be so cruel.

Silence. A rigid back. Bowed head. No words. No move.

There was no pain. Not now. But she wrapped her arms around her waist as if to hold herself together.

She wasn't a coward. It wasn't her way to walk away from anything that mattered to her.

But his silence defeated her.

She started to back away, then spun around to leave him. She wouldn't run. Couldn't. All she thought about was needing time. Time to figure out what was going on with him.

She couldn't have been so wrong about the man she trusted, the one who made love to her. She just could not be wrong.

*But what if you are wrong? What then?*

Now she ran, through the hallway, up the stairs with that odd, choked little voice asking those same questions over and over again.

# Chapter Nineteen

The heavy, brooding quality to the overcast day suited Sarah's mood perfectly. She had a strong feeling that it suited Rio and even his sons, too.

Lunch was finished, and she was no closer to finding an answer to what had made him turn and lash out at her. She was not about to give up. *Quit* was a word she had banished once free of Judd.

She looked up and out the window to see that Gabriel, lost in his own imaginary game, worked his way over the planks that formed a path to the barn. His arms were straight out at shoulder height, one foot set directly in front of the other, every step punctuated with a body wobble that set his arms to waving to keep his balance.

Beyond him, the horses milled about the corral while Rio worked to muck out their stalls.

For a few minutes she indulged herself in a flood of resentment that he had taken over her chores, especially the care of her horses. Then she chided herself. If he felt anything like she did, busy work, separated busy work, was all that prevented them from a shouting match.

Or maybe it was just her that it stopped.

"Sarah? Sarah, there is no more to wash."

Lucas's voice jerked her from her thoughts. She looked down at the dishpan of soapy water to see that he was right. There was nothing left.

"Thank you for helping me, Lucas." She did not look at him, he reminded her too much of Rio's face. It took a while before she realized that he was still there.

"Did you want something? Ask, Lucas. If I can help or give you whatever it is, I will."

"The drawing paper. You have more?"

"No. But as soon as the road dries out a little bit more I'll go into town and get some for you."

She glanced at him then, puzzled to see his head lowered, his shoulders hunched. He looked as if she had beaten him in some way. Looking down, she saw the way his hands clenched the dish towel.

Sarah lifted her hands from the water and, rather than take the towel from him, wiped them down the sides of her pants. She hesitated before she lifted his chin.

"I know you're disappointed, but I have a feeling it's more than that. I have no right to ask you to tell me what it is, but Lucas, the offer to help you still holds."

She had to fight the urge to draw him into her arms. If ever a boy needed a hug, needed more than words, Lucas did. His eyes were painful to look at. Wounded, confused. Sarah wasn't even sure what she was seeing. She had the growing feeling that something was terribly wrong.

Her hand fell back to her side. "Tell you what, why don't we take a walk. Maybe then you'll feel like talking."

"He does not want you to leave the house. He said it is not yet safe for you."

Mentally she backed up and smothered the flare of anger his words brought. There was no question of who *he* was—Rio, of course. Rio giving orders about her and what she could do.

A deep breath helped calm her. Rio had a right to worry about two killers who still could track him here. She understood where his concern came from, but it didn't sit easy on her shoulders. He didn't want her, and she didn't want any man to be accountable for her well-being.

None of which was easy to explain, even if she had an urge to do so. Especially not to Lucas.

Where did that leave her? She couldn't take the boy to task for his father's well-deserved fear, she couldn't make an issue of it at all.

About to say as much, she caught a flash of misery in Lucas's eyes before he glanced away.

"Since you and your brother helped me get the house in order and the soup's on for supper, why don't you and I sit and have a talk."

Sarah ignored the lack of response and took the towel from his hands. She snapped it free then folded it over the bar to dry. Moving toward the table, she encouraged him to join her. She found herself having to ignore his sullen glance, because he did come over to sit near her.

"Something is troubling you, Lucas. I'm not the wisest woman, but I know how to listen. I'm not related to you, but I can be your friend. I'm not a stranger in the sense that I know a little of what has happened to you, your brother and your father.

"I also promise you, Lucas, that whatever it is I won't say anything to anyone unless you want me to."

"You want me to trust you?"

Sarah sat up straight, her gaze directly on the boy. She opened her mouth, then closed it as she quickly changed her mind about what to answer him.

"How 'bout I talk, and you listen?" His curt nod did little to reassure her that some minor thing was bothering him.

"I know how you lost your home and your mother. And I'm not saying that to be cruel. I lost someone dear to me, too. I *do* understand how the hurt stays, how you can feel guilty that you didn't do enough, or that you did something to make it happen. In my case that's true, but not in yours."

He frowned, watching her with narrowed eyes. Sarah felt out of her depth here. But all she could do was try.

"You don't want to tell me. Fine. What about being at the mission school. From the little that Gabriel told me—"

"He had no right."

"Please," she said, reaching over to touch his

shoulder. Lucas shrugged it off, and she didn't try again. "Gabriel told me how it was for him. He said he hated it there. Hated being with boys that taunted him because he wasn't a full-blooded Indian, and because he was Apache. The boys were cruel, but all children—" She broke off. "Go on, say it."

"I'm not a child."

She looked into his eyes and slowly nodded. "You're right and I'm wrong. You were forced to stop being a child. But still, Lucas, your brother is one and he found some comfort in talking to me. There is nothing I can do to make the past go away. I can't bring your mother back, or your home. I can't give back the pride that was stolen from you."

"Never. They took my clothes, cut my hair and forbade me to speak a word of she who is gone, or to speak the words of her people. I didn't care when they punished me. Their feeble little stick could—"

"What little stick?" Sarah demanded.

"The cane. All the mission women had one."

"Oh, Lucas. I'm sorry. So sorry that you had to go through that. They didn't know—"

"They knew." He glared at her, his teeth clenched, one hand folded over the other that formed a fist. "It was as the others said. They took all that mattered to us and punished us when we fought back. They wanted us to learn their way. They wanted us to forget our people, forget all we were taught.

"When I asked why they wanted to do this to us, I was hit. I tried to understand why. I didn't want to be like them. I had a...a brother and a father. I was not like the others who had no family.''

''And you missed your father,'' she said, hurting for him and not knowing how much talk or touching he would allow.

''No. I didn't need him. He did not want me. He did not want Gabriel. He only wanted his whiskey.''

Sarah saw through the lie. The wounds were there. Lucas had been taken from his father's side, stripped of his learning of two worlds, forced to behave against what he had known and act against all he'd been taught.

Oh, yes. The wounds and the anger still burned deep and bright.

''Lucas, someday you'll be a man, and hope to love a woman as your father loved your mother. And I hope that you'll both grow old together and keep that love. But when someone you love more than life itself is taken from you, long before you believe it is right or time, the hurt that you feel can make you forget there are others that love you, others that need you.

''I'm not saying that's what happened to your father. But I think it's true. I think he loved your mother so much that he forgot how much you and your brother needed him. That's how badly he was hurting. He knows now that the whiskey didn't help and never will. Now he hurts because he has to face what he did. He can never bring back what was. But he can try to begin again with you and Gabriel.

''But Lucas,'' she pleaded, reaching over to cover his hands, ''he can't do it alone. He needs your help.

He needs you to talk to him. I know he loves you. I know that he—''

"How?"

"Lucas, he told me. I can see for myself that it's true. I think you know it, too. He never stopped loving you, he stopped loving himself. You can't give love to someone else unless you care about yourself first. It would be like..." Sarah paused. She struggled to find a way to chase the bewildered look he wore.

"You love to draw. But if you draw your pictures and never showed them to anyone wouldn't that make you selfish?" By his look she was not reaching him. She frowned and tried again.

"Do you love Gabriel?"

"He is my brother."

"And that's the only reason you love him?"

Lucas looked away, then back at her. "No. He makes me laugh. He pesters me with questions that I must find answers for and that makes me think and be stronger. He is younger and I must protect him. Sometimes...sometimes he is stronger than me. He has never shamed me. He tries to be brave like me, he said."

"And it would hurt Gabriel very much if you turned away from him? It would hurt you, too."

"Never would I do this to him!"

"No matter what he did? No matter if he tried to take something or hurt you?"

"Never! He is my brother!"

He jerked his hands away from her only to grip the edge of the table. There was fire in his glare.

"Then why, Lucas, would you think that your father ever stopped loving you?"

"You know nothing. My...she who is gone was leaving him. She was taking us to her people. She no longer wanted to live on the rancheria. He didn't fight with her to keep us. He said he would let us go. This is the love you tell me he feels? You know nothing!"

His shout jarred her as he suddenly broke off. His eyes dark and miserable, he shook his head at her and then pushed the chair away from the table.

Sarah, shocked by what he said, was left with her mouth open. In seconds the missing pieces of Rio's guilt and actions following his wife's death fell into place for her.

But she couldn't think about Rio now. Not when his son stood staring at her with his pain etched on his young features as clearly as one of his drawings.

"Lucas, I wasn't there, but I think if you look in your heart you'll know that he would never have abandoned you. Maybe he meant to let you go for a little while, but never for always. He loves you and your brother too much. You know that. I know you do. I also know that you're hurting. Please, give him a chance. For your sake and for his."

He spun away. She saw his shoulders begining to shake. The first sob was muffled as she rose from her chair.

Sarah hesitated. Then she went to him and wrapped her arms around his thin body. The child's tears widened the crack in the wall she had built around herself.

She fought back her own tears, but when his arms came around her, she felt them fall.

They held each other for long minutes. She heard the boy's sniffles as he attempted to stop crying. She tried to stop herself. When he pulled free of her arms, she let him go and then had to watch him stumble away.

It was time for him to be alone with his thoughts. And time for her to do the same. She became aware of a dull ache at the back of her neck. She closed her eyes and absently massaged her neck.

She couldn't confront Rio about what Lucas had told her. And what did it matter to her? This was something between him and his sons.

But as she opened her eyes and forced herself to stir the soup and think of what else she could make for supper, she was hit with the realization that Lucas had never intended to tell her about that.

There was something else. Something that prompted him to ask if she had more paper. And then her response of going to town to get it invited a feeling that it would be too late.

Too late?

As in too late because they wouldn't be here?

*Grasping at straws?*

Maybe, she answered herself.

Could Rio think of leaving? Silently she ran the thought of the possibilities of such a move. If he left now the floods would cover his tracks.

If leaving was his intent, this morning's cutting speech made more sense. He had to know that she would argue against him going. He had to know that she wanted him to stay here and make a stand.

And if he believed he was protecting her by taking off…

"Oh, Rio," she whispered, glancing toward the door.

He had to realize that since the rain had stopped not only would the killers travel, but others, too.

She knew there would be someone coming out from town to see how she fared. And what could she say if Rio and the boys were seen?

Sarah drummed her fingers on the table. She could sit here all day and try to figure out what Rio was planning. How much easier if she confronted him.

She sighed and leaned back in her chair. She would not make one move without thinking it through.

She had no right to argue with Rio if he did plan to leave, not when he had the lives of his sons to consider.

But she couldn't help feeling that she had a stake in them, too. Gabriel's sunny smiles and incessant questions. Lucas's more serious mein. Their presence brought to life the painful loneliness of her own, but they also filled the empty places. Still, she would never do anything that put their lives at risk.

Rio would need supplies. He could wipe out the little she had remaining, but somehow that didn't seem the act of the man she had come to know.

Yet…he couldn't be thinking of going into town to buy what he needed. Or could he?

And where would the money…

Sarah tensed, then leaned forward. The man he killed. Rio must have searched him. And just thinking about what the killer had done, and almost did to her, brought no accusation against whatever Rio had done.

And he had no one else after him but the last two killers.

Or did he?

Could the law be looking for him? Could he have lied about that? He never told her that his wife was planning on leaving him and taking their sons with her. What else hadn't he told her? She then remembered that he'd mentioned the territorial jail.

Sarah absently rubbed her forehead as the ache grew in intensity. She had two choices. She could sit and wait for him to tell her what was going on, or she could confront him and demand to know.

Still she remained where she was, battling off the growing fear of facing that cold, hardened stranger she had met this morning.

Why? Why had he done that to her? Why tear apart…the memories of last night came rushing back.

She refused to believe him. There had been need— mutual need. But there had been something more, some stronger emotions. And when he'd attacked her this morning she had been shamed that he'd so easily aroused dreams and desire of what might be.

All she would have now was the strong reminder of her aloneness once he was gone.

If she believed the man who had spoken to her this morning.

Only if she believed him, and not the man who had loved her last night.

What drove Rio to feel guilty? She struggled to remember all he'd told her. Guilty because he wasn't there. Guilty because he couldn't stop them from killing his wife, destroying his home and stealing his horses.

And the man who had held Sarah while she cried out the black secret of her heart, the man who kissed her with a tenderness she had never known would see only the need to protect her.

By leaving…

By making her so hurt and angry she'd be glad to see him go.

And if anyone came looking for him, she could in truth tell what she knew, all with righteous anger coating every word. Every damn believable word.

Sarah made her choice. She couldn't be wrong about Rio. She had given him what had never been Judd's after the first year…her trust.

And without that, she thought as she shoved back the chair and stood up, without trust, there was no chance of building on the feelings they stirred in each other.

Now she didn't hesitate. There no longer was a reason too. And she knew as she went to the door, that she wasn't wrong about Rio.

# Chapter Twenty

The air outside was cool, but without the bite of chilling wind. The sky remained a scudding mass of gray clouds. Sarah lifted her face and closed her eyes. There was no smell of rain.

As she looked about again, she wore a small smile, for there were other potent smells. The churned mud held a musty earthiness and pungent odors rose from the mucked-out leavings from the stalls.

She walked on the same board pathway that Gabriel had entertained himself on earlier. With every step, she refused to allow doubt to come creeping back as she crossed the yard to the barn.

The horses crowded the corral fence. The mare's nickers and the stallion's snort to attract her attention failed to distract her from the open door. She took several deep breaths, exhaling the last slowly, as if this could bring up the level of courage she needed.

Sarah was not aware of the silence within the barn itself until she stood on the threshold. No cat came to greet her. No chicken squawks. No cow rattling the stanchion.

She lifted her right foot, about to step into the barn when she stopped and retreated a step. It felt as if something had pushed her back outside. Her mouth was dry as straw stubble. A chilling tremor snaked its way down her back.

For all that she felt stopped by some unseen but strongly felt barrier, she was also pulled toward going inside to discover what was wrong.

And something was wrong.

She was afraid to go in. And the fear was a stomach-tightening, weak-kneed sensation that strengthened with every second she delayed. She had felt fear like this before, fear that her accounting to Rio had dredged from memory.

She felt split in two. With her right ear she could hear the horse's restless stampings, with the left, she heard the painful silence.

Swallowing repeatedly did not provide moisture for her mouth. She could not call out, then, she realized she didn't want to. It was a few seconds' work to call up the layout of the barn, but harder to believe that Rio had not replaced the tools used to muck out the stalls.

She had to hope. There was nothing else. If Rio had been interrupted, he would not have had the time to put away the hay fork or the manure hook in the tack room.

And she needed one or the other for a weapon.

Doubt had disappeared. She needed a weapon.

The first step into the shadowed interior of the barn was the hardest.

What if those two men were just waiting for her? If she was caught, or killed, it wouldn't be long before Lucas would come looking for her.

Once more those killers would get away with murdering innocents.

Not while she had a breath left.

Sarah scanned the center aisle. No Rio, no Gabriel, and no cow. Those men wouldn't have bothered taking the cow. Maybe she was being foolish beyond imagining. Rio would have turned the animal out in the pasture behind the barn. He could be there with his son right now.

She wanted to believe that. Wanted it with every tense nerve in her body.

All she could do was listen to an inner voice yelling that she was wrong. There was no easy way to find them safe.

Safe. She locked on to and clung tight to that thought. She sidestepped toward her left. With her hands extended behind her, she felt along the wall for one of the long, wood-handled tools.

Sarah suddenly froze. Her breath was caught in her chest. What her fingers encountered was the long cool barrel of her rifle. She released her breath in a rush as she snatched up the rifle.

She should have been thinking herself lucky. But all she could feel was despair. Rio had no weapon but his knife. He had refused to wear her handgun. That was hanging beside the door in the kitchen.

If those killers…

*No!*

She refused to think about it. She cradled the rifle and took courage from the fact that she now was armed with a weapon she knew how to use. Once more she inched along until she peered over the wall of the first stall. Empty.

Sarah climbed the ladder and searched the loft. Nothing. The stalls below on the left side were empty, too. In the tack room, she used the rifle barrel to poke at the pile of empty sacks. No sign of disturbance.

Standing in the doorway of the tack room, she wiped cold sweat from her brow. Her rapidly pounding heart allowed her no more than panting breaths.

No sign of Rio or Gabriel.

It was then she noticed the smell. It was not one she could identify. Stepping out into the barn again, she found she clutched the rifle, one hand on the barrel, the other positioned to fire. The total silence sank into her bone marrow.

She forced herself to think of what could have happened here. It was the last thing she wanted to do as a tightness rose in her chest.

What was that smell?

She didn't realize she sidestepped to avoid going closer to it. Her mind was filled with the fact that two people couldn't disappear as though they have never been. Not when one of them was a small boy excited at being free for the first time in days.

Or was all this anxiety she felt mere imagining?

Could that be it? Just imagination?

It didn't feel right, and there was no sense of relief. If anything, the fear increased with a force that left her shaking.

She had to find them.

The foul odor made it hard to breathe. She started forward, thinking to get Lucas and keep him with her. She even managed a few steps before she felt pulled toward the middle stall. One of the ones she hadn't checked. The smell of something foul was stronger and her stomach churned. She was breathing through her mouth, and as much as she wanted to stop, to flee, she found herself slipping the latch.

Rio had mucked out all the stalls. This one had brown-stained hay covering its flooring. An unusually thick layer of bedding.

And she knew what she smelled. Knew it as if she had lifted the hay. Tried not to think of what awaited as her stomach rebelled and emptied itself.

She was still gagging when she turned back. She had to be sure. She pushed aside the hay. Red comb. Glassy eyes. Little brown head twisted and limp.

Sarah backed out and slammed the stall door closed. She didn't need to see more. No chickens. No cats. Now she knew that Rio had spared telling her the worst of those two animals. Animals, not men.

What if those weren't the only dead things concealed beneath the hay?

Sarah backed away. She couldn't look. Not now. She refused to give in, give up any hope that Rio and Gabriel were still alive. She had to get Lucas!

She ran across the yard. She cursed her need for

privacy and lack of close neighbors. The road was still flooded, she could never make it into town and bring back help in time.

Had Gabriel seen what those wretched, evil creatures had done? Please, Lord, I hope you spared him that.

"Lucas," she called out the moment she opened the back door. The kitchen filled with the aroma of the soup simmering on the stove. Sarah took a few breaths and then found herself hunched over the dry sink, heaving, but there was nothing left. She washed out her mouth, patted cold water on her face and called out for Lucas again.

She heard him coming down the hall as she loaded her pockets with bullets.

"What's wrong, Sarah?"

"Take the gun belt, Lucas. We've got to find your father and brother."

"Why?"

She closed the cupboard drawer and turned around to face him. Within his dark eyes she saw that he already knew the answer.

"There's no time to waste, Lucas. Nothing is going to happen to them. We'll find them. I swear to you we will." Inwardly she shuddered for what she was about to do.

"Can you use a handgun?"

"Rifle," he choked. One hand swiped across his eyes. "I hunted with a rifle."

"Then take it." She snatched the gun belt from its hook, wrapped it around her hips then belted it.

"Lucas, one thing. We stay together unless I say otherwise." He stood waiting while she loaded his pockets with extra ammunition.

He grabbed her arm. "How...how did you know?"

Sarah thought about lying to him. The feel of his fingers digging into her arm, and his pleading gaze, would not allow her to lie.

"There's no sign of them in the barn. I saw Gabriel go in, but not come out. So they're alive or I...Lucas, you don't want to—"

His grip was fierce, his eyes more so. "Tell me."

"They killed the chickens, likely the cats, too. I didn't...couldn't look at more. These aren't men, they are monsters. I don't know how they caught your father. I don't know why they didn't kill him if that is what they want."

"Gabriel," he whispered. "They will use him to hurt Father."

"Sick, evil creatures. Not men. Let's get going, Lucas. We don't have time to waste."

Sarah grabbed hold of two small kitchen knives. She wanted the largest one, but it was too awkward to carry. Lucas slipped into one of her wool shirts, the sleeves rolled up, tails trailing his knees. She squeezed his shoulder as they stepped outside.

"Do you know where they are?" the boy asked.

"No. They needed shelter from the storm. Fuel and fresh water. They didn't take any of my horses. Something tells me they're close by. There aren't many places they could be."

Sarah set off, wishing their pace was faster, but the

muddy earth slowed them down. She saw that Lucas was studying the ground but didn't think he'd have luck. There were too many puddles.

She led him around the pasture fence toward a clump of cottonwood saplings. In the distance were the bronze-red hills, thick with shrubs and trees.

"Sarah? Sarah, there's the cow."

She looked over her shoulder to see he was right. The cow was in the pasture, at the far end. She appeared to be unharmed. Rio had likely taken her out when he released the horses.

They worked their way over soft, muddy soil that added the handicap of being rocky. The sparse growth of creosote bushes and flattened grasses yielded no clues to help them search.

Approaching the ancient cottonwood, she recalled being there with Rafe, and their discovery that someone had watched the house, waiting for a chance to kill him. The memory made her shiver.

A little way beyond, they were forced to slog through calf-high water. There was no dry ground. The narrow stream that ribboned over Sarah's land had widened, overflowing its banks until she could not tell where its boundaries were.

Water was the least of Sarah's problems. The land changed to rocky outcroppings, some taller than her, others wide enough to conceal more than men and horses. The surface changed, too. Gone was the level earth, it dipped and rose, making for slow progress.

"Sarah," Lucas whispered, tugging on her jacket to get her attention. "Wait. Look over there."

Sarah backed up a few steps, her gaze directed to where Lucas pointed. The land rose hill-like. She could see where the recent storm had tumbled mud and rocks. But it was the darker spot midway up the rise that held her attention.

Despite the overcast day, the area she stared at was darker than the sage and tree-strewn land. Thickets of walnut, cedar and pine lay before them.

She wasn't aware that she crouched down until she looked over at Lucas.

"I've never seen that before."

"It looks like a cave, Sarah."

"A cave. Yes. Perfect shelter. Hidden away, but Lucas, do you see any sign of their horses?"

"Not from here. I will go—"

This time she grabbed his arm. "No. Stay right here. Hard as it may be to wait, we need to be sure. That climb won't be easy. If we go up and we're wrong, we'll expose ourselves to them."

He stared at her for long moments, his eyes far too old for a boy. "You ask me to wait? You didn't see what these killers did? They will kill my father. And my brother. You wait. I'll go."

He jerked his arm free of her grip.

"Lucas, please. Think about this. If you go up there without being sure and are right, you could endanger them more. Those animals won't hesitate to kill them. Then they'll come after you."

"You say nothing of yourself."

She gnawed her bottom lip. "I'm afraid. I won't lie

to you. I just want us to have a good plan, a plan that gives us a chance.''

She shivered at a sudden drop in temperature and glanced skyward. No sign of lightning in the distance, but the clouds appeared darker. She hoped the rain would hold off.

She had to wait for Lucas to make up his mind that to rush off could prove fatal to his father and brother. If they were even up there. The more she studied it, the more she was certain the storm had torn loose enough rock and earth to reveal a hidden cave. But how deep was it? How was she to find out if Rio and Gabriel were there?

She should count it as luck if they were above them. But one opening meant one way in and one way out. How could she protect them with two killers holding them?

''We can't go in there, Sarah.''

''I know. I was just thinking about that. We need to figure a way to lure them outside. If they are in there.''

Sarah shivered. She was fighting fear and panic that she and Lucas wouldn't be strong enough or smart enough to save them. Lucas shifted and glanced down.

''Not a good place to wait. Too wet.''

His remark brought her attention to the cold damp that had seeped into her boots. Again she gazed skyward. It would be getting dark soon and colder. She shifted her position, wrapping her arms around herself as if to ward off the chill. But the true cold came from somewhere deep inside herself.

Sarah hadn't realized she closed her eyes, images forming, her own sense of helplessness coming back.

When she turned to Lucas, she couldn't believe he wasn't there. His name was a soundless cry from her lips. She strained to see where he had gone.

It was minutes before her gaze picked out his slithering body, heading upward, right toward the dark mouth above them.

There was no time to waste cursing him for taking matters into his own hands. She had to move and move now.

# Chapter Twenty-One

Deep within the abandoned mine shaft, the only light came from the fire set against the back wall of stone. Firelight danced on the blade that snaked toward Rio. Only his wrists were tied, held chest high before him. He spun away. Not too fast. And not too far.

Rules.

If he had any hope of winning, of taking down the killer that taunted him with his own knife, of gaining freedom, it was crushed with every flickering glance he spared toward his son.

Gabriel had courage. Even fighting for their lives, Rio managed to separate part of his mind to see that. The child stood rigid, as he had been ordered, another killer, another knife at his throat.

More rules of the game.

Killers' rules.

Killer games.

He weaved and dodged the blade again, this time slamming his shoulder against the pointed protrusion of rock.

Pain flared from his shoulder down to his nearly numb wrist. He blocked it out. Just as he had been forced to block out all that came before this moment.

He was losing track of how long it had been.

The time was lost, but not the image.

He would never lose that.

Stepping over the threshold of the tack room, seeing a knife at his son's throat…no, nothing would wipe the sight from his mind. Not even the blow to his temple that stunned him while they wreaked their horror for Sarah to find.

Sarah.

No. He could not think about her. Or Lucas.

Yet they were there. Worry for them rising despite his own effort to block it, too.

The distraction cost him. At first he didn't feel the slice of the blade across his raised forearm. At least it was his own knife the bastard was using. Clean blade, honed to a deadly edge.

Quick death.

Rio skirted the fire. His moccasins allowed for better purchase on the rock-strewn floor. But in other places, sand was thick, almost ankle deep. He had to avoid being trapped.

Stay alert!

Dodge. Weave. Duck. And sway. He sucked in his stomach. Close call. He'd almost been had.

How much longer?

He flexed his fingers, the rope around his wrists tight, cutting off his blood.

They were going to win. Get away with the spree of killing that both of them taunted him with.

An end to his life.

And his sons.

Sarah would be at their mercy.

*Animals. Remember? They have no mercy.*

Move.

Keep moving. Provide their sport.

Bound. Gabriel was helpless.

Weaponless.

Dart to the right. Back bowed. Another slash from the tip of the knife. Jump over the fire.

Move. Again. Don't think of your child held hostage. Don't think at all.

"Finish him. Finish him off, Harson. Gettin' damn tired jus' standin' an' watchin'. Ain't no fun for me. You promised me fun. I wanna go get the woman."

"Shut the hell up, Boorum. You'll get yours."

Rio ignored Boorum's whining. But it was steady now. Impatient. He had the appearance of a small shaggy bear, his light eyes twin pinpoints of evil in his heavily bearded face. Greasy strings of dark hair sank to his shoulders. The once-glossy bearskin vest carried the same rank stench as Harson. Rio had learned the hard way that the smaller killer's bulk was not fat. He swung a mean fist. Big, meaty hands that liked to punish.

Especially anyone smaller than him.

He learned, too, that his home was not the first they had ravaged. His wife not the first savaged and killed. His prize stock not the first they had run off and sold.

He stood their failure. He had taken revenge.

They were the only two left.

He had killed Harson's brother at Sarah's.

So now he paid for that. Now he provided sport.

Rio's gaze flicked from the knife to the eyes of the man who wielded it. Harson was not without skill. Rio continued to dance away from the blade.

Harson had a few inches in height on him, his body rope-lean. But he had long arms, and that made him dangerous.

Rio stumbled. The knife flashed. Another slice. This time only cloth was cut.

He stared at the scar that ran from the corner of Harson's left eye across his cheek to his chin. Some-one, somewhere, had cut open his face. The hands bore other scars.

"Com'on, breed. Come an' get me."

Silence.

That was a rule, too. No answer to taunts. Rio darted to the other side of the fire. One minute. A small dis-traction. That's all he needed. If only there had been time to talk to Gabriel. To warn him to watch for a chance.

The one thing he could and did do was to keep his gaze from the fire. Beyond all was a deepened gray. But even as he kept his gaze away from the light so not to impair his vision, he kept moving close around it, or jumping over the flames, to force Harson's eyes toward the light. A twist into the shadows, Harson following, his eyes not as sharp as they adjusted from light to darkness.

He could make it work.

He had to make it work. His strength was ebbing. Thinking, breathing, both were becoming difficult. He had to stop listening to the hammering voice that promised him and his death.

Sweat soaked his clothes. Dripped into his eyes. Stung. Shoulders hunched, he swiped at the sweat, arms raised to protect his face.

Harson sliced off the last button holding his shirt closed.

Rio squinted.

He could not look away. Harson's eyes held a deep, cold hardness that was unmistakable.

He was getting ready to finish him off.

Dark eyes where violent energy darted around as if it were trapped and had to come out. Had to kill.

The thick, coarse features that promised it would not be quick, not clean, but ugly.

Sarah!

Her silently screamed name jolted Rio. Once done with him they would go after her. He had lied to her. Made her hate him. Cast the lovely gift of herself aside as if it meant nothing. It had been everything.

She would never know. Never hear the words from his lips. He was stumbling now. Sand and rock traps for his feet. Sweat blinded him.

Whimpers from Gabriel.

Growled orders.

Silence but for the pop of sap in the fire.

Harson edging him toward the back wall. Trapping him.

Rio seethed with violence all his own. Feeling the muscles of his body loosen. Ready for anything.

Ready now to make his move.

Sarah no longer saw Lucas. He had had a head start. She had watched him, elbows crooked to hold the rifle horizontal to the slithering moves of his thin body. She lost sight of him halfway up the rocky, brush-strewn slope. She had started to follow after him. Even took a few crouching steps in his direction, then changed her mind.

She had no skill to move surely and quietly, more certain with every breath she took that Rio and Gabriel were up there. In danger.

She was chilled to the bone. The cold brought with it a numbness that encased her body and stopped her from thinking of what she had to do when she reached that opening.

Sarah could not avoid the sharp, jagged edges of rock buried beneath the thick layer of mud that made the last few feet of her climb treacherous.

In the distance thunder rumbled. The threat of rain brought a new fear. The storm had washed all that had hidden the cave, would more rain hide it again?

She inhaled, trying to sense how close the rain was. But the darkness, the overpowering sense of danger blocked her. She tried to moisten her lips, but they remained as dry as her throat and mouth. She was breathing too fast, like someone who had run a long distance beneath the desert sun.

She looked up. The opening was about five feet

high, no more than three or four feet wide. The darkness descended and made details hard to see. But she had the impression this was man-made. Almost like a mine.

The wind freshened, chilling and damp. She had to stop thinking about the threat of rain.

Just as she drew up into a crouch, prepared to lunge toward the opening, she felt someone's presence.

"Sarah," came Lucas's whisper. "Wait."

She froze, unable to speak as he worked his way alongside her.

"I found their horses. Set them loose."

She squeezed his hand. "We need to hurry. I feel...I..."

"Yes. I feel the danger, too."

Sarah shook her head. Her fear was playing tricks with her hearing. Lucas sounded older, steady where she was still uncertain of what to do. But they were both standing, ready to go beyond the blackness that loomed before them.

They were three or four feet inside when the glow of fire was reflected on the stone walls. The opening curved away from them and slanted downward.

Not knowing what they would find, Sarah led off, her back to the uneven wall, taking side-to-side steps that allowed her to avoid most of the small rocks that littered the floor.

She heard the low, taunting sound of a man's voice. A few inches more brought a child's cry.

Gabriel! She glanced at Lucas. He nodded. She

reached for his hand, courage flooded her. Both Rio and his son were alive.

Then there was no more waiting. She stood at the edge of the fire-lit cave.

Deeper and wider, as if the hillside had been hollowed to make room for this hidden place. There was a drop of about four feet to the bottom.

No matter what Sarah thought to see, nothing came close.

Little Gabriel, his body shaking with the wide, long blade at his throat. The grinning lips on a killer's face. His gaze on the scene before him.

Firelight, flickering as it threw shadows on the cavern's walls. Shadows distorted by the natural jut and curve of stone.

The hulking form, knife wavering, taunting Rio.

And Rio himself, hands splayed, wrists bound before his body, all sinuous moves directed by the threatening knife.

Thin red ribbons sliced Rio's arms, chest and thighs. It took her seconds to realize they were all knife cuts.

Lucas's breathing beat loudly in her ears, a beat that pounded like her heart. Terror held her upright as her knees weakened and threatened to give way. She barely felt the boy's hand grip her upper arm.

A whisper rose in her mind, gathering force, then screaming a warning she had to heed. She looked down. She had drawn and cocked her gun.

"Don't fire." Sarah whispered the words in Lucas's ear. "Stone walls. A ricochet could kill them."

The boy nodded his understanding, needing no explanation from her with regards to *them*. He knew she was only concerned with his father and brother.

Their gazes locked and held. Sarah sensed what Lucas wanted from her. She knew what she had to do.

"Drop the knife and let the boy go!" she yelled.

She had grabbed the killer's attention. His head snapped to glare at her as she moved out into the opening. But she hadn't counted on Rio being ready to make his own move.

As she repeated her order with the gun held steady in her hand, Rio fell to one knee. His hands swept down, sand flew upward in a spray as Rio lunged toward the hulking body before him.

Filthy curses filled and echoed in the cavern.

Sarah repeated her demand, this time backed up with a single shot. She saw Gabriel reel free from his captor.

"Lucas! Get your brother out of here."

She didn't look to see if he obeyed her. Her eyes watched the flash of the knife aimed at Rio. Once more sand flew high. She saw the bulky body staggering away from Rio.

She sensed Lucas moving away from her. But she couldn't be drawn to look. She had to help Rio, had to protect him.

His graceful, powerful body twisted and turned, avoiding every thrust of the knife. But he was being forced back against the wall.

Sarah steadied herself. She knew there was no choice. Shots rumbled. The noise rivaled the outside thunder. Bright blood blossomed as the killer half turned to shout at her.

She couldn't hear him, for Lucas was firing right along with her.

Their guns were empty. She kept triggering only to hear the empty clicks. Someone was screaming in pain.

Sarah fumbled at her belt, sliding cool bullets into hot metal. She lifted the gun, sighted it and found no one standing to shoot.

The noise suddenly stopped. There was only Gabriel, sobbing in his brother's arms.

Sarah stepped forward to the very edge of the drop. The fire had been scattered over the sandy floor. Wood still burned.

"Rio?" The cavern's walls threw her cry back at her. An aching, desperate sound that would not stop. She kept calling him. Her voice rose with panic when he didn't answer her.

Lucas and Gabriel were suddenly beside her. Both boys' faces were pale with shock, two pairs of dark eyes moist with tears.

"Where? Where is he?" she screamed, then pushed them aside.

Rio came up from the floor slowly, using the stone wall at his back for support. His breathing was harsh, almost too loud in the sudden silence. He stared down at his knife, then shifted his gaze to the body wounded by bullets, but dead by his hand.

"Rio?"

Tears blocked her throat. She watched him, praying

silently, pleading and screaming for him to come to her. She saw his staggered first step and fought herself not to go to him. She knew, without knowing, that he had to do this on his own.

She could only wait.

# Chapter Twenty-Two

Sarah saw that her agony of waiting was shared by his sons. They crowded close to her as Rio made his way to them. Lucas bent forward, arms extended to help his father climb up to where they stood.

Rio looked back, then stared at his sons. His hand shook as he reached out and touched first Lucas's shoulder, then Gabriel's.

The scattered fire still burned. In the wavering light, she saw Rio's eyes, dark, bottomless, glimmering.

She felt his hand touch her cheek, his thumb brush her lips. The horrors of the day faded in a sudden, dizzying rush of love and desire for this one man above all others.

"Sarah." Rio swayed where he stood. Lucas came to support him. Gabriel clung to Sarah.

She started to walk, willing weak knees to hold her upright, but Rio stopped her.

"Wait. If I died this day..." His voice broke. He flung his head back, gulping for air. Lucas had slipped

an arm around his father's waist and urged him to
walk on, but once more Rio hung back.

"No, son. I need to speak."

"Later, Rio," Sarah pleaded. "You're hurt and this
place—"

"No, Sarah. Here it must be. My sons know my
love for them. The threat to their lives is gone. But it
is to you I say these words, Sarah. It is you who must
know that had I died this day, I would have died loving you."

Sarah stared at him. Her breath caught for the moment. She wasn't fully aware of turning her lips into
the bruised palm of his hand. She could not hold the
aching intensity of his gaze as a sweetly heated healing
balm flowed through her heart and her body. Tears
flowed, too, but neither she nor Rio made a move to
stop them. They were healing, too.

With vision still blurred by tears, she took in the
faces of the young boys and the man before her. It
was hard for her to speak. When she finally did so,
she hoped Rio fully understood the importance of the
few words.

"Let's go home."

It was a weary group that reached the house before
the rain came. A gentle, misting rain that Rio called
female rain, so unlike the unleashed storm's fury akin
to a man's rage.

Sarah found wisdom in the Indian naming of the
rain, for it was sky tears, tears of release like her own.

She made no apology, nor could she stop crying for

more than minutes at a time. She had only to see a new bruise on Gabriel or clean a scrape on Lucas to begin anew.

Rio asked that she tend the boys first. He headed for the barn. She knew it was pointless to argue with him, but burying the animals could wait. While the boys ate a little, she brewed tea to help them sleep.

Neither boy wanted to make up a bed upstairs, so she replenished the fire and waited until they were almost asleep before she left the parlor. Their silence bothered her. Too much violence in their young lives, but then she thought of Lucas's words as she tucked the quilt around him. "It's finally over." And Gabriel, tight against his side, whispered, "We are safe now."

Rio was waiting in the kitchen.

"There were thanks to be given, Sarah," he explained. "And I wanted some cleansing before you touched me."

And touch him she did, not only to salve small cuts, or stitch larger ones, but to reassure herself that he was here, that the words he had spoken were not idle, but from his heart.

She was on her knees beside his chair, having cut through the pants to clean the wound on his thigh. Sarah worked quickly, feeling the power of his muscles and the sleek texture of his skin that drew forth the desire to hold him safe. But when she looked up, she saw another desire fill his eyes. One that found an answering chord within her.

"Sarah, what I said this morning...a lifetime ago, I did not wish to hurt you."

"I know that. I won't lie to you. What you said did hurt me. But I understood why. You needed to push me away. You were going to leave, weren't you?"

He could not look away from her. The answer to her question was revealed in his eyes before he spoke.

"Yes. I planned to leave."

"You said the threat is gone, but I sense that you haven't changed your plans. You still intend to go. And that, despite telling me that you loved me."

It was not a question, but he responded as if she had asked him one.

"I did not make promises, Sarah. How can you think I would stay after what happened? Did nothing of what I told you make you understand? I am a half-breed by white man's law. I cannot own land. I am not to have claim to whatever my labor brings to me. How can you believe that I would love you and ask you to risk—"

"But you haven't asked me, Rio."

"And I will not."

He pushed back the chair, standing with an effort but moving behind the chair. He gripped its back with hands that showed white knuckles and glowered at where she still knelt on the floor.

Sarah took a deep breath and released it before she stood up. She set her workbasket with its salve and linen strips on the table. She tucked the scissors beneath the linen, buying herself a little time. She knew whatever she said to him now mattered more than any other words.

"Sarah, you see how it has to be for us. There cannot—"

"Don't say that. Don't put words in my mouth. If you did not want me, did not tell me that you would have died today loving me, I could let you go.

"But you can't take back what you did say. You can't take back the physical loving we shared no matter what ugly words you used to hurt me. I said I understood, Rio. I meant that.

"When I said for us to come home, I meant that, too. I want you to stay. Does it matter so much that the property is in my name? The only thing that matters is what is between us. If you can't see that, can't believe it, then nothing more I can say will make it happen. You know what I feel. If I need to say the words, I will."

She moved then, coming to his side, forcing his hands free and holding them with her own. She lifted each of his hands to her lips and kissed not the hand but the rope-burned wrists.

"Rio, we have shared ourselves—heart, mind and body. If that is the kind of love you can walk away from and be at peace with, then I will not stand in your way. Take the horses and your sons and leave me."

She held her eyes steady and direct on his. "But if that sharing meant to you what it does to me, then stay. Love me, help me build a home, a place for our family, a refuge from those who will never understand that a man and woman who love know that strength is built from that love. No one can ever destroy it. No man or woman can come between it. Two, not one alone.''

Sarah made no attempt to pull away from his hands now holding hers. She saw the struggle in his eyes, open and clear to her as never before. She willed him to agree, but knew that nothing would be so simple for this man to whom she had given her heart. He would think, he would worry and argue with her and himself, so she had to pray that in the end love would win.

"Sarah…Sarah…" The murmur of her name came between kisses scattered over her face. His lips were gentle at first meeting hers, but they had been through so much this day that life required a more potent celebration.

Need to hold and touch brought the desire to lose themselves in passion.

Sarah ached with the need to love him, to comfort him. A lonely man struggling to survive, just as she had been alone, and lonely, struggling to survive.

She lifted her arms to his shoulders, drawing closer to his warmth. His sleek, bare skin against her clothed body brought erotic sensations alive.

And the hunger he had shown her.

"Sarah, lovely, lovely Sarah, I am not good for you."

"Hush. You are all that is good for me." Passion made her bold. She pressed a kiss to the skin over his heart.

Rio brushed her black hair back from her face. His hands cupped her cheeks and tilted her head back. The air around them stilled and he gazed into her eyes, searching them before he spoke.

"You are the most giving woman I have known. You offer all that you are, and yet find more to give. You make me want to take and take from you, Sarah, and in return offer you all the man I can be."

He pressed his forehead to hers, kissing the tip of her nose.

"I have only to look at you to see the passion that waits for me. You do not know what that does to a man to know that his woman is as helpless as he is to stop the need that burns within.

"And when I touch you," he whispered over her parted lips, tasting, cherishing a brief kiss, "you come to me with all the woman you are, with nothing of you held away from me."

"And I need you to kiss me. Now, Rio." A softly worded demand, but a demand nonetheless, for hunger was a fever in her blood. His mouth crushed hers, and she delved into the swirl of pleasure that his hungry kiss offered for endless minutes.

When he drew his head back, his breathing harsh, she closed her eyes, took a deep, shuddering breath and released it. Her lashes lifted slowly, her eyes searching his, finding his gaze dark, intense, almost fierce. She could not hide her need from him. Her mouth molded to his, opening to the slow stroke of his tongue. The taste of him filled her, melded with her own, and became one taste to share.

Rio sensed it, too. His mind and body were so attuned to Sarah's, he drank her love and his much-needed gentleness from her lips. But he sensed, too, an underlying tension as a result of the day's terror.

He held her tight, as if he could bring her inside himself and thereby protect her from any harm. He felt every tremor of her body. He stroked her, almost petting her as if she were a wild creature he sought to soothe and tame. He silently cursed the violence he had dragged into her life.

He kissed her again and again, whispering his need of her. Slowly he felt the tension seeping from her body. He caressed her arms, fingers massaging knots that kept her muscles tense. She moaned, her body restless against his. He kept up the litany of meaningless sounds as he lifted her into his arms.

"Rio?"

"You are safe now, Sarah. I am taking you upstairs."

"And staying with me?" She pressed a kiss to his chin. Beneath her knees and across her shoulders she felt the strength of his arms.

"And I am staying with you."

She ignored the feeling that he wanted to add to that. She knew she didn't want to hear him declare a time limit. She had meant what she told him. He was free to go. She was not about to beg him, no matter how right she believed she was. They could make a good home here. She understood his dream, it was close to her own.

"I don't think you should carry me, Rio. Your wounds will open."

"I will carry you."

And that, she thought, was that. The man had a stubborn streak. Hadn't she noticed the squared cut of his chin from the first? Didn't she warn herself not to argue?

Ah, well, a small skirmish's victory to him. She had a larger battle to be won. She draped her arms around his neck and snuggled her head on his shoulder. She felt his lips on her hair and sensed a smile on his mouth as he climbed the stairs.

When they reached her room, he set her on her feet. Sarah blinked when he lit the lamp and turned it low. The light made her feel shy with him. She didn't know why, but it did. About to tell him so, she stopped herself when he turned around to face her.

There was a fierce hunger in his eyes, a look seemingly more intense because of the shadows. She reacted with a small tremor and a curl of heat that spread through her body.

Rio reached out, grasping her shoulders. He pulled her close and kissed her with a quick, hard meeting of lips that betrayed the tension he had hidden so well.

"By all the Irish saints, and every god of the Apache, Sarah, I swear I had never been so glad to see you and Lucas, and at the same time, wanted to shout you both out of there."

With her arms wrapped around his waist, she leaned her cheek against his bare chest. "I think I know exactly how you felt. I was never so afraid in my life. But it's over and I don't want to think about it now."

His hands tightened painfully on her arms. He could

not rid himself of the memory of the danger she had put herself in to save him.

"Stop it, Rio. You know it's over. Don't let the memory of what happened—"

"You are right, Sarah. Wise and strong. And now—"

"Now, you want to hold me, and kiss me and want me as much as I want you."

She suited action to words and drew his head down until his mouth hovered above hers. She kissed him with a fierce desperation that spoke more truly than words how deep her fear of the day's events had penetrated.

But passion had awakened, and passion left no room for fear.

Rio caressed her hip, his hands sure as they opened the tie to her robe. With his palms flat against the upper curves of her breasts he parted the cloth, watching her as she watched his hands slide the material off her shoulders into a puddle at her bare feet.

"Now you, Sarah."

She needed no coaxing as she moved to the buttons holding the ragged pants, nor did her hands tremble with the emotions that stirred awake. She wasn't at all shy to touch his flesh, palms lightly skimming his sides, his slim hips, powerful thighs. But her hands shook as she curved them to cup his erect flesh, hot and satin smooth, telling her more potently than kisses or words how aroused he was, and how much he wanted her.

And when Rio felt the tremors that shook her, he

drew her closer. He caressed her from her bare nape down her slender back to the slight flare of her hips. He repeated the touching a second time, less gentle, deliberately arousing her and himself as their bodies pressed tight.

Their lips met. The stroke of his tongue heavy, deeper. He held her hips, finding a cradle for his swollen flesh, feeling the heat from her breasts pressed against his chest.

Sarah broke the kiss. She stepped back and drew him with her toward her bed, into deeper shadow. The air was cool on her bare flesh, quickly warmed by his touch, by a brief kiss and the heated murmurs of lovers still learning the other's desire and need.

She felt the press of the mattress on the backs of her legs and sat down, ready to roll closer to the wall and make room for Rio.

He surprised her, holding her still as he went to his knees before her. A touch and her legs parted to make a space for him. His warm lips scattered kisses over her breasts, his hands cradling her lower back.

A string of tiny love bites made her cry out. She grasped his shoulders, restless now that she knew what would come, what they could share.

"Rio...Rio," she whispered, her voice broken. She felt both strong and vulnerable to him.

"Do not ask me to stop, Sarah. I cannot. I see and feel your need as my own."

"Yes." A mere murmur, all she was capable of, for she did know that the same need clamored in his blood, in every taut nerve of his body.

"Lovely, lovely Sarah," he said in a passion-rich voice, dark with promise. His head lowered and his heated lips claimed first one taut peak then the other.

Sarah's fingertips bit into his shoulders. His gentle suckling tightened every nerve in her body.

"I awoke with the taste of you on my lips. A sweet and spiced, heated fire, Sarah. A fire that burned for me, with me. I carry the memory of your crying my name in need. Will you cry my name again?"

Sarah closed her eyes, unable to answer him. She never knew a man would think such things, much less speak aloud of them. But this was Rio, a man apart from any other she had known.

And his name was cried from her lips as her hands raced over his body. Deep inside she felt the sensual pull that had drawn her to him. His heated mouth bathed her flesh until she believed she was afire. A fire that burned for him, with him. A hungry fire that demanded his flesh be joined with hers.

Each touch of his lips, each gentle tracery of his hands drove a fever to new heights. She was lying back, naked, open to him. For a moment there was fear, dispelled by his intimate touch. All but disappearing as his mouth trailed his own brand of fire down across the taut skin of her belly.

She fought the instinctive need to protect that most feminine core. His hands slid from her hips to her thighs, gentle caresses soothing the momentary tension that gripped her.

Sarah tunneled her hands through his long hair, uncertain of what he meant to do. And she heard his voice whispering, a dark passionate voice, words she did not understand. It was the tone, and the touch of his mouth that made her think of praise and sweet cherishing. All brought pleasure to her, and she knew she would deny him nothing that he asked of her.

Rio was caught in learning new tastes of this woman who gave so much. Skin warm and sweet like cream, heat and trembling and the fire that waited his claiming.

His hunger for her grew with every touch, every kiss. He longed to be gentle, to be a tender lover, but the small cries, the restless moves of her body all urged him to hurry.

The graceful, feminine twist of her body almost made him lose control. His tongue dipped into the tiny indentation of her navel. She stilled as he rubbed his cheek over her skin, his warm breath another caress to her flesh. She arched upward, needing to touch more of him as badly as she needed him to touch her. She lifted her hips to the heat of his hand and barely heard his harsh, approving whisper at her readiness.

She welcomed the intimate caress of his fingers, a feeling of urgency communicating itself to her. She nearly cried out when his mouth tasted her. The sensations ran through her, twin assaults that left her with panting breaths. She barely felt the edge of his teeth, shuddered almost violently from excitement.

"Rio? Please. I can't stand any more."

But he didn't stop. She clutched at his shoulders, crying out.

Rio deliberately deepened the passionate intimacy

he had never shared with another woman. Sarah's cries, the heated scent of her, every move of her body was surely going to drive him over the edge.

He felt the way her whole body tightened with unbearable tension. Her fingertips dug hard into his shoulders. Her voice was tight and husky and suddenly she tremored against him, releasing a plea his own body refused to let him deny.

It was long moments before he heard her whisper for him to come to her. Her hands smoothed the skin on his chest, gently rubbing the hard, pebbled tips that drew new hunger from him.

"I want you. I want you inside me. All of you. Everything. Isn't that what you wanted? No holding back this time."

She entwined his fingers with hers, bringing his hand to her mouth. She held his gaze with hers as she gently bit the fleshy pad at the base of his thumb. The shudder that raced through his body brought a smile to her lips. She kissed where her teeth had touched as he moved upward and covered her with his body.

The knowledge that she would make his body feel the same trembling excitement that held her own added a potency she had never known. She loved the way his aroused body pressed against her. Her every breath was filled with his scent.

"Rio?"

"Yes, Sarah, my Sarah," he whispered, seeing the dark, fevered look in her eyes. His body was rigid with desire, his hips thrusting against her. He nipped her lower lip roughly, possessively.

"I need you, Sarah."

"As I need you." She tossed her head from side to side, unable to control the shaking that took hold of her body. She was desperate now for the promised fulfillment.

*"Varlebena iszáñ. Varlebena."*

That word. She had heard it before. Sarah gave up the struggle to remember before it truly began. Her response to him ran as deep in her blood as his response to her was.

Rio groaned and pushed himself against the damp core of her body. Sarah cried out, her hips surging to meet him as he entered her deeply.

A ragged groan came from him as he drove into her. And Sarah knew that this moment of possession bespoke the ultimate surrender. For her. And for him.

She cried out then, swirled into a gentle savagery that bound her to him, and he to her. Wild, and yet free. There were no questions, only acceptance of its reality.

She heard the shout of her name on his lips, his own a whisper from hers as they raced toward the shuddering union that celebrated both little death and the renewal of life. She stared into his eyes. She loved him. Only him.

## Chapter Twenty-Three

When Sarah finally came back to her senses, she was aware of Rio lying beside her, his fingers toying with her hair. Her head was on his shoulder, and she moved the little needed to see his shadowed face. He looked so serious that she found herself alarmed.

"What's wrong?"

"I did not hurt you?"

"No." She stretched a little, then winced. She wasn't able to hide that from him. "Well, maybe I'm a little sore. I have a feeling that's not all that is worrying you."

"Wise Sarah. I cannot stop from remembering the sight of you coming into that cavern. If I had lost you…"

"But you didn't. Not me. Not your sons. Leave it be, Rio. And when I finally thought of the risk it was too late. I had to do something. I couldn't let you die, couldn't let Gabriel die. Just don't say that wouldn't have happened. You and I both know those men intended to kill you."

She touched his cheek and drew his head down to her. She kissed him lightly, but with her newfound love.

"If we are going to talk about risks, then let me take you to task over yours. I know you would have left here, Rio. With the storm they could never have tracked you. If you want, we'll both claim the other took far more risk with their life."

He gathered her closer within the cage of his arms, ignoring the few twinges of his wounds. He shook his head. "Sarah, what is a man to do with a woman who thinks clearly, simply, and then speaks her truth?"

"I have some wonderful ideas." She fought a smile. He really sounded vexed with the idea that she was not only ready but able to brush aside what had happened. She didn't know how to explain to him that what she found was worth any risk. The thought of losing him, losing the boys brought a chill to her flesh.

Rio, of similar thoughts, drew the quilt over them. He kept her tight to the warmth of his body.

"Would you promise me never to—"

"Only if you would promise the same to me."

"You are a stubborn woman, Sarah."

"I don't want to fight with you, but yes, I am. Especially when I'm right. And when it matters so much to me."

"Go to sleep, *iszán*."

"I'm not at all sleepy."

"There is no need to fear, Sarah. I will keep you safe. This time and for some time to come."

It was as close to a promise of staying that he would

make. She knew it, and as he called her wise, held her tongue. She wrapped her arm around his waist, needing to hold him. She closed her eyes and refused to allow one frightening second of the day to come back. She'd have to deal with the events of the day, and the knowledge that she had caused death. But not now, not tonight. Tonight belonged to her and Rio.

But Sarah dreamed. She knew where that lonely gray place had come from. She had first found it in nightmares after she had buried her baby. An absence of color, of sight and sound, a ghost world. Alone. None there to taunt her, none to accuse her. She even remembered the burning of tears that would not cease.

But that cold, empty place had become a place of refuge. A place without pain, a place where she could lock away all emotion and be numb.

Alone. She always came back to that, being alone and lonely. A price to pay to retain sanity. After nights without end, she came to understand that if she sealed herself off from feeling anything for anyone, she could never be hurt again.

Mary and Catherine had cracked her walls.

Rio came and tumbled them down.

And that revelation was a gift. She was free to love again. To never be alone.

Sarah remained unaware that she turned from Rio in her restless sleep. Just as she remained unaware of the tears that soaked into her pillow.

She stood enraptured with the knowledge that she no longer needed that icy place within herself.

Rio had given her a gift. Love. Love would allow

her to be Sarah again. Open and loving, as she had been once.

It was then that she remembered the Apache word Rio had whispered to her. *Varlebena*. And it's meaning rushed into her mind. Forever.

*Forever*. A word and meaning to savor. She clung to the promise implied in that one word and fell into a dreamless sleep, wrapped in the warmth of her love.

Morning stole her peace. She found herself fighting a new battle.

"You can't be serious, Rio. Why let the sheriff know about those men? The cave can be sealed. I've already told you that I never knew it was there. And no one mentioned it to me in all the time I've lived here. Why take the chance?" His idea brought to mind that he had been in the territorial jail and she still didn't know why.

Sarah appeared to cradle a cup of coffee between her hands, actually she clutched it. She leaned back against the cupboard's edge, her booted feet crossed at the ankles, her posture seemingly relaxed. Inside she was drawn tight with tension, afraid to breathe deeply lest she fall apart.

Calm reason was the only way Rio would continue to listen to her. She knew that, yet it was so hard to keep a lid on her temper. This was one argument she never expected to have with him, and she wasn't at all sure she would win it.

"Sarah, please." Rio, seated at the table with the light from the winter sun warming his back, rubbed the back of his neck. He broke off staring at Sarah to stare at the circling motion he made with his empty cup.

"We've been over this, Sarah. Those men are dead. I'll tell the sheriff I alone killed them. You had nothing to do with it."

"No. I'm not some fragile piece of china that needs your lies to protect it. I did kill—"

"Sarah!"

She closed her eyes for a moment, biting her lip. When she looked at him again, it was as if those terror-filled minutes lived in his gaze. She had to look away.

"Do you truly want me to stay, Sarah?"

"You know I do," she answered in a choked voice.

Rio fought himself not to go to her. If she was near, if he held her in his arms, he would give in to her pleas. And it would always stand between them.

He told her that, then added, "Try to understand that, agree or not, I am going to town. I do not want to live with this lie and the fear that will come with it. Fear of someone finding out. Sarah, please, you must see that I am right."

"All I see is that you are too damn stubborn and honest for your own good!"

"And would you have a man that had no honor?"

She was chilled by the softness and the coldness of his voice. She shook her head, not trusting herself to speak.

"Will you not trust me?"

"Are you still giving me any choice, Rio?"

"About this, no. If you want me to take my sons and leave afterward—"

"No!" She moved then, coming toward him, carefully setting down the cup, then rounding the table to stand beside him.

But Rio had already pushed his chair back to stand, and caught her close.

"Sarah. Oh, Sarah, I would not bring sadness to your eyes. Let me do this. Let us try to begin with truth between us. If there is justice nothing will happen to me." He cupped her chin, tilting her face upward. He met her searching look with a steady gaze.

"I'll agree to this madness of yours on two conditions. One, you let me come with you. I told you that the sheriff here is new, but I know him, and others in town." She held him tight, her fingers digging into his shoulders. "Say yes, Rio, or I'll just follow you."

"You give me no choice."

"I can't. I won't lose you. Besides, we need supplies. Do you think we should try the wagon or packhorses?"

"Packhorses. The wagon will get mired in the mud. What else?"

"I want to know why you were in jail?"

"You trusted me without knowing."

"That was then. Now I want to know." To her surprise, he closed his eyes, his face turned away. "What is it? How bad…"

"Not bad, Sarah. I still feel shame when I think of that time. When I was drinking, drunk until days ran together. I stole a bottle of whiskey. Some men from

town came after me. I ended up in jail and they took
my sons to the mission school. I was sober and angry
by the time they let me go. No one would tell me
where they took my sons. So I hunted for them. The
rest…"

"The rest becomes our beginning, Rio." She kissed
him quickly, smiling when he finally looked at her.
"There's no place for shame between us. Thank you
for telling me. I honor your trust in me."

"As I do you, Sarah." Relief washed away his fear
of losing her. And if shame lingered, her smile light-
ened it.

Hillsboro showed the ravages of the storm. The mud
was hock deep on the horses, the wooden sidewalks
with their swollen planks were covered with the debris
of the floodwaters. Most of the storekeepers were out
with brooms, sweeping the areas clean in front of their
stores.

Sarah called out answers to the questions fired at
her over how she had fared. She thought about going
to the bank first. Buck Purcell had seriously tried
courting her after Catherine's marriage, but then, he
had been halfheartedly trying to marry one of the widows for years. Despite Sarah's rejection, she knew he
stood as a friend to her. Support for herself and Rio
was all that she wanted.

Mentioning it to Rio was a mistake. He shook his
head and kept his horse to the center of the street,
heading for the newly built jail.

They dismounted and tied their horses to the rail.

"Sarah, I wish you would allow me to do this alone."

"No. Together or not at all."

"And you compare my head to stone? Who is the stubborn one now?"

She didn't answer and busied herself knocking the mud from her boots.

Sarah went inside the jail first. There was no sign of the sheriff. She had never been inside, not even when the town held the dedication for the new building. A potbellied stove stood in one corner. Centered in the front room stood a massive desk and chair behind it. One wall bore the gun rack, another was filled with Wanted posters. The room was neat and clean, not that she expected less from George Vaughan.

She hurried to the door, calling out for the sheriff. The cells were empty.

"Likely he's in his workshop. George was a cabinetmaker before he tried his hand at mining. He's a good man and a fair one. Wait for me and I'll go get him."

"Sarah, do you remember the story of Ruth?"

She frowned at Rio. "Yes but what has a Bible story to do with us?"

"Where you go, I go. I will hear what you say, and speak to this fair, good man myself. I will not have you lie to protect me, Sarah."

"I had no idea I was thin as a piece of parchment to you." She smiled to take the sting from her words but couldn't help shaking her head over her man's stubbornness. Her man...she liked the sound and feel of that, even if Rio wouldn't allow her to stand before him. Men! Rio's idea of honor was far different from hers. She had a strong sense of honor, but would protect what she claimed as hers no matter the cost.

Directing Rio around the back of the jail, she knew it was a good thing she had come with him. He'd lay his own head in a noose for his precious honor. She had no intent on lying, but that didn't mean that she would not use everything she could to make sure that Rio came away unbranded by those men's deaths.

Standing in the doorway, she glanced around at the workbenches lining the walls, furniture-making tools scattered over flat surfaces. The air was sharp and pungent with the smell of varnish.

She watched as George used a pointed metal tool to carve out a design in the wood length that spun on the lathe. Thin curls of wood shavings fell to the floor as the man's large hands directed the tool to yet another place.

Sarah didn't know where the sudden patience to wait for George to be finished had come from, but she was glad of it. When George was done, he greeted them with a smile.

He was a large-boned man. A thick shock of brown hair curled over his head, a mustache every bit as thick, covered his upper lip. Bright brown eyes softened the craggy face as his puzzlement turned to recognition.

"Miz Westfall, isn't it?" he asked as he came toward them.

"Sheriff." She stepped aside so that he could see Rio and introduced them.

George extended his hand. "I was hoping this wasn't an official call, but since Miz Westfall mentioned my office—"

"Yes, it is the sheriff we need to speak with." Sarah ignored the glare from Rio's eyes. She wasn't going to waste time.

In short order George had them in his office, his offer of coffee refused as Rio, without sparing himself, told the tale.

Before Rio reached the end, Sarah's store of patience disappeared. She made no apology as she interrupted.

"Sheriff Vaughan, I killed those men. If you intend to arrest—"

"Sarah, stop it. You had nothing—"

"Now hold on, you two. Let him finish, Miz Westfall. Then I'll hear you out."

"They were going to kill him and his son. I had no choice. They were animals. One of them attacked me. You know how the town would feel hearing that."

"I'm none too happy hearing about it myself, Miz Westfall. With the storm and the flooding there wasn't much I could do as sheriff. There's too much riffraff running loose as it is. Best thing to do is ride out with you and see for myself."

"Don't you believe me?" Sarah demanded.

Rio grabbed her arm. "Sarah, we agreed to tell him, now let him do his job. As a matter of fact, you stay in town and wait for us. You said you needed to buy supplies."

Sarah gaped at him. There was an audible click of

her teeth when she closed her mouth. She didn't want to be separated from Rio. It made no sense, for she knew George to be a fair-minded man. It was the reason the town council had chosen him. He had listened, really listened to Rio's story. But she didn't want to part from him.

"Trust me, Sarah."

When he spoke to her in that soft, dark voice and looked at her with unspoken love in his eyes, she had to agree.

"All right. I'll meet you back here."

She watched them go, then roused herself. It wouldn't hurt if the tale spread and spread quickly. She'd have Rio come out a hero by the time he returned.

Nita Mullin, like most of the shop owners in town, was sweeping off the drying mud from the wooden walk in front of her store. She appeared as spry and ageless as the first time Sarah had seen her. Nita was a good friend, a practical woman whose sage advice had aided both Mary and Catherine. Sarah took a deep breath and released it as she looked into Nita's kind eyes.

"I need your help."

It took no more for Nita to set aside her broom and whisk Sarah into her dress shop, straight to the back where she had her private rooms.

"Set and talk. You look like there's a heavy burden weighing you down, Sarah. Don't tell me Buck is pressing you for an answer. You could do worse. Then again, you can do better."

Sarah waited until Nita settled on her rocker while

she perched on the edge of the settee. "This isn't about Buck. But it is about a man."

"Land's sake, woman. We've had nothing but stormy weather for weeks and you found yourself a man."

"Well, not exactly, Nita. He found me. Please, this is important. Let me tell you what's happened."

Sarah had an avid audience for her tale. She made no mention of her own grief or what she had shared with Rio, but little else was kept secret. She was exhausted when done. Seeing Nita bite her lower lip, Sarah wondered if she had made a mistake. Nita's first words disabused her of that thought.

"We'll tell Caroline, of course. And Dolly. That will do for a start. Why you're so worried I can't figure. You did what had to be done. So did he. Unless there's more you're not telling me?"

Sarah picked at her pant's seam. "I want him to stay, Nita. I want to make a home for him and his sons."

"Child, oh child, do you hear yourself? I don't care what the man is, and maybe there's more folks that feel that way than I know. But you've never been a foolish woman, Sarah. You know what you're up against here. There's too many folks that can't forget the raiding and killing the Apache did. I know—" she hurried on to say with a lifted hand to stop Sarah's interruption "—that's true for both sides.

"But you can't change the way men think, Sarah. And women, too. Especially those who lost family and friends. If you want to stay in Hillsboro, I can't see how you'll manage if he stays with you."

Sarah leveled her very direct gaze on Nita. "Help

me to free him of any taint over these killings. As for the rest, he might not want to stay with me."

Nita rose in her own brisk way, smoothing the apron front of her gown. "Sarah, if you want this man and are sure he wants you, then don't let anyone stand in your way. If you can't live together here, go find a place where you can."

"Leave? But—"

"Give me no buts, woman. You know what you'll face here. And lots of other places, too. But there's God's country west and north of here. Think about it. That is all I'm telling you. Now, let's go see Caroline and Dolly."

Nita proved right. By the time Rio and the sheriff returned with the bodies, most of the townsfolk had heard of the attack on Sarah and her rescue by Rio Santee. Nita was the only one in whom Sarah confided Rio's Apache heritage, and she saw no reason to mention it to others. It wasn't something to be hidden for long, but Sarah took whatever time she could.

Sarah stood with Caroline near the sheriff's office. She had the packhorse loaded with some supplies, the rest Marcus Jobe promised to send by wagon as soon as the road dried up. Caroline slipped her arm around Sarah's waist and leaned close to whisper her approval of Rio.

Happy and secure in her love and marriage, Caroline patted her thickening waist. "Lord, Sarah, if you get him to the alter you won't be far behind me. That is one armful of man."

"But he's not a man to be led where he doesn't want to go, Caroline. Still, pray for me. I think I love him. I really think I do. He's got so many good qualities—''

"Qualities? What are you saying, Sarah? You're not buying one of your horses." Caroline cupped Sarah's cheek and forced her to turn toward her. Shaking her head, she then smiled. "Listen to yourself. No lies. A woman knows when she loves a man. You're one of the strongest women I know. Mary told me that part of your strength comes from never lying to yourself. I believe that. He's handsome as sin," she said with a laugh in her voice.

"You'd need to be dead not to notice, Sarah. Of course he has redeeming qualities or you wouldn't look twice. And I've never yet met a woman who wouldn't fight with every weapon she has to keep hold of the man she gives her love to."

Sarah never answered, for Rio and the sheriff came outside to join them. Rio appeared calm when she looked at him, but George made it clear for her benefit that there would be no charges.

"Wouldn't surprise me none to find them hombres wanted for something somewhere. If I find out, I'll let you folks know."

With that Sarah was content, and thought that Rio was, too. But as the days became weeks, worry ate into that contentment.

# Chapter Twenty-Four

At first, Sarah bloomed as she reveled in her new-found love. Her days began and ended with a kiss, with laughter, with overflowing joy.

Rio proved to be a passionate lover. Sometimes fierce, hot emotion marked the night, at other times tender, gentle loving wrung soft cries before they were joined. Still other nights were marked in memory for the teasing and laughter that brought them together.

Looking back over those weeks, Sarah believed with all her heart that they were good for each other. The boys, too, appeared to thrive, their bodies filling out, pranks and laughter a part of their days.

She thought of all as shared joy in the signs of spring coming, the newly expected foal, the work and the play they shared. But underlying all this were signs she could not ignore.

There were the moments when Rio thought himself unobserved, and she would see a distant look on his face, his gaze directed toward the south as if he were once more contemplating his earlier plan. The signs of restlessness were there, though she had to admit he tried hard to cover them.

She tried to break through to him, but he would walk away before an argument began. A few times he seemed about to speak of what bothered him only to gaze deeply into her eyes, shake his head and walk away.

Something inside stopped her from questioning him. She admitted she was afraid to know, afraid of what he would say.

Since the day they went to the sheriff, he had refused to go into town with her. His way of protecting her from gossip, for true to Nita's prediction, there were many townsfolk who pointed and stared at her. For the first time since Sarah had bought her home she found herself with few friends to defend her. Despite the effort to hide the knowledge, word spread that Rio was part Apache.

Sarah hid the hurt of turned backs, of the whispers and those who loudly complained of her being allowed to shop where they did. Cooler heads prevailed to stop any outright violence, but she sensed it was not far behind.

She couldn't even blame them for their small-mindedness. Nita was right. Many had suffered at the hands of the Apache, and it didn't matter that Rio and his sons had nothing to do with it.

Sarah took her stand. No one was going to dictate how she should live her life. But how much longer could she hide her growing isolation from Rio?

Much as it pained her, she stopped taking the boys

into town with her. She no longer stopped at Caroline's or Nita's to share a letter from Catherine. Everything she could do to avoid calling attention to herself and her remaining loyal friends, she did.

The price paid brought her other joys. Rio had deepened his relationship with his sons, and her own with them.

The moments of seeing three dark heads together, maybe hearing a burst of laughter, or seeing arms slung around shoulders brought a gladness to her heart and reaffirmation that she had made the right choice.

She had given them a safe place to build their new bonds, to share love, to have a home. Why couldn't people see this? They hurt no one. Why would anyone want to destroy what they were building together.

There wasn't a man in the county who could match the driven way Rio worked. No chore was left undone, no repair unseen under his hands.

The land and house, the barn and animals took on a well-loved luster.

But it was still her home. Another unspoken bone of contention. One she wasn't sure how to handle. Her land and home meant everything to her. She had paid in blood for it. This was her nesting place, her refuge, her security.

Did she want to give it up for the love of this man and his sons?

Would Rio even let her?

More often than not, she awoke to find him gone from their bed. At first, panic filling her heart, she searched for him, fearing this was the night he had left her.

She knew there would be no scene, no chance to change his mind, no tears, no pleas. He would leave as he had come to her, in the silence of the night.

She discovered that he would not be in the house, but out in the darkness near the corral. She would stand and watch him, her arms wrapped around her waist, the curtain on the kitchen window tucked aside so as not to hide him from her view. She envied the horses for whatever confidences he shared with them. And she cried, too, for the way he shut her out of what troubled him.

This could not go on. She knew that.

But the fear, that deep, gut-twisting fear of knowing Rio, knowing that if she pushed him, if she pushed for confrontation with all that she sensed, she would lose him, was enough to keep her silent.

She couldn't lose him. Rio made her happy, and this despite the fear. She knew that he loved her, that he would never deliberately hurt her. When she managed to push aside the fear of his leaving to protect her, the happiness she felt brought a glow to everything around her.

She prided herself on being strong. She had survived so much that would have left another woman broken. Now she was alive again. Truly alive and willing to fight.

Rio had given her the gift of easing sorrow and replacing it with his love. If unexpected tears hovered in her eyes, he was there to hold her, no questions of why, just simply holding her until the tears were gone.

These moments were healing and cleansing, and in their aftermath, the physical loving between them was long and slow until he wrung a soft cry of pleasure from her that was his name, and he, in turn, cried out hers.

But having opened the doorway and fully explored her fear this night, she could not lock it away.

She refused to awaken one morning to find him gone.

She couldn't let it happen. There had to be a way out. There had to be a way to overcome the biggest obstacle of all.

Rio's pride.

She had her own measure of it. She understood more than Rio knew what pride could drive him to do.

She needed a way to have it all.

Such a greedy woman she had become. She didn't want to settle for half or maybe someday. No. It had to be all.

And by the morning's light creeping into her room to chase the night's shadows, she found the way.

All she needed now was time.

But time was against her.

At midmorning, Sarah was scraping the last of the dried bits of dough from her breadboard. Before the sun had fully risen, Rio left with the boys to check on their snares. Survival lessons that meant taking nothing but their knives with them. She sent them off with a smile, one that couldn't reach her eyes, for the worry that someone with more temper than reason would find them. She had to trust Rio's skill to avoid any trouble.

She was about to dampen a cloth for the final cleaning of the board when she heard a buckboard coming around to the back of the house. Wiping her hands on her apron, she went to the kitchen door.

Spying Nita on the buckboard's seat brought her running from the doorway.

"What's wrong, Nita? You never—"

"Listen to me," Nita shouted, yanking on the reins with a vicious jerk to bring her horse to a standstill.

"You've got to get out, Sarah. You and Rio and the boys. There's not much time. There was a meeting last night, another this morning. I tried, Buck and Caroline tried, to calm things down. You know we've got horses' asses that won't listen to reason. They want you and that man of yours gone. I'm afraid for you."

For the longest minutes, Sarah couldn't breathe, couldn't move or talk. She silently denied what Nita said. But Nita wouldn't lie. She would not have come here if this wasn't true, wasn't serious.

"Ain't never seen the lot of them this worked up, girl." As if to bear out how frightened she was, Nita grabbed hold of her double-barrel shotgun. "I'll be standing with you, and what's more, we won't be alone."

"No, Nita! I don't want anyone to get hurt."

"Girl, you ain't listenin' to me. Got a feelin' in my bones this is goin' way beyond talkin'."

"How much time do I have?"

"Well, Buck got Ross Durvarey to water down the drinks over at the Red Horse. George, he took hold of Marcus and Ollie to keep things calm over at the Paradise saloon. Your guess is as good as mine if they can keep tempers from flarin'. Damn fools, the lot of them."

Nita leaned down to place a gloved hand on Sarah's shoulder. "It's real bad, honey. There was talk of burning you out. Seen my share of ugliness in folks more times than I can recall. Never thought to see it here. So don't be tellin' me to go, Sarah. Ain't gonna turn my back on you."

Sarah reached up and grasped Nita's hand. "You have been a wonderful, true friend to me, but I can't…won't let you put yourself in danger for me. I already planned to leave. But not this soon. I needed more time to talk to Rio. And yes, Nita, I can see by the look in your eyes that you know I'd rather stay and fight them, but I won't lose what I've found."

"No, don't, Sarah. But I'm afraid for you."

Sarah glanced away from Nita's naked fear. "I need you to buy me time. Rio's gone with the boys until dark. I have things to pack. I just wish…" she said, turning to look at her friend once more.

"What? If you need money, I took care of bringing what I could. Buck," Nita said with a wink, "was right helpful."

"No. Money's not what I need. I want you to say my goodbyes to those who matter. You know who they are. And thank them for standing up for me. Maybe, just maybe, there'll be a day when folks will look at a person and judge them by what they do, and not what they are. Keep the house safe, if you can, Nita. One of us will be back."

Sarah squeezed her hand once more then stepped away from the buckboard. "Go, dear friend. Say a prayer for us."

Nita stared at her for a long moment. Her nod was abrupt. A quick move to slap the reins and turn her horse helped to hide the moisture in her eyes.

"Gonna miss you, gonna miss you all," she cried out, but she did not turn around for a last look.

It was just as well she didn't, Sarah thought. She could barely blink back the sudden surge of tears. She heard a silent clock ticking away the precious minutes, yet she stood there in the yard. Her fists were held down at her sides and anger roiled through her. She did nothing to stop it.

She had fought hard to have a home, a place of sanctuary. She knew she could stay and fight them. You could do it, a small voice whispered in her mind.

Sarah uncurled her hands. She blinked a few times, then took a long look around. Slowly then, she shook her head.

No. She wouldn't stay. And she wouldn't waste another moment on regrets.


If Rio was shocked by the sight of Sarah waiting on the trail with packhorses, he hid it from her.

"It's time for us to leave," she said before the boys could ask questions. "I know a place, a safe place where we can make a life together."

Her breath held for the moments he studied her. She sat tall in the saddle, meeting his direct and most penetrating gaze with her own.

"Are you sure, Sarah?" he asked.

"Do you love me, Rio?"

He smiled then and whispered, "*Varlebena*, Sarah, *Varlebena*."

*Forever.*

Rio urged his horse forward the few steps to Sarah's side. He leaned over and cupped her chin. He let her see the silent message in his eyes, and he leaned closer still to brush his lips against hers.

And Sarah knew she had made the right choice, for she had left behind a house and found a home for her love.

"Let's ride," she said, taking the lead.

It took five days before Sarah found what she was looking for. The flat ground stretched out before her. She glanced over at Rio and saw the way he studied the land around them, then focused on the canyon wall opposite where they rested the horses.

"It won't be much longer," she said, uncapping her canteen and taking a long drink. "See that twisted pine and the boulder?"

"Sarah, there's no way—"

"Yes. There is. I've been through here before. Trust me. There'll be welcome for us and for the boys."

And still she waited, needing to be sure that way ahead was safe. She remembered everything that Rafe had told her about the Apache thinking the place was haunted, but times changed, as well as people.

When it was close to dusk she motioned them to move out, skirting the flat land until they came to the twisted pine. She let her horse pick her own way up and around the boulder to the bare trail that climbed up. She glanced back now and again, for they had to ride single file and dark was closing fast on the land.

The rich scents of pine and cedar filled the air as the first echoing footfall of her horse told her how close they were.

She waited for Rio and the boys to ride up close.

"This is a natural tunnel. When we come to the end don't be surprised by what's waiting."

"Sarah, this place holds—"

"No ghosts, Rio, just friends. My cousin and her husband live here with their children. You'll see. We will be welcome here."

One whinny from the packhorses was all it took to warn that they were coming. A thunder of hooves could be heard long before they cleared the end of the tunnel.

"Rafe, it's Sarah," she shouted, then nearly was unseated as a match at her side flared and a straw torch sprang flames.

"I've been watching you for a while," Rafe said, still in shadow while the torch he held illuminated the faces of Rio and his sons. "Anyone following?"

"No, Rafe," Sarah was quick to answer. "We needed to leave Hillsboro and—"

"And Mary has coffee on and hot food waiting for you."

Rafe held out the torch to Sarah and was about to turn for his own horse when Rio stopped him.

"Wait. You don't know me. Yet you offer welcome and turn your back on me?"

"That's right. Sarah brought you here. Don't need more than that."

And later when the tale was told, Rio realized that Rafe had spoken the simple truth. He and his wife needed no more than that.

It was late, nearer to dawn when Rio roused Sarah from her bed near the fireplace. He motioned for silence as he led her between the pallets where his sons slept and drew her outside with him.

The crisp night mountain air brought Sarah to shivering until Rio wrapped his arms around her and walked away from the house.

"There are words I need to say to you, Sarah. Words of promise." He placed his hands on her shoulders and turned her to face him.

"From my heart I give these promises to you, *iszán*. I will be your shelter for the days to come. And I will be your warmth. You will never spend another hour of being lonely for I am here for you always. We are two, man and woman, but from this day forth we have but one life to share. We will spend our days together, bound by the generous hearts that share their love. And our days, Sarah," he whispered, drawing her close so their lips just met, "all our days will be good and long beneath the sun. I love you Sarah. Love you and honor you as the woman of my heart.''

For Sarah it was more than hearing words as he locked her within the strength of his arms, his lips tender and seeking as they sought hers. A rainswept night had brought a stranger into her home, into her arms and into her heart.

And she vowed to keep him there—forever.

# Epilogue

It took nearly three years before the once merry widows were able to come together again. The first few days of this spring meeting in the hidden valley were spent sorting names and children and a flurry of cooking and catching up with one anothers' lives.

Three radiant women looked on as their husbands went down beneath a tangle of shrieking children. Shaded beneath the giant cottonwood tree outside of Sarah's new cabin, it was the first time they found themselves alone. A warm breeze ruffled the thick grass and whispered through the leaves overhead as the sounds of children's laughter filled the air.

There really wasn't a need for words between them, but Sarah put their thoughts into words.

"I never knew happiness was something I could hold and touch every day of my life. I have only to look at Rio and—"

"And love is waiting there in his eyes, in his arms and his lips," Catherine finished for her.

"You know," Sarah said, looking at her.

"Oh, yes. It is the same for Greg and me and Mary here," Catherine said with a short laugh as she poked a finger into Mary's side. "She knew it first."

There was more laughter then, for Mary merely winked. She rose and stood on tiptoes to see that Beth was standing. Tall for her age and already showing hints of the lovely young woman to come, she managed to extract little Robert, a sturdy four-year-old the very image of Rafe. Mary smiled to see them, blessing each day for the love they had given her, but the smile went to her eyes when she saw her handsome husband rise and tower over the tangle of bodies.

"I have been blessed," she shared with the others, knowing they felt the same.

Catherine came to stand beside her, slipping her arm around Mary's waist just as Sarah joined them to do the same. "My twins won't want to leave here. The girls don't have this kind of freedom back home."

"Then stay with us. Greg could make money anywhere. Rio and Rafe have done very well with the horses they're breeding. And Rafe still has other business interests, doesn't he, Mary?"

"Some. He's sold off quite a bit. Contentment, or so he tells me, does that to a man."

"So think about it, Catherine," Sarah said.

"Well, we have," she answered softly, her gaze picking out the honey blond heads of her twin girls. Gabriel already had MaryKate by the hand and Lucas was lifting Sarah Beth into his arms. Moments later she saw Greg offering Rio a hand up.

They watched their men coming toward them, the

children close by their sides, faint sounds of voices reaching them.

"Actually, we can't give Greg too much choice. You see I want you two with me this time."

It took Sarah a moment to tear her gaze from Rio's lean, hard body coming closer and looked into Catherine's eyes. Mary reached the same conclusion she did.

"A baby, Catherine? You're going to have a baby?"

"Yes."

The word was almost lost in the squeals of joy and laughter that followed, for the children reached them, crowding close.

Over the children's demands to be told the news, the three men stood apart, whispering among themselves.

"You're real sure about this, Greg?" Rafe asked.

"Look at Catherine. I can't deny that woman of mine anything she wants."

"Nor I, Mary."

Rio was silent, for his gaze had locked with Sarah's. Then he smiled. He understood what Rafe and Greg meant. A heart overflowing with love could refuse the giving woman nothing. Nothing at all.

"We'll stay. But, true to tell, I don't know if I can survive all this togetherness."

Rafe, laughing, slapped Greg on his back. "We'll show you. Won't we, Rio? It's all a matter of knowing when to run. Disappear. Like now."

And while their women were distracted by bending

to answer smaller children, they made good their escape.

"Where were you, Rafe, when I was trying to escape Catherine's wiles?"

"Busy loving my wife," Rafe answered as he led them around to the nearly completed barn.

Only Rio paused as they entered the dim interior and made for the loft's ladder. He looked back to see that Sarah watched him. She blew him a kiss, her dark eyes sparkling with joy as she mouthed the words. "I love you."

Escape? Rio didn't think so. He never wanted to be without his woman, his Sarah and her love.

No silent mouthing for him. No whisper would do. He shouted out the words to her.

"Sarah, I love you."

And the warm breeze carried the words throughout the hidden valley.

\* \* \* \* \*

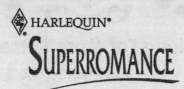

# Harlequin® Historical

**After the first two sensational
books in award-winning author
Theresa Michaels's new series**

July 1997
## THE MERRY WIDOWS—MARY #372

"...a heartbreaking tale of strength, courage,
and tender romance...."
—*Rendezvous*

and

February 1998
## THE MERRY WIDOWS—CATHERINE #400

"Smart, sassy and sexy...one of those rare,
laugh-out-loud romances that is as delicious as
a chocolate confection. 4☆s."
—*Romantic Times*

## Comes the final book in the trilogy

July 1999
## THE MERRY WIDOWS—SARAH #469

"Extraordinarily powerful!"
—*Romantic Times*

The story of a half-breed single father and
a beautiful loner who come together in a
breathtaking melding of human hearts....

You won't be able to put it down!

*Available wherever Harlequin books are sold.*

# HARLEQUIN®
*Makes any time special* ™

Look us up on-line at: http://www.romance.net          HHWEST1

HARLEQUIN · FIVE DECADES OF ROMANCE · CELEBRATES

In July 1999 Harlequin Superromance®
brings you *The Lyon Legacy*—a
brand-new 3-in-1 book from popular
authors Peg Sutherland, Roz Denny Fox
& Ruth Jean Dale

# 3 stories for the price of 1!

Join us as we celebrate
Harlequin's 50th Anniversary!

Look for these other
Harlequin Superromance®
titles wherever books are sold July 1999:

**A COP'S GOOD NAME (#846)**
by Linda Markowiak

**THE MAN FROM HIGH MOUNTAIN (#848)**
by Kay David

**HER OWN RANGER (#849)**
by Anne Marie Duquette

**SAFE HAVEN (#850)**
by Evelyn A. Crowe

**JESSIE'S FATHER (#851)**
by C. J. Carmichael